SPILT MILK, BLACK COFFEE

HELEN CROSS

BLOOMSBURY

LONDON · BERLIN · NEW YORK

First published in Great Britain 2009

Copyright © 2009 by Helen Cross

The moral right of the author has been asserted

Bloomsbury Publishing, London, Berlin and New York

36 Soho Square, London W1D 3QY

A CIP catalogue record for this book
is available from the British Library

ISBN 978 0 7475 9790 2
10 9 8 7 6 5 4 3 2 1

Typeset by Hewer Text UK Ltd, Edinburgh
Printed in Great Britain by Hewer Text UK Ltd, Edinburgh

The paper this book is printed on is certified by the © 1996 Forest
Stewardship Council A.C. (FSC). It is ancient-forest friendly. The
printer holds FSC chain of custody SGS-COC-2061

FSC
Mixed Sources
Product group from well-managed
forests and other controlled sources
www.fsc.org
Cert no. SGS - COC - 2061
www.fsc.org
© 1996 Forest Stewardship Council

www.bloomsbury.com/helencross

For Cleo

PART ONE

PART ONE

AMIR

It's a cold Christmas Eve in city centre – six weeks after our Jackie left her young daughter home alone while she ran off to Greece to follow a bloke.

Like magic it's snowing. Tinsel collars hang round each snow-coated lion, and a golden veil of lights encircles the stone pillars. I can hear the tinkle of rides in the German market and a drift of oil and sugar; perhaps Jackie was going round on the carousel, a bratwurst stuck in her giggly gob. On the town hall steps carol singers were gathering. Joy to all men. Which about summed up our Jackie.

It's also the morning of Jackie's wedding, to a completely different gora, one she had met in The Bar just weeks back. 'Wine? What wine you want?' Tony, the gimpy stranger, had asked, coming over to our Jackie with a letchy grin. 'Whatever wine goes best with gin, love,' Jackie had replied. And, perhaps to let me know that she was unchanged, still happily filthy, despite everything that had occurred during the last disastrous year, she said she'd given tosspot her muckiest smile – the one I'd once told her lingered in the air like smoke.

Meet Jackie, come away with smiles soaked in your clothes, twisted through your hair.

Some snaky bloke's taking photographs; perhaps just a manky relative, though I fear a tabloider.

I'm becoming a gimp: imagining all the time. Perhaps she'd just forgotten she was getting married today. Another headline Ashfaq, my 48-year-old newsagent brother, had drawn my attention to said, OOOPS WHERE'S MY DAUGHTER, and a picture they could have used as the dictionary definition of dizzy: Jackie full-colour red-face, ice-creamy hair, grinning, sucking on her little finger, dumb as daylight. Though she's smart as a whip really.

And she looked good, real friendly, even in the BOOZY BLONDE MOTHER OF ONE exclusives, though she was a real tough Yorkshire lass, slamming towards middle age, and there were faint lines that ran from the corner of her nose down to the sides of her mouth, like fine cracks in plaster, and sometimes when she was laughing and crying at the same time you got this sparky rainbow spread over what she called her 'old fizzog'.

''ave we met before?' Tony had asked Jackie later on that night they first met.

'Perhaps you've seen this old fizzog in the papers, love,' she said, tapping her pinkish wine-warm cheek, and Tony laughed, never considering she was telling the truth.

Because of this non-stop truth-telling she isn't a woman people trust.

TROUBLE AT TILL FOR BUSTY MUM was how one local rag greeted the news. Or, in another, DUMB BLONDE 'FORGETS' DAUGHTER, 12. All this would have been in the weeks before Jackie and Tony met. And the old perv would have been high on her, at first, and perhaps in no state to read papers.

That's if he could read.

And who could have tipped him off? Few of Jackie's mates had even met Tony, let alone got to know him. Those that did know Tony Shoe did so only in his capacity as one of our store's many shoe reps. No one knew his real surname. And there'd been no time even for proper invitations.

Thinking never got in the way of her fun, though. I've heard all about her punk days, her acid-house days. Her disco days. All the slutty disasters. She loved making fools of men, and yet she craved their love and approval, which was the cause of her chaos.

So the first many even heard of this do was when they received Jackie's text: Tony and Jackie request yr company @ a Winter Wedding: 2pm Sat 24 Dec @ City Register Office. Drinks and dancing l8r – venue tbc.

Orla said the timing, on 'the biggest day in the retail calendar', was deliberate. Still, despite 'huge sodding inconvenience', Orla had, to everyone's surprise, arranged the rota as if around an important funeral, and most of those who wanted to attend could.

But there's still no limousine and I think I might gimp out and cry so I put on my shades. Glance up at the CCTVs, cotton-woolled with snow. The traffic is caught in a slow weave, all the cars stuck together and then all the buses. A few single lashes of rain streak windows of vehicles and a few moments later the wipers begin. There was a tug on my elbow. 'So where is she?' Tony Shoe, fiancé, says, real nervous. The guy's a complete half-head. But. But if she's happy . . .

'I can't say, mate. She's just not here yet.'

'Is this normal, mate?' Tony says, in a conspiratorial man-to-man whisper, which blows the words out the corner of thin dry lips. 'We've not known each other long. Is this just like regular female lateness?'

'No,' I say. 'This is completely out of character.'

I'm chuffed that she's making this tosspot sweat. It was obvious what Tony saw in 'busty bubbly blonde' Jackie Jackson. But what did she see in him, the girls gossiped?

5

Again. Perhaps Tony Shoe was a secret lottery winner, as Leo had suggested.

Leo. It all started sliding after Leo. Who yesterday said he wouldn't begrudge Jackie an easier life – as long as it wasn't Leo himself who had to provide it, because Leo's had women, 'flashy birds, local lasses', who expect, after a few shags, him to fund them, knowing all the time that he has a mortgage and a family of his own back home.

Generally, I'd say Marilyn's right: most men don't risk much for Jackie.

After the end of the affair with Leo, Jackie told me she'd stopped going out, because it was when she went out sharking that bad stuff happened, and I'd thought how it sounded like my own ma, who at that time, last April, was just losing her reading glasses hourly, and innocently asking the exact same question several times a day. 'So it's right boring, is it, this snow-white life you're living?' I'd asked Jackie. 'Ah, but I imagine I'm not living the life I am living, Amir, just reading about myself in a book,' she said.

Boooook: I had to laugh at that Englisher accent, teeth-achingly cheap-jam-sweet so when she said book, it rhymed with spook. 'And that helps?' I said. 'Well, it gets me to sleep, love.' 'You so wouldn't be the kind of book to put anyone to sleep,' I'd said, not thinking. 'For a few years I was the kind of book you could only read with the lights on, Amir,' she whispered – sweet lips bang on my ear. 'So no way,' I said, total dry mouthed, 'you'd be a page-turner. One with a great plot, gripping, thrilling.' 'But kind of throwaway? A beach read,' she said and pretended to sigh sadly, and she was half right: I was infected back in April, at the start of all this, no matter how hard I tried not to be, by the way my ma and bro thought of the boozy goris.

DASH OF A SALESWOMAN: SEXY SHOPKEEPER DESERTS DAUGHTER – that was Ashfaq's favourite header. Though he normally gets all his news online, because he hates all papers and journalists and says he won't read the rags he sells because of what they wrote about us lot round here, but about Jackie he'd broke his rule, and read every article, leered over every bosomy photo, even sniffed the pages so he had ink on the end of his nose. Even if I'd tried to buy up and burn all the papers, it'd not have saved her from our Ashfaq, because my bro proudly owns Fags 'n' Fings, and plans to build a Fags 'n' Fings empire. First throughout Yorkshire, then across the world.

'It'll be you next,' Leo gruffs with a grin. He's checking his watch, looking round for the limo. He only has a few hours before he has to be back on the shop floor. I bluff on about no way, though the truth is that I was probably going to do as my ma had hoped, and Ashfaq had insisted, and ask Harpreet to marry me on New Year's Eve, because it wouldn't be long for Ma now; last English winter she'd see maybe.

So. Harpreet. And therefore a week left.

Jackie has done everything from postwoman, chambermaid, barmaid, waitress, nursery worker, cleaner, right up to telesales operative. All the white-trash jobs that Ashfaq says the gorehs happily do because they have no entrepreneurial spirit. Which is why they are on the bottom rung of the ladder, and then get jealous of us lot, and why they spray-paint misspelt slogans on Ashfaq's shop.

No matter how hard I try, my dumbass mind turns back to Ashfaq or Jackie. The two who've brung me the most trouble.

Particularly those pool-cool orbs – that steady blue magnet holding your gaze – even after half a bottle of whisky. Even my avowedly bird-blind brother had noticed that, the first time she trotted into his shop and flicked her silver mane. 'Turn to Allah, mate,' he said, with a shake of his head after he'd looked into those two sapphires dropped in snow. And I did, I tried – and it's not the first time it's occurred to me that what's happened to my own ma over the last six months is punishment for what I said, did, and truly felt I couldn't help, with Jackie Jackson.

But I got away; here I am, free. As rain and ice falls in my face like a handful of nails so I have to screw up my eyes and just listen. 'She's a great woman,' Leo was saying to Tony. 'I used to be her boss, and I can assure you she's very reliable.'

'She told me she was sacked. And had been interviewed by the police,' the half-head replied.

'Well, that's right, but . . .' Leo said.

'I never knew what for, except she said something about a fight. A fight?'

Another old bloke going completely bananas, despite having only known her a month.

I pull at the suit Harpreet has pressed for me. Now I don't work at the store I think I look a bit of a prick in this fashion attire. Looking like a twat was something I grew used to during my days working for Orla as a fashion assistant at the flash store, but nowadays even Ma doesn't notice what I wear, and I wonder if soon I'll have a stiff polyester suit and a pair of comedy cufflinks – when I'm a husband and newsagent.

'So what were they scrapping about?' Tony asks and I wanted Leo to leave it there, not to mention Jackie's drinking or sacking, but half-head was looking puzzled, needing more, so I turn into the snow-hail, refuse to listen, think instead of Harpreet by my side day and night.

Apart from Danuta, I didn't recognise most of the people bent under coats and umbrellas climbing up the great stone town hall stairs, going into the wedding. Despite Orla's guilty generosity with the rota, there were several staff who'd been invited but who'd refused to go near. Several hated Jackie, especially gori birds her own age who, since the news had come out about Elle being left alone at home, mocked her, said she was hanging around with pensioners; and even before the flit she'd lost Elle, and she'd brought the depresh on herself because she drank too much, and she was a slag – that was the most common – and some of her best mates were wickeder than my own ma about lasses like her. Those cream-fleshed, half-dressed weekend women, who our Ashfaq called 'the vanilla tarts'.

Of course that wasn't the real Jackie, though she spent much energy and caused much chaos by pretending it was. 'Perhaps we could help one another out?' Leo'd told me he'd said to Jackie early on when he'd started to get ideas about her, middle of last year. 'Do each other a favour, maybe?' 'Are you talking one sex addict to another?' she'd replied. And: 'It'd be like dating my own child,' she'd laughed once when Danuta suggested something about us – me and her. 'You should give Jackie a go, Amir,' Danuta had continued. 'She'd give you a run for your money.' 'It'd be fun, honey, but it'd get me arrested.'

This was roughly a year before she did get arrested.

It is snowing now in thick soft feathery flakes and more people are getting edgy, wandering out of the register office, weaving around the grand stone pillars, looking over the icy road for our boozy blonde mother of one. Gone. Perhaps all females have a desire and ability we blokes simply don't: to hide. Like a few months back when my own ma started her disappearing acts, and had half the street out searching, the police on alert and our Ashfaq going round like a gold-chained, gym-heavy parliamentary candidate – in an open-topped car with a loudhailer.

Perhaps hiding is the smart thing to do, because she really is very clever. 'The staff discounts are amazing!' Danuta had told us all one day, and Jackie, who, at that time, had worked at the store for ever, replied, 'No, love, it's just another way of getting you to buy your own uniform.' And when Danuta did use the wages, which she was meant to be saving to buy a house when she returned to Poland, to buy discounted designer gear in the store, Jackie sighed and said, 'What you gonna do next, love, rent out your forehead for advertising?'

Look at Tony: it should be illegal for a granddad to propose to a girl. Especially when she was drunk. Especially when she was lonely, and only pretending to be that kind of woman.

'Her phone's switched off. Poor guy,' Orla shouts, crossing the road towards us. 'You should see him. Poor Tony Shoe. Where's her father?'

Blackened bus-smashed snow was stacking up in the gutters now and I think of my ma earlier this month, barefoot in the frosty garden, and Harpreet's tiny feet pressed into the high gold shoes; them ones she bought to impress me. 'He's dead. He died at the beginning of the year,' I say.

'Perhaps it's all too much for her. It sounds like it's been a very long year. What with her dad dying and the custody thingy.'

'And you sacking her,' I say quietly. A few times when she was drunk Orla'd tried to hug me; she was about as cuddly as a pencil, and now I no longer worked for her I no longer had to fear her.

'If it was my wedding . . .' she sighed. 'I'd want to make sure someone made me come.' Not sure if the double entendre was intended. Probably, though Orla usually only makes risqué comments of this nature when she's lashed. 'What about her mother? Have you called her?'

'Her mother isn't here. They don't get on,' I say, and like a perfect photograph I remember that bleachy council semi, gravy clouds over that flag-flapping ice-white estate, their crumby tea-warm house, and me looking on as they roared at each other, carving, in slices, paper-thin, a skinny chicken.

I should never have gone there. That was the start of it for me. The lust I could handle, but when I saw how she managed her old ma it crushed me.

'I heard that the mother was dating that old coach driver too,' Orla exclaims. 'Imagine mother and daughter both screwing the same bloke. You must think it's a classic white-trash tragedy, Amir. They've probably written it up for *Chat* magazine.' Still I don't reply. Snow like confetti coming down still. Like the only confetti there'll be this day, I feel sure. Because I can see no white limousines, no crimson bride and blush-pink fur-trimmed bridesmaid. 'But, I guess, attending your daughter's third wedding when she's barely forty isn't quite what any mother had in mind.' Orla stamps her shoes angrily into the lacy snow.

This makes me remember another morning, and Jackie in our shop, looking at Ashfaq, then at her own tits, and then at Ashfaq again, and eventually saying, 'They're just like shoes, love, they come in all shapes and sizes.' Ashfaq looking like he'd been hit with a brick.

But Orla knows zero about me and Jackie. No one knows, except my ma, who, for the first time in my life, I can tell totally everything to – now that she remembers absolutely nothing. I stroke back my hair and feel the gel that Harpreet had tenderly applied this morning, now stiff as glue. Jackie had invited Harpreet to this wedding, but I'd not passed on the invitation. Can't imagine going public with her; it'd be like parading wearing fancy dress.

But I guess I'll get used to it.

Jackie had even invited my old ma to her wedding. Like the two were proper pals.

'She's thirty-nine,' I say, real quiet, and then was well annoyed that I had been provoked into a conversation with Orla, when I no longer got paid for it.

'Well, no bride, no bridesmaid and no mother of the bride, plus a groom who swears he was too pissed to care. It's crazy, eh,' Orla says, and despite the staffing crisis the event has caused her, she looks very excited to be here at the start of something terrible. Tony comes up to join us again, and we all look up at the high stone steps, climbed by thousands of hopeful Yorkshire brides over hundreds of English years. I stare at tall old windows too, expecting Jackie to just appear there princess-like, grinning, waving, with a laugh to melt a stone lion's heart. 'Perhaps Ellie's playing up,' Tony says, 'I took her with us for dinner last night and she's actually quite a handful. Didn't give me an easy time at all.'

'Elle,' I say. 'Her name's Elle.'

'Women, eh? I don't think I'll ever get the 'ang of 'em.'

'It's not like learning how to ride a pony,' Orla snorts, though with my ma and Jackie that's exactly what it's like, clinging to the side of a wild beast, falling off and getting back on again immediately. Not with Harpreet, though, that'll be a safe, calm, leisurely ride, a comfortable lifelong journey. A wise decision. Plus my three sisters, Samirah, Wahida and Yasmin, and my ferocious sister-in-law, Halima, all agree on Harpreet – so it'll keep everyone happy.

'Elle had been looking forward to the wedding,' I say, because when Jackie had, in the last few weeks, talked of the expensive wedding it'd always been about what Elle would want. What Elle would wear. What Elle would like at the reception, the disco, the buffet. She loves that little lass so much, and the lass loves her mam too. I think of the way she said, 'Mummy won't be long,' that night I found her. For I was the one who first discovered that little lass home alone, there in the house, camped out with candles and a few fags, a sheetless mattress dragged down on to the living-room floor, just the purple-blue fish tank humming, casting the room aquamarine.

Tony breaks the snowy silence to say, 'Well, if she's not here in ten minutes I'm giving the chance to someone else. I'm serious. Is there any reliable lady out there who wants to marry me?' Do I imagine it or does Orla blush? Then Orla is telling Tony how once she'd seen Jackie in the lap-dancing bar. The one with the slogan 'We've the best bouncers in town'. Luckily before Orla can complete the lap-dance story Marilyn comes over. Now those two are true best friends and if Marilyn doesn't know where Jackie is, no one will. I have a stinging memory of the staffroom one day last April, a few days after Jackie had come to work drunk and slept all morning on a mattress of bubble wrap in the store cupboard. Marilyn was holding the crying Jackie in her arms. The two friends kind of cuddled there, intimately, their soft cheeks wet against one another, hot. And as I watched, Jackie turned, smiled, wiped her red eyes and said, 'Amir, darling, it's not what you hope.'

Mucky fox.

Eyes up and snow fizz-melts on my too-warm cheeks: even memories of her burn me up, and it's only the thought of Harpreet at home brushing Ma's hair that takes the temperature right down.

'I've just been over to the hotel, but there's no sign of her and the receptionist says the limo left half an hour ago,' Marilyn pants. She is a heavy woman, unfit, and seemingly unconcerned with how her body pleases others, which is unusual in the store. Every few months she announces that she wants to leave and use her surveillance skills to protect people, not thousand-pound handbags. And can you blame her? It's a wonder any of us survived that store.

'I hope there hasn't been an accident,' Marilyn whispers.

'Very likely. There usually is around Jackie Jackson,' Orla replies.

Marilyn says, 'She does know how to cross the road on her own.'

'She knows how to, yes, but can she be trusted not to walk in front of a bus just to get the driver's attention, that's the question,' Orla says. 'We know she has a thing about bus drivers, don't we?' Then Orla starts raving about the rota and how she will never alter it again, ever.

'She's probably getting Elle ready,' Marilyn says. 'I think she's doing this whole thing for her.'

I try to remember more slutty, seedy, immoral moments from Jackie's so-called life.

Still snowing, and if you look up you are lifted high into a drift of feathers. 'Unless she's left her daughter up there in the hotel room and flown off on honeymoon alone,' Orla laughs and walks away, and I fiddle with the expensive watch that Harpreet has just bought me. I can picture her wrapping it, tongue up over her thin upper lip, folding and stroking the silver paper like an excited girl. It's heavy, a real businessman's item, and it's making my wrist sore. Like the handcuffs Jackie said she wore when they brought her home on the aeroplane. 'Drama queen,' Halima snorted when she read about those handcuffs – while I thought: goddess in chains.

A different bride floated up the town hall steps, her long hard beige face like the wooden stick poking from a ball of candy floss. Since Jackie, all other women seemed like fools.

'You know,' the husband-to-be says, coming up close to me and Marilyn, 'the night I met her, I thought she was . . . working. You know, *working*.'

We stare at him. I just think of a word: smutty. 'You did?' I say, and Marilyn looks away, with something like a tear in her eye. Marilyn had confided in me earlier in the week that she thought management were trying to get her off the shop floor and into the CCTV room. I'd told her to think of it as a promotion. 'But Security Control is for the freaks, Amir,' she'd said. 'It's where they put you when you start to scare off the customers.' She was right.

'And there was this powderiness to the drink, a chalky aftertaste, you know. I still wonder about it. If she really was a . . .'

'That's what my brother thought,' I say, before he can say the word, fixing this simpy half-headed salesman with a look

I'd learnt from Ashfaq's martial-arts movies, that says I am Lord; taller and younger and fitter. 'But then again, my brother hates women like her.'

'That's your wife-to-be you're talking about, dickhead,' Marilyn tells him, and marches away up the steps.

Once Marilyn had told me how when she'd told Jackie that she had breast cancer Jackie had held her in a huge hug and said, 'It's only when our bodies go wrong that we realise how perfect they were before. Poor bodies – we're nicer to our nasty boyfriends than we are to our perfect bodies. Sorry, body,' and later during the illness Jackie had cooked meals from scratch, lasagne and soup and chilli, and brought them round for Marilyn's freezer and brought vintage comic novels in from the charity shop. Just the right kind of books, apparently, just the right kinds of conversations.

The register office is high-ceilinged, cold, and because of the flowers it stinks like a funeral parlour – just like Cosy Retreat on a Monday morning, when, over the weekend, the rellies have brought in reduced-price, garage-forecourt bouquets. I never take Ma grapes or flowers, I take her magazines and books and a bit of what my three sisters say every woman wants really – conversation and understanding – and I wonder if you can give those true things to a woman you don't love, or even really know: if I can give them to Harpreet.

Through the high windows I see the snow falling thicker, doing its damnedest to muffle and wrap this devastating year.

Only half the polished seats are filled – with frowning guests. Behind I can see another wedding party peering in at the door, and they too are edgy, checking their watches. Then an official in a dark suit arrives and goes to speak to the father of the groom, who laughs then nods rapidly. 'We'll wait another ten minutes,' says the official real wearily. He has no doubt had this situation before. Brides regularly do not appear. How often? Maybe once or twice a month. Maybe more. I would like to know. Nowadays probably every week; lasses changing their minds, following their hearts, and, according to my ma, when she was normal enough to be angry at the outside world, 'leaving the rest of society to pick up the pieces'. Mama, I can picture it: Jackie on her knees in that manky estate kitchenette, quickly wrapping the most dangerous pieces of her ruined life in thick layers of Fags 'n' Fings newspaper.

Poor baby.

Tony is in a pinstripe huddle with his mates. 'Sorry, everyone, the show seems to have been slightly delayed. If you would kindly remain in your seats,' the groom's father says and then continues, 'And if I'd known I was the entertainment for the day I'd have brought my ukulele.'

Marilyn touches my shoulder and whispers in my ear, 'Amir, I think she's not coming. I think she's changed her mind.'

And I had to hold on to her forearm to stop myself punching the air. I'd arrived at the wedding feeling like a total gimp, and I could be leaving feeling like a samurai warrior.

ELLE

'You must never give up on love,' my mum says, and just when I'm about to say something smart in reply she presses her fingers hard against my lips instead and says, 'I mean it, Elle. Never.' And she dabs at the sore patch where I've bitten my lip bloody.

'Even if it means I end up like you?' I say, because she is totallysentimental.com, because she is hungovered and wanting another drink, and I start whistling a merry tune, because it's very annoying when someone whistles.

'Yes. Even if it means you end up like me.'

And I gulp hard and grimace, go cross-eyed, then stare out the windows of the limousine at the snowy city. I am kind of chuffed to be with her, though I still feel car-sicky, and even at my age Dad has to let me go in the front. The Steps, Cherub and Caprice, nearly spewed up with jealousy when they heard I was gonna be a bridesmaid. The counsellor told me nothing was my fault though I still felt it was – me and that Asian. We made Mum news, we got her arrested, we made her the legendary Boozy Blonde Mother of One. 'Stop biting your lip, love,' Mum says, and I carry on until she swats at my bleeding gob with her sequined bridal purse.

'So. Where you wanna go?' I say, and when she doesn't reply I lift up her lacy white veil and see that she is, surprise, surprise, crying, but not necessarily unhappily. She has glitter on her eyelids, like frost has settled on her in the night, and closer, she smells damp and flowery, like she's just out of the bath, and I want her to keep smiling at me. 'You look like a freaky ghoul,' I say, 'a total spook. Didn't anyone ever tell you not to cry when you are wearing enough mascara to open in pantomime?'

'It's not exactly fair to leave him standing there,' she sighs, taking a ball of snotty tissue from up her leg-of-mutton sleeve and pressing it to her red and black eye. 'Poor Tony.'

Tony smelt sharp and sweaty, and smoked finger-thin cigars from a slim square tin. The memory-smell and the roundabout was making me dizzy. I am wearing Cherub's new thong knicks and she's absolutely no idea and I want to ask Mum if we can go ice-skating or on the big wheel, though of course I know we can't, so I look at her angrily. Everyone was angry with Mum; not just her family, like with Marcel before, but now, because of that Asian, everyone in the country hated my mum. I scowl at her and say, 'It's not fair to marry him, Mum, is it?' She strokes her hands over my red cheeks and her fingers so soft and clean I wanted her to keep doing it. Until I push her away and say, 'It's not fair for you to marry anyone, Mum. Not with you in this state.'

'Don't you think so?' she says, but I don't answer because I refuse to be the one who takes all the decisions in her life. We were still circling the ring road not far from the town hall and the driver is eyeing her up in the mirror, and suddenly Mum cries out, 'Oh my God!' I don't respond immediately. Remember I have known this woman all my life. 'Oh. My. God. No. Elle! No!'

She won't let anyone else anywhere near the centre of attention.

'Hmm,' I say eventually and comb my hair with two fingers, and wish it was curly. I wave to a little lad going by in the fast lane; he waves back at me then is speeded off ahead. Mum is making horrified gasps and I start thinking about hedgehogs and that I know for certain they exist. Ashanti thinks they don't exist and has said that I have to prove it by the end of the Christmas holidays. I have to find a hedgehog, dead or alive. It's mad. Our teacher will name the spiky creation and then it will be settled for ever.

'Elle, I just realised I left my make-up bag in my room.'

'Well, hell, Mum, stop the car and call the cops.'

I'd put blue mascara on, which probably looked like you came from Freaksville unless you were real pretty and skinny, so now I feel truly utterly hopeless. 'I'm serious, love, I've only got a lippy with me. I thought we'd be going back to the room. What have you got with you?'

'Mum, I'm not old enough, I don't wear make-up.'

'I was wearing a bra and full make-up at ten.'

'Like that surprises me.'

'I was hoping my mam wouldn't recognise me.'

I just lick the sore dip in my lip so it stings. She always said she hated handing me back; said I was a video, which she had to return immediately after she'd viewed, or pay a fine. Like I had any choice!

'When I was younger, older than you but still youngish, I was really into Madonna. Do you know her?'

I say not a word, just stare at her blotchy mug for a long time and wish we could stop and get chips. Then I blink three times and I say, 'You mean you cheated on Olivia with Madonna?'

'Oh, this was long after Olivia. I liked Olivia when I was your age. Madonna was later.'

'Still, it's not nice, Mum, innit.'

'Elle, don't say innit! You sound like a horrid teenage lad.'

'Well, you should know,' I say, because Marcel was always there between us like an embarrassing smell that made you want to leave the room or hide your face.

And because I'm about to be sick I concentrate on the horizon and see tower blocks like huge graves, and beyond that hills and fields and wide-open Yorkshire. I wonder if she is going to tell me off for mentioning Marcel, but she just goes on, 'Well, the rumour was that Madonna made her way to New York City and hopped in a taxi cab and she said, "Driver, take me to the centre of everything."'

'I can just imagine you liking that, Mum,' I sigh. And for a while I narrow my eyes, straighten my arm and mime pointing my fingers like a gun. My pink bridesmaid dress was so not me, but it fitted, even when I raised my arms. I quite liked it, the sequins and the colour, though I was known at school as a laddish girl. Elle-boy they called me.

My stepmum Claire thinks I will grow up to be a lesbian because Mum is such a slut. But Dad said that Claire should leave me alone and let me wear what I liked, and if I wanted short hair and trousers and blue sweatshirts that was fine by him. Claire said, 'You might not think that, Paul, if she's driving a truck at seventeen.'

Actually I can imagine it: me, the open road, the dusty mountain-backed highways of America. Me alone, or just me and Mum together.

The limousine driver is still eyeing Mum and making my heart thump at my shame-flat chest like a stick on a drum. I hated men leering her. Mum was saying again that she was sorry about what had happened, but how I could have called Dad at anytime and he and Claire would have come to get me. Though that counsellor said I should not have to feel guilty, and should remind Mum that it was her who came home in handcuffs with sunburn, and was charged with child neglect. Not me.

So I did.

Still Mum doesn't mention the Asian though she knows I know. She said, 'It was nothing to do with him, Elle.' But Claire's right, Mum's usually wrong about what's to do with what.

Claire wants me to call her Mum, but I don't, and I always won't.

'Amir just wanted to see if I'd come home in one piece, love,' she said, but I know also that one of her problems is that she always trusts blokes, so I have to be very careful with what I know. I wish I'd nicked Cherub's bra-top as well, and when I get home tonight I will and I whistle more loudly, so Mum pinches the top of her nose and bites her lip, like she used to when I practised the violin.

Every night when I was alone in her house I thought she might just come home, and I listened for that slow rising pop of her uncorking a bottle – her signature tune since I'd been a baby – and I'm whistling 'A Spoonful of Sugar' now, though I don't think you'd recognise it if you didn't know, and she's still going on about why I didn't call Dad. I keep whistling, then I suddenly shout: 'I didn't call Dad because he worries too much. Understandably.'

'Hmm,' Mum says and I know she is trying to stop herself from saying something mean.

'Mum, he's a good dad. He cares about me,' I say, pushing her to say the mean thing.

'Poor Tony,' she sighs instead.

'I thought you said he was loaded.'

'He has very high aspirations,' she says, 'in that direction.'

'You mean he's another greedy nutter, up to his eyes in debt, who worries about his body like a girl.' Again I was mentioning hunky teen Marcel, in a roundabout way: I couldn't stop myself. Perhaps Dad and Claire and the counsellor were right and I was deeply damaged by it.

'Perhaps I should never have said yes to Tony,' she sighs.

'Just out of curiosity, Mum, have you ever said no to a guy?'

I am slumped right down in the slippy seat and I want her to hoick me up but she don't, and I won't move because I'm sulky, thinking of Tony. Last night, the wedding eve, we had had to eat with him at the hotel. He didn't say much, though you could hear the wet chomp of his dentures chewing. Mum tried hard to be encouraging and chatty. It was the first time he and I had met. When Tony asked for the wine list I leant over to Mum and said loudly, 'Yeh, right, like he can read!'

To be honest, I only liked to be with Mum when it was just me and her. When there was a bloke involved I started getting worried. I don't know why. And she did too; perhaps because when she had her kid with her she couldn't pretend to be seventeen. 'Wait until you get a boyfriend,' she'd whispered, tickling me under the ribs, and I could tell I'd made her totally shamed of him.

'Like he's a lad, Mum!' I shouted, so loud he could hear. 'It's like you're marrying a granddad.' Then when she didn't say anything I said, 'It's like Marcel but in reverse.'

'You should have seen George,' she said.

I didn't laugh, because I had seen the pictures of bald George in the newspaper: runaway Mum and her OAP lover. I just hit my head down on to the table and wrapped my arms over. The funniest most slap-heady picture of George was taken at his allotment, where he had hidden when he returned to England, after escaping Mum in Greece. You had to laugh – along with the rest of the nation.

All the time Tony stayed hidden behind the menu, pretending not to hear our argument. He was blanking us both, not even a raise of those fluffy eyebrows, and I wanted to tell Mum that if she married Tony this is how their whole marriage would be: thirty years of hiding behind the wine list.

If Tony knew about me being left home alone he had not mentioned it. 'He's not into the news,' Mum had reassured me when we were getting ready for the meal.

'That's because he can't read,' I replied, and she said quietly that I was being unkind, and anyway she didn't want him to know because it might hurt him. Not until after they were married at least, then she would tell him everything. 'Poor bugger,' I say.

'Look, love, it's a fairytale wedding for Tony,' she says, trying to be stern with me, 'and I don't want to screw it up at the last minute by telling him stuff that's not even relevant any longer.'

'Yeh, fairytale, right. Like when the wolf dresses up as the freaking grandma. Poor Tony's gonna feel like Little Red Riding Hood for the rest of his life. Gobbled up by a sex-wolf who dressed up as his bubbly blonde housewife.'

'Don't you ever use words like that!'

'What!'

'Housewife,' she says and I almost let out a little laugh, because it's so mad that what Mum hates most about Claire is that she's got a nice house and is a good wife.

But now as I whistle and look out the limousine window and feel sick-dizzy, I think Mum's kind of right – Tony doesn't really need to know. It's good and bad how quick fame passes. Only a few girls at school even mentioned Mum now, and six weeks later she was forgotten entirely by the lads. The teachers might still mutter about it in the staffroom, but not in front of me. Though I would long remember Mum in that front-page photo wearing a glittery teen-top, grinning by a mountain of Bacardi Breezers: GOOD-TIME GIRL GOES AWOL.

When I first saw that I vommed up in the toilet with shame.

'So what do you think I should do?' she asked again, just like, 'Come on, darling, tell me really what you think about Tony,' which she'd asked twice this morning before breakfast. Hoping I'd make all the decisions for her.

'Think and Tony are not two words you should expect to hear often in your marriage, Mum,' I replied. Tony even smoked his skinny cigars while he ate, and because of that I'd refused breakfast though the buffet was lush, and I was well hungry.

'OK, Elle, perhaps he's not the sharpest knife in the box,' Mum had said, nursing her black coffee and frowning anxiously. I felt loved when I made her worried, though I knew this was childish and wrong.

'He's not even in the box, Mum,' I exclaimed, 'he's a lump of rock cavemen use to beat corn.'

'When I first met him, a few months back in that bar in the store . . .'

'Weeks, Mum,' I sobbed, surprised by my sudden hot spring of tears, 'you've only known him a few weeks, and before that you were in love, madly, with someone else. By the time we get out this hotel you'll probably be engaged to the doorman.'

She blew air down her nose and closed her eyes. I'd wanted to ask if we could go to the cinema at the weekend, but I knew we couldn't because that's no honeymoon. Which made me remember Tony. 'Elle, I was going to say that he kind of reminded me of someone on the television.'

'Yeh, in *The Flintstones*,' I'd said and stormed off to a table at the far corner of the breakfast room, and tried to work out how I could have the mega full English without enduring shame.

'I had been drinking when I met him,' she confessed later, when we were about to get into our dresses.

'Really, well gee that is shocking,' I said with my eyebrows up in my freaky fringe. 'Imagine you! Drinking!'

She stroked my face and I slapped her away and she looked hurt and said, 'He's one of the best sales reps in the entire Yorkshire region.'

'How fascinating.'

'He's kind.'

'Mum, you get a kitten for kind.'

'Kittens don't bring home a wage packet, love.'

'The ones in advertising do.'

'You're saying I'd be better off with a pretty pet than with Tony?'

'You'd be better off with a brain injury, Mum,' I cried, and very dramatically I put my head on the bed and wept – as much for my lost breakfast as anything. 'Haven't you noticed how much time he spends looking in the mirror?'

'That's no bad thing in a man, sweetie.'

'It is if you look like Tony, Mum.'

'He's better looking than George.'

'A road accident is better looking than George.'

'I thought George was very sweet.'

'Yeh, for someone dug up from a cemetery at midnight.' Then I say, 'Mum, why have you turned to the oldsters?' And suddenly, because of the way she smiles sadly, I know.

'One day you'll understand,' she says.

A lad at school had said that if I called a newspaper myself I could sell my true story of my life with Mum. I'd say how she went from loving a teenager to loving an OAP. WHORE'S DAUGHTER TELLS ALL, the lad who'd suggested it had said.

'I won't marry him if you don't like him,' Mum sniffed as the limo took another sharp turn, and I looked up and said, 'OK, I don't like him.'

'Well then, that's it.'

'Oh, yeh, right. Like I believe that. Remember I'm the kid who battled against abandonment and fear, without a penny for food . . .'

'You had a freezer full of pizzas and you know it . . .'

'. . . for a whole week!'

The best headlines in the papers had said: HEROINE IN THE NIGHT, LOYAL DAUGHTER DETERMINED TO SURVIVE. And my favourite: TOUGH LITTLE COOKIE SITS IT OUT. Soon I would take all my cuttings and put them in a scrapbook, maybe get that last headline blown up and strung above my bed, or, as Ashanti had suggested, tattooed on my backside for all eternity, because Ashanti is usually my best friend though every few weeks she says, 'I'm not talking to you. I'm not your friend,' and goes off and refuses to even look at me, and some days she makes fun of what Claire puts in the lunchbox, but Ashanti's still the best Barbie clothes-maker you'll ever meet. And I was chuffed she was jealous of my headlines. 'Tough little cookie sits it out, right there on your arse,' Ashanti said. 'God, I wish I had headlines.'

'Because of you I've got headlines,' I say, pressing my thumbs into my eyeballs so I got a flashing headache and yelped with the pain.

'Well, because of you I've had head lice three times,' Mum said, and I remember Mum squealing as she combed them out of our hair, drowning them in a glass of water and then lining them on the edge of the bath and counting them up, like they were a haul of sharks. Unlike Claire, who snaps on rubber gloves and splashes on the chemicals, which burn off our scalps.

We're still going round and round the ring road, and I'm still whistling *Mary Poppins* tunes because I refused to be the one to decide if she should marry or not. She'd have to learn to say yes or no for herself. I had already given her my wisest wisdom. I want her to say no. Otherwise I would never have her to myself, alone together, ever again. And I was not just being selfish; I also knew the troll was not good for her. Earlier this morning, as we were almost fully dressed in our freaky bridal outfits, the furry rims stitched to our sleeves, I'd looked at us both side by side in the mirror and said solemnly, 'You have to stop leaping into things, Mum.'

'I'm one of life's leapers, honey.'

'That's why they worry about you.'

'Claire and Dad worry about me in the way people worry about UFOs, because they've made their lives so flaming lily-white they've nothing else to worry about.' Then she surprises me by saying, 'That's why they made such a fuss about Marcel.'

Now, because I remember this, I say, 'They think you could have caused the death of me.'

'What, death by pizza?'

'No, by child neglect,' I say very sombrely, pronouncing the words as the policeman had, and trembling my bloodied bottom lip. 'I am that neglected child. If that Asian hadn't . . .'

She sighs and lets her head hit the window heavily. 'His name's Amir, Elle. And I've said how sorry I am. And yes, I was crazy at the time, I can't explain it. I was in love. But how many times do I have to say it: I didn't know you were there!'

I look hurt, heartbroken and sad, but have to balance this, so I don't set her off crying, or flick her switch to loon. 'We think you're so impulsive that you risk your life and other people's lives,' I say, repeating what Claire had said to Dad as the two of them looked through the pile of newspapers. Claire has them all saved. Clips from my mum's tragic life are the inky heirlooms she'll pass through the generations.

Some days, most days, I wondered if Mum and Dad might even get back together but they probably never would – so it was up to me to save her. But how could you save someone you didn't understand? 'You make me sound like a drunk driver,' Mum sighs.

'Precisely, drunk in charge of a . . .'

'Heart.'

'Oh, purlease, Mum!'

'I don't know any other way to live, darling, except in the fast lane.'

'Well, Mum, now you've lost your licence, and so you'll have to start taking the bus.'

'But that's what I'm trying to do! By marrying Tony. I'm taking the bus!'

'Not that bus! Any bus but that bus!'

A posh people-carrier full of dirty football lads goes by backwards in the slow lane and I watch them go and one sees me, smiles, then is gone, and I feel suddenly hopeless and begin to cry and when she reaches out for me, I turn away and remember how a few hours earlier, as we had put on our wedding make-up, I had slammed down the blue mascara and screamed at her in the mirror, because even then I knew the freaky blush-pink dress looked well wrong. Elle-boy wasn't the kind of girl that the lads went for, not like the perfect Steps, and I felt miserable when I tried to change my face. It didn't worry me usually, though when I looked at Mum it worried me that it would worry me one day. One day soon, and every year it would get worse, until I looked like Gran. That ancient relic had been pictured in the paper with her crunchy chin pulled so far in that it crumpled her neck all tortoisey. Below the picture it said, 'She's made her bed, now she can lie in it.' Another paper carried an 'exclusive': MY LIFE WITH RUNAWAY MUM, BY THE ONE WHO KNOWS HER BEST – HER OWN MOTHER! When Gran read it she was so shamed she even rang Mum to almost apologise.

'I wish I'd been a better mother,' Mum says, and then turns away and apologises because even for Miss Manipulation that was too much, too like things that Gran says, so Mum changes and says, 'Help yourself to champagne, darling.'

'Oh, are you out of cocaine?' I say and roll my eyeballs. 'Mum! I can't drink yet. Even if I am Daughter of Troubled Alcoholic Jackie Jackson, the law still applies.'

'Well, I know that, honey, I just want you to know it's here if you want to try it. And it's not every day we are tearing around in a limousine.'

'Round in circles, waiting for you to decide what to do – to say yes or no, I do or I don't.'

I look at her with huge pleading baby eyes – *just say no.*

'Who else is going to drink it? I'm off the booze, I've told you that.'

'You. Later, I bet. That's who. You. When you are back on it. In about an hour's time. Don't forget you have "a history of alcohol misuse and a string of failed relationships".'

'You really have a fantastic memory, darling.'

'You are the original Boozy Blonde Mother of One, for now and for ever.'

She closed her eyes, rested against the window and said, 'Yep, I want that on my gravestone: Here lies the Boozy Blonde Mother of One, bad wife, bad mother, bad daughter, bad friend; a string of failed relationships and a long history of alcohol abuse.'

I wanted her to hold my hand but she doesn't even try.

Worst were the quotes that came from friends and family, because it was like they weren't even describing a living person; instead my mum was just a locked door they had battered down, only to find a room filled with rotten food and flies. One 'close friend' said, 'Jackie Jackson has never had any trouble finding a man, though she's no oil painting.' Another 'neighbour' said, 'Men just go for her, every time. I've no idea why.' A 'former colleague' said, 'Despite the fact that she's hardly a beauty she is an unstoppable man magnet. It's scary to see her in action.' 'She's pushing forty but I've seen her eating up blokes half her age,' another 'family friend' had said.

I wondered which 'friend' was really that Asian. And how much cash he'd got for it. She could probably sue that bastard, though she'd probably not even try. She was probably wondering instead what Marcel would think, if he was reading it, wherever he was, and I feel car-sick again because the driver was going round the ring road faster now and looking at us annoyed in the rear-view mirror. I looked at him and shrugged then mouthed the word 'sorry', and pointed a finger at my mum. 'This is making me dizzy,' I say and it's true, and that my eyelids feel sticky with the weight of wedding-day shadow, and I can feel a little crackle around my mouth when I smile through the putty-thick foundation. I needed a cigarette or a gun, because in the papers they'd gone for very innocent babyish pictures of me, set alongside Mum's peroxide-slut bar-room grin.

'So where are we going?' Mum said, turning to me as if I was the most adult person there. 'We won't get a place in a hotel anywhere. It's Christmas Day tomorrow.'

'You really are going to just leave him there! Usually if you are in doubt as to what to do, you just go along with things.'

I wanted to ask her more, so I could try to understand, but instead I just fold my arms super-tight and scowl.

'Leaving as in liberating, love.'

'Leaving as in dumping,' I say with a very shocked gasp and snap round of my head.

'It wouldn't be right to go through with it,' she says quietly. 'You're right, I'd be the wolf pretending to be the wife. That's wrong.'

'Just because something's not right doesn't mean you shouldn't do it,' I say. 'Isn't that your motto, Mother?'

Claire says Mum isn't in control of her life, which is why I can't stay over midweek because if I did I'd be late for school. I know if Mum lived with Tony I'd probably only see her about twice a year.

'We won't find anywhere to stay tonight, Elle.'

'Perhaps we could go to a bar and pick up some guys and ask them if we could stay the night at theirs,' I say. I keep thinking that Asian might turn up at the wedding; he might come after her again, angry that she got out on bail and wanting her punished properly. If I see a red Vauxhall car by the time I count to five then we will be OK. If I don't we won't.

'It'd be better than our house,' she says, rubbing at her forehead, which is pencilled in a wavy pattern. 'It needs a tidy up. But I never have the time.'

Time, Claire says, is the most important gift you can give another person. When I'd asked Claire what she wanted for Christmas she said, 'More time with my family.' Though she doesn't work, and is in the house all day. I think Claire said this as a way of getting at Mum, but what she said was true too, because people often tried to get away from Mum after they'd gotten what they wanted from her – sex, secrets, shocks – and they hardly give her any time at all because they are afraid of her. So I say, 'I'll stay over with you tonight,' when I see a red Vauxhall nip past us on the inside lane.

'But it's Christmas Eve, Elle,' she says, surprised and happy, and I wonder if getting wed to caveman Tony on Christmas Eve was simply so that she would not be alone again on Christmas Day. Last year, after it all burned up with Marcel, she came to our house and sat drunk on the carpet, until Claire had to make her lie down on the settee, where she snored until lunchtime when Claire freaked and sent her home in a taxi.

When I'd asked Dad what he wanted for Christmas he'd said, 'Peace and quiet.' Which is why he probably couldn't live with Mum again, even if she did want to get back with him.

'I want to stay with you this Christmas, OK,' I say. And for a while she goes all wet-eyed and sniffy, and I have to fight her off because she's trying to kill me with cuddles.

'Perhaps I could make it work with Tony,' she sighs, ignoring the driver who is making annoyed gestures, but pulling me firmly against her dress, so my head is tucked against her warm soft bazookars.

'You could have made it work with Dad.'

'If I'd been a different person.'

'Yes. If you'd been Claire. If you'd been a bit tidier and a bit stupider. Is that a word, Mum? Stupider?'

'Only where Claire's concerned,' she says and strokes my cheek, grinning. 'Only then is it exactly the right word.'

'If you're not turning up, Mum, we need to get out of this city.' I say this with a wide-eyed and serious grimace. 'In case he comes after you.'

Him and the lousy Asian.

PART TWO

AMIR

I'd only been to her house a couple of times, before that day I called round in October and found little Elle home alone. The first time was early one morning back in April. I was nervous, perhaps because Ashfaq had been insisting I make a decision about Uma. So I popped over just to take my mind off because, boy, could Jackie witter; she'd chatter the troubles out of you. And I liked the idea of peeping where slutty Jackie lived, get a better all-round look at Motormouth in her natural setting, unmade-up, without heels, drowsy in a silky see-through, maybe an edge of lacy underwear, dirty off-white dreams in her smoky eyes, and the wicked morning smell of her. Just remind myself of how right Ashfaq was. About the dangers.

That April my brother had been back from Pakistan for three days, but it felt like three years, and though we tried not to argue in front of our mother, me and him were always inches from a whack in the chops. He had his own big pad above Fags 'n' Fings but he preferred to live like a hotel guest in my small family home where he was constantly online, with me and Ma and Halima bringing cups of tea and generally skivvying round his royal personage. Which he's puffed out by hours at the gym so his steel biceps were bigger than my thighs, and his neck's an iron barrel. Of course the asshole couldn't understand why I didn't like having him around, because he might be more than twenty years older than me, but he's centuries behind in IQ.

As I tell him, he has the money but I have the brains – and the looks.

That April morning he'd called me into our kitchen and stood there before Ma, stroking the head of his little Halima, like the wife was his mascaraed show dog. Ashfaq was holding a measly computer picture of the latest 'cousin', fat little Uma. 'Look at this beauty,' he said as he held the picture up high, like he wanted me to kneel down and pray to the grainy mutt. 'You won't know what happiness is until you're married, bro,' Ashfaq said, pointing a chubby thumb at Uma's technicolour cheek.

'Yeh, but then it's too late, bro,' I said and he grabbed me by the tie and pulled me purple though Ma was yanking her hair and yelling for him to stop and Wahida was shouting that she was refusing to get involved, because Wahida says being sister to me and Ashfaq is like being an extra in a scary movie.

Ma wasn't proper ill then, just forgetful and repetitive, but she got bothered, shouty and confused if Ashfaq and I got fist fighting. So I flew straight out, and before I knew it wandered round on buses to where hollow-cheeked, brown-toothed lads in tracky bottoms dragged on sorrow on street corners, and flags of St George chomped from chimney pots, slapped on mossy rooftops, letting us know whose manky patch this was. Where the ratty lasses with tank-sized pushchairs wore track-suits and gold chains, hair scraped back from grey faces into limp rodent tails. Some of the low council houses still had gardens with those tiny-leaf emerald hedges, spreading rose bushes, a few heavy perfumed blooms, yellow or red, thicker than fists, but most had been crashed over into car parks, not even paved, just rolled over and over until every rusty car was kissing a rotten windowsill.

And life was more weathery there, rain wetter, wind harder, and the sun took just moments to burn. No wonder Jackie had cooked up the way she had. Still, walking there, to her, I see spring trees clouded pink with blossom and I think: confetti.

Confetti, there, where I have to remind myself of what Ashfaq says, how all the mothers are single and the mini-motorbike-riding ASBO teens are on crack and the tiny fatherless kids have well-dirty slogans on their T-shirts and sugar stains mapped on their lazy pinky faces. Though I didn't care because Jackie's the kind of lass who makes you go places you shouldn't, wouldn't, but couldn't not, even if you feel a beat of fear, glimpsing addicts in every bush, knives in every fag-stained thuggy hand. I listened and looked – but tried not to stare – and I thought I really might get stabbed in that godless place. Then again, getting murdered would save me from getting married.

Soon I found my naughty knuckle tap-tapping on a red rattly door. I prepared a few casual, yet hot and witty remarks. Then she opened the door dressed in her feathery You Crazy Chick! skirt.

My life as a tarty chicken. Fake-tan roasted. I gasped. Felt faint. Because it was the first time I'd seen with my own pervy eyes what I'd heard so much about: the day in question being the beginning of the store's 'chick-themed fun'. This required the store's female staff dressing up in tight buttercup-yellow tops with yolk-coloured fluff around the plunging neckline, and a feathery lemony mini-skirt, extra short. On their backs, strapped with glittery elastic, just a pair of gossamer wings, fluttery-filthy.

'Huh, hi,' I said and behind me I could hear a wolf whistle.

'Huh, hi, hon,' she grinned, and leant over to kiss me on the cheek. 'What you doing round 'ere, love?'

She smelt like she had just bathed in beer. She pulled a couple of times on her skirt hem. Pale thighs sandwich-bread soft. 'Hi,' and the only thing I could think to say was, 'hard-boiled egg.'

She left me brain-dead every time. Because there she was – the plumped-up big bird, stuffed with smiles – wearing the mad store outfit at home. Typical. She dressed like she was nineteen. Orla insisted the store presented its 'youth, style, sexual confidence and internationalism on all levels', which Jackie said was 'more likely to make us a terrorism target than a retail powerhouse'. Still. Spectacle was her second name. No wonder no man had been able to live with a woman like that.

She was mental, and so purely chick that I look down at her silver high heels expecting webbed feet.

I should have listened to Ashfaq and never come. Though I always knew there was treasure submerged in her, some precious wreck undiscovered by any other living man, and maybe this is what sent me diving down into her dark depths again and again. 'Amir, love, what on earth are you wearing?' she said, and smiled as I fell for it and looked down at my black work suit and she bit her bottom lip as she tickled me hard in the belly, warm fingers pressing my aching skin. She made me laugh in the way no one else could: suddenly and even when the joke was on me.

Actually for once, Orla had spared the guys – we were not to be 'crazy cocks' as Jackie had told us a week earlier. Nattered on and on about it. 'You have to strap on a great phallus and walk around the store going cock-a-doodle-doo every forty minutes,' she'd insisted to Leo. 'But I guess you won't find it that hard,' she'd smiled at him, my boss and her ex.

Dirty bugger.

And she kept the tease going for an entire week, so by Friday Leo had passed the crazy-cock information on to us all, his entire team, and we were well ready to strap on our cock and crow, but, no, it wasn't true, we just had to wear our regular all-black store uniforms, and display an arrangement of 'exotic chocolate eggs' on our till point.

Still, I thought of Ma watching the crazy chicks, every young-enough woman in Womenswear, who had to parade around the store every forty minutes, wiggling their arses, shaking their wings and smiling while tweeting. And I thought of Pa too, forever wondering why I'd chosen to join the circus rather than settle down with Uma to make chubby brown bairns.

'Tweet, tweet, love me, I'm not a real mad, bad woman at all, I'm just a baby chicken, Amir,' Jackie said when she first heard about the promotion. Like a traffic roar female non-stop chat rattled through the day and I couldn't get a joke in edgeways – even if I'd been the jokey type. Though I knew well enough that if you made birds chirp you had it in the bag. 'Tweetie, you're a fashion specialist in one of Europe's premier stores,' Marilyn had sighed. 'Fashion specialist, my arse! It's like being on the till in the supermarket only you can't get cut-price bread at the end of the day, love,' Jackie had replied.

I was just panting at her, as if I were a dog under a spell. She pulled at her hem again, wiggled her shoulders and said, 'Basically, Amir love, it's just another is-she-isn't-she naked malarkey.' She was plenty naked, and she knew it. She'd stuck with the same tarty style she had as a girl, tight dresses, cleavage, heels, make-up, plenty of hair and bare. And she'd not gone the way of the clean, neat, busy, big-handbaggy, middle-ageing mams I saw roboting around the store, spinning urgent thinness. No. Plump, blonde Jackie still looked young, sexy, energetic and deeply darkly.

Dangerous, remember.

And as I stood on that doorstep, where above so-perfect white clouds were coming over super-fast, I thought I might be carried up into the air because around that wicked lass my man's heart was ruined, turned into one big pink, gimpy-soft balloon.

'I just needed you to bring some hard-boiled eggs in. For the promotion,' I said and grinned – for, yes, I was the original village idiot.

And then there, behind my chick, back in the manky kitchen, I saw that little girl, Elle, for the first time, eating breakfast, scowling at me – not even a kitchen really, just a scratchy wood table in the side of a living room that also featured a cooker and fridge and a bank of cupboards, the air singed with toastiness, a pile of bills on the cheap table, heap of washing up. 'What does she spend the money on?' I asked Marilyn later in the year, when I heard about Jackie's debts. 'Living for today,' Marilyn had replied, and Ma said this was the problem; instant gratification, like all Ashfaq's godless Englishers; no hope for the future, unable to face their ruined pasts. Like Ma now, no memory, no plans, just the wild moment.

Fifty per cent of me loved Jackie for it, and fifty per cent hated it. 'How hard do you want it?' she says. This is it. 'The egg, love,' she said, and for what seemed like hours her and I discussed how to do it perfectly: boil an egg.

I decided she'd been dressing up to amuse her daughter: probably, she was likely to be that kind of hormone-crazed, over-energetic madcap northern single mam who dyes blonde hair red for charity and wins all races at sports day and before long will be snogging her daughters' little lad mates at teen parties.

How wise I would be to choose Uma.

Then I noticed all the house plants were dead. It was startling to see so many dry brown skeletons in pots, when my own ma had once had good green fingers (what a sorrow, what an insult, my youngest sister Samirah said now, that the forest of ferns in Cosy Retreat was dusty plastic). In Jackie's house the plants were dying on the window ledge, dead on the sideboard, a great yucca crinkling to a khaki ash by the gas fire. The money plant had shed its leaves in a pool of pats like wizened palms. Even for plant life that lass was lethal; could make you blossom one minute, wilt down dead the next.

'I think they needed more water and less nicotine,' Jackie said when she saw me looking. She smoothed down her silky yellow feathers and leant against the pale doorway, and dragged deep on her fag like a – it's wrong but . . . chicky hooker. 'I kept meaning to give up for their sake, Amir.'

By Jackie's sink an empty bottle – of gin probably. She was a drinker, that chatterbox; big noisy trouble. Keep back. Ashfaq was right: those estate gorehs were in the estate they were in because they'd forgotten the importance of family; of mothering and homemaking and cooking and . . . Yes, I would have nothing more to do with them. I would go home immediately and propose to Uma because Ashfaq's right again: we have to find someone dependable and kind: some good woman to help us, soon.

'Yep, all your plants are beyond saving, Jack. There's nothing anyone can do.'

'Don't say that, Amir!' she cried, pressing her warm moist hand over my dry mouth, 'surely there must be someone who can help.' And I laughed, but immediately I stopped and knew it had been a mistake to go there, to the house, the kitchenette, the washing drying, the sewerage smells seeping from the downstairs toilet, which had a chipped beige door open on to the kitchen. Like at Cosy Retreat when you stumble off that bright main corridor into a skanky cell that rellies were not intended to find – mops, potties, incontinence nappies, chemical sprays stacked up – and the throat-lump sad of seeing how things really are, not how you want to pretend they are.

Then when it felt real bad, it got badder – I peeped from the corner of my eye a movie prince watching me from the bottom of the stairs, so sheepish he could have been going baaa.

Oh, the dirty dog. Though I'm still whammed every time by how shamelessly those gora guys use her. And how she can't see it. Or can see it and doesn't care. Or does care and so pretends not to see it.

He curls a snowy paw in my direction, like a total dickhead royal. 'Amir, this is Daniel, he found me on the internet,' she said and the pair of them laughed like bullies. 'You make it sound seedy,' the prince oiled, and I noticed that our Jackie had a bloom on her that might have been chick make-up but was probably morning sex, though she'd told me that since she'd stopped drinking she'd had to stop going out and so all fun had ceased – though in staff meetings Orla sometimes offers a piece of wisdom: 'Women are judged on haircut, nails, handbag and shoes; nothing else matters.' 'Remember that, Amir,' Jackie had whispered to me in the briefing meeting (like some bad school lass, if she couldn't talk out loud she'd whisper and if she couldn't whisper she'd mouth the words, and if she couldn't mouth the words she'd write little notes with bubbles over her 'i's and 'j's and ten question marks), 'when you storm your brains to think of what your Pakistani brides want.'

'I don't want a fashion dummy for a wife,' I'd whispered, as we pansied around the store, getting our daily orders from Orla, 'I know that much.'

'Oh, I don't know,' she'd pouted, and pretended to luridly squeeze the plastic crotch of a nearby mannequin. 'Consider for a moment, this strong silent type, Amir.' And then she rubbed noses with the mannequin and tickled its chin, though she knew Orla was watching hard.

'Is that what you lasses want in your blokes nowadays?' I ask seriously, because I'd read something like it in one of Ashfaq's magazines. But Jackie sighs and shakes her head and walks away from the mannequin. 'Not for me, Amir. Been there, done that. No, now I want a real flesh and blood thinking man, who I can really talk to, who makes me laugh. I don't really care what he looks like. How symmetrical, tall or toned he is. I definitely don't want rock hard and plastic. No, as long as he's honest and open and funny and kind I'll leave the muscles, tans and chins to another lass.'

'That's the problem with the brides anyway,' I said quickly, burning up a blush.

Jackie and I look at each other then, eye on eye, wet lipped.

'They don't answer back, Jack. I like a woman with a bit of fire in her.'

The white glittering store was as quiet as a mountainside. The whole Fourth Floor Customer Service Morning Team were ear-wigging, but Jackie just carried on, like it was a privilege for those losers to listen to us. 'Ah, you think that now, love, but wait until your house is burning down, Amir.'

Now I looked at the handsome fucker by her side and realised all she'd said back then had been lies. 'I used to know his brother,' she said. The movie lad came up and put his arm around her and she was stroking him, just as she had the store dummy. He held her, grinning, like our Jackie was a cuddly toy he'd just won on the hook-a-duck. And as he stroked her white hair I thought of Ma's hair, wired up like a scouring pad, and I repeated my dicky excuse about hard-boiled eggs for You Crazy Chick! month and she promised that she'd boil one up, extra hard.

It was sad, wrong and one hundred per cent despicable but knowing another bloke had her, well, it affected me and as I was turning to leave I mumbled about how well the costume worked, and she said softly, so I could hear, and her mincing pimp could not, 'How did we come to this, Amir? Screwing dummies and wearing freaking fancy dress for work – and quite happily! Without any extra money! What happened to unions? Someone must have removed our brains in our sleep.'

She looked vulnerable, and because of that I believed she was being honest.

'My brother thinks the store's done it,' I said, 'he thinks I'll burn for working there.'

'Now, tell me how is your brother and his beard?'

She no longer looked vulnerable – just a moment, then gone.

'Ma and I are just relieved neither of them are in Guantánamo Bay,' I say, but already she is turning and moving back to her blond mannequin in the dark hall, and I felt as I often would around Jackie: that I had betrayed myself and my family. She had all the fashionable prejudices about us lot and I shouldn't have been surprised because she was just a regular slutty white lass from a bad part of town. 'Is Ashfaq out of bed yet?' Ma had asked me that April morning. I told her Ashfaq was at work, and she asked me again and then again, and the last time she said, 'Because if he's not he's going to be late for school.'

I wanted to cry.

'Guantánamo Bay!' Jackie shouted back to me. 'Now that's an idea. That would keep me out of trouble.' And I heard the white prince laugh and there was a whoop and giggle and the sound of her falling and the little girl shouting out, 'Muuuuum!'

This was seven months before prison became a real probability.

ELLE

Right from last April I knew life was going totallytrouble.com. Picture the scene: we two walking down an unfamiliar blossomy street and I see Mum's freshly done fingernails flashing like tiny flames. 'Hey, I've just remembered,' she says, 'someone I know is having a gathering round here today.' Then she moves her shoulders up and down, smiling, 'Oooh, Elle.'

'A gathering?' I said, voice flat as my lousy chest. 'What's a gathering when it's at home?' Which is one of Dad's annoying phrases but Mum doesn't even notice I'm quoting him.

'Exactly that, love, people gathering – at home.'

'Why?'

'Hmm. We'll just pop in.'

'Is it a drinking party?'

'Nope honestly, Elle, this liver is now safe,' she said and clutched at her half-naked upper body and laughed and promised that if anyone offered her a drink she was going to tackle her hardest word: n.o. If anyone even offered her a liqueur chocolate she would gasp in shock, and *no no no*. But I'd got a sulk on by then, and suggested she say something simpler: 'My name is Jackie Jackson and I am an alcoholic.' So she looked at me like I'd pinched her hard with the badly bitten stumps I call fingernails, though really I wanted her to stroke my cheek with the shining red discs of her nails. But she don't, and so, 'OK,' I said, rolling my eyes, 'I'll come with you to the *gathering*, but not for long and you have to promise you won't . . .'

And she gives me her cheeky-minx wiggle and says, 'Well, I can't be woozy at work again, not with Mr Coriander about.'

Er? Excuse me?

'Oh no,' she continues, 'not again, not with Mr Chutney looking at me like I am the reason for all that is wrong in the West.'

Ladies and gentlemen, put your hands together for Mr Chutney! Who will this latest charmer be then? Yes, I think that April walk was the first time she truly mentioned the Asian to me. She wanted me to be chuffed and to ask about him, though she knew that after the business with Marcel I asked no questions when she mentioned a man. Still, she mentions Mr Chutney, or Mr Coriander, a few more times, so I have to spin my eyeballs about and shout, 'Mum, I'm not interested in your sex life, accept it and move on.'

Though I'm jigsawing it all together super-quick, because this weekend Big Marilyn came round while I was there, and I heard them in the kitchen – on about something to do with new stock-control guidelines, and then about how Mum had made the mistake of telling some man about the reasons for her hangover. He flinched when she spoke, and then put on 'his Taliban stare' and said, 'Why do you go out on an evening and act like the worst kind of English bloke, Jackie?' 'Would you prefer to keep me under curfew, love?' Mam asks him.

Anyway Cherub says coriander tastes like water from the swimming pool. But then again she's also started lying on the settee for hours, just occasionally saying things like, 'Shit, time is really dragging her heels in the sand.' And Mum once said that she imagines living at Claire's to be like being in hospital; sunny, white and bleachy-smelling, quiet and hygienic, safe, nutritious meals at regular times. Well, not any more, not now Cherub's a teenager; now it's like living in a boarding school in Freaksville ruled by one extremely vicious head girl.

We keep walking, and I want Mum to suggest we go to a restaurant for burgers and chips but I know she won't because she's almost skipping along to this gathering, so I have my hands deep in my pockets, and I'm picking at the fluff. Luckily I am also wearing Cherub's grey sweatshirt, which I just filched out the washing basket, and feel well chuffed because I don't know who'd be more effing angry, the Steps for me nicking it, or Claire for me wearing something dirty and crinkly. Claire is very into ironing. She is also very into never leaving washing up in the bowl. And not just tooth brushing but dental flossing. Claire says, 'People notice these things.' That's one of her phrases. One of my mum's phrases is, 'Let 'em think what the bloody 'ell they like.'

So I was fizzing up about the mysterious Mr Coriander and about having to go to the gathering, and about the Steps hating me, and kind of upset too because Mum's cash card was saying no, wouldn't give out a penny, and I'm remembering all kinds of horrid things. Like yesterday Mum asking Gran to lend her some money and Gran saying, 'You've had two husbands, Jacqueline, shouldn't one of them be paying something towards your upkeep?' Mum replies, 'You make me sound like a stray, Mam.' 'If you were a stray, Jacqueline, someone would have deemed you a public nuisance, if not a health risk, and put you down long ago.' And then I'm remembering Dad refusing to pay the maintenance and shouting, 'You will just have to accept you are not getting any of my bloody money, Jackie.' And then the flash-thought of her and Big Marilyn talking about this bus-driving mate of Danuta's. 'The one you shagged at the bus stop,' I heard Big Marilyn say.

'You were intending it as a laugh.' 'Well, it certainly made the bus stop!' Mum shrieks.

'Jackie Jackson: same old queasy story,' that's what Claire once said when Dad was telling her the latest.

I fold my arms, and try to make my shoulders touch my ears and think that if I see a black cat by the time I count to ten Mum will be OK and won't die until she's really old. The Steps' dad died. That's really, really sad, obviously, and a bit unfair too, because everyone feels sorry for the tragic orphans and no one cares about me.

Though I should admit Mum didn't think I was staying over. That's why she smelt different; warm and oily. I had only at the last minute, when she was already zipping up her dress, said I was staying for another night. She paused in her zip-tugging and looked off into the distance, crunchy-headed, like she's doing some very complicated maths. 'Oh,' she said, 'I wish you'd said that before, love.'

Cherub says my mum looks so much like a tart she should live in the baker's window. Though I don't cry any more when they say stuff like that.

Then she's taking off her dress, and putting on a different one, though the warm and spicy oil smell stays.

It was a half lie that I'd only just decided to say. Actually I have a very clever plan. I tell Dad I'm staying over with Mum for three nights and I tell Mum I'm staying with her for two nights. It helps that they are what the judge called 'still two very hurt and angry people utterly unable to communicate on even the most basic level'. This means if Mum's so-called life is stressing me I just go home as she expects me to, but if I'm having a good wild un-Claire time, with restaurants and shopping and DVDs, I stay, for what she thinks is an extra day. And it works for everyone – because if I come home when Mum thinks my time is up, Dad thinks I'm coming home early, and is so chuffed by the thought that I'm choosing him over

Mum. And if I come home at the time Dad thinks I'm coming home, Mum is so chuffed by the thought that I'm choosing her over Dad. Win win; one side always happy, the other side often monster happy.

Though I sometimes think that if they do ever get back together then all this daft plotting will come out. Though probably they won't. And if they do, I won't worry any more about anything, certainly not everyday lousy shit like getting told off.

We keep walking, not noticing the rain flicks on our bare arms, and gee, the hours just fly by as she chats about her job and her plans for the future. I'm staring in the opposite direction, but listening keenly for another mention of Mr Coriander. Mum just brushes her hands over my hair and my T-shirt, smoothing me out, and I like it though I push her away and sulk on, stroking at Cherub's top myself.

Mum's told me many times how it makes her feel, seeing me wearing things she's not bought. Like it's my fault I'm from a broken home! And then there's Claire, who don't like me to wear stuff Mum's bought, and only irons the stuff she's bought, so I have to smooth Mum's stuff out with my bare hands. It's actually a bloody miracle I wear any clothes at all!

Ashanti says she's seen one of her mum's boyfriends naked, but it's probably a lie.

'Always sober, always calm; that lad thinks he's a god-damned superhero, Elle,' Mum sighed, as we turned off the main road and down a smart cul-de-sac. 'And if those big brown eyes were fingers they'd be constantly wagging.'

She says Mr Chutney's always frowning at her in case she takes a smile or a friendly word as encouragement. 'I mean, Elle, I honestly don't want to think of the Asians in the way your gran does but when they won't talk to you as an equal then it's hard.'

I start whistling a tune to the trees.

It's true that Gran dislikes many people, but particularly the Asians. She blames them for rising house prices, for litter on the street, for drugs, for terrorism, for not saying hello at the market, for getting down the supermarket extra-early and buying up all the special-offer two for ones. For being too religious, and for having cocainey shags on a lunchtime in the car park near her house. Some days she thinks they are all too strict and hard and other days that they are all too dirty and loose. Sometimes because she can't see them behind those spooky veils, and sometimes because she can see them everywhere.

'You know, Elle, every break time when he goes to get a cappuccino he brings me one back too! Without me even asking!' Mum says, dreamily.

Most of what I know about the Asians I've got off Gran. Until she explained I thought Muslim was that white cloth Claire puts round the Christmas pudding. Now I know all about the Taliban and how Asians keep their men and women apart and how the men go after tarts like Mum because their own lasses aren't allowed to be sluts.

'It's as if he thinks frothy coffee might save me, Elle.' And then she gives me a raised-eyebrow smile which I can only translate as meaning: you've either got it or you haven't, love. 'Though actually Amir's brilliant with his sick mother. He wraps up meals every evening, ready for when he's out at work, and gets up in the night with her. He does everything, even though he has three older sisters and a sister-in-law. A lesser man would leave everything to them, don't you think? But he really does his share. He really cares for her.'

'Aww, bless,' I say, and then hope it came out right – I tut and roll my eyes to be sure. I wasn't meaning it in the sicky pet-loving Christian way, like Claire when she encounters any tiny drop of human innocence. I was meaning: you sentimental goddamned fool, Mother.

I just can't imagine it, what it must be like in their families, where I guess there are about twenty folk under one roof babbling and funny music, candles maybe, religious shrines, goats, satellite TV beaming in news from the East, incense, chanting, mumbly praying and the stink of tandoori all around. Maybe a scraggy monkey on a rope. I wouldn't say this to anyone at school, even though there's hardly any Asians there, but that's how I imagine it.

We are looking for the door. I am worrying that we are on the wrong street. Or that the party is over and she doesn't know. Or that she's been invited as a cruel joke and when she opens the door blokes will fall over laughing. She really has got her teeny outfit fully co-ordinated and it's tight and sexy. Cherub is getting a body now too; and I fear it's gonna be fantastic, though I don't ever dare to stare long enough to be sure. Then again poor Claire has teeny tits, and I'm the one likely to inherit enormous bazookas. Though there's no sign of them yet.

I wonder if Mum's borrowed the outfit from work, and if that's allowed and what if she gets sacked and has no money at all to live on, and I want her to hold my hand, but she won't, and I'm remembering now how I'd heard Mum discussing outfits with Gran, and I'm thinking how this 'gathering' is something she's been planning for ages. Gran said she didn't know what Mum should wear, then added, 'At your age lighting is all important. You should try and keep to the shadows.'

Though I've been into that posh shop where she works, and it's the opposite; so light and white that some days it's like sitting on a cloud and it's no wonder Mum acts the fluffy floaty way she does. Still Gran said that at Mum's age she needs to work in a shop lit only by candles. Mum got angry at this and said why was Gran always wanting her to know that she was old? There was a long pause, while Gran considered

Mum, like you might a child murderer on TV, trying to see exactly where the evil was in so ordinary a face and body. 'Actually you've not changed much in twenty years, Jackie.' Mum said quietly, 'Thanks.' And Gran replied, 'I don't mean your looks, Jackie. I mean your attitudes.'

And then, even worse, on the table this morning, while I was waiting for her to get over-dressed, I saw a letter she had been reading. It said: WHY WAIT FOR THINGS YOU WANT! Personally addressed, a proper letter from John Dugg, Head of Personal Loans for the Halifax. *Wouldn't a shiny car look great parked outside your house? Or perhaps a new fully-fitted kitchen would add the finishing touch to your home?* It had details about complicated bank stuff, and then said: *So what would be the finishing touch to your home?* By this Mum had written in small blue letters: *It is love.*

How sad.com is that?

And I thought of another thing I miss about her, the way she covers her daft face for the scary bits on TV, the way she loves prawn-cocktail-crisp sandwiches. And if there's any hope of her getting back with Dad it's because she still wants to be in love, she's not given up on that. Then, throat-lumped and disgusted, I threw the letter in the bin, because according to Dad they were really never going to get back, not ever. Though it kept going round like a dizzy spell: it is love, *it is* love, it is *love.*

The blood was pinking my knuckles again because we had arrived at the right white door, and Mum hurried across the garden, her spike heels sinking in the grass, and then she tugged a few times at her tiny skirt, and then knocked. How do I know her heart is racing? Because part of her blood-red heart is in me. Same way I know her knees feel a bit wobbly as she waits, and her palms are warmy wet, as an old red-eyed, no-haired granddad opened the door. 'Jackie Jackson,' Mum said. 'Though I don't know if you remember me, and this is my daughter.'

I feel suddenly ashamed, like I'm not, and never will be, pretty and titty enough, and I truly wished I was a lad; then again when Ashanti calls me Elle-boy I hate that too. Cherub says you have to dress up older than you are if you want lads to like you, and even Caprice tries to look like fifteen though she's only ten.

The door man, who is wearing a black smart suit, smiles at me sadly, and I give a tragic gaze back, accepting my misfortune at being Mum's daughter. I can smell his armpits too, and they smell nothing like my father's – and maybe this is some important clue as to why Mum sits herself in the baker's window. While Claire is mad on air-fresheners, which is why Cherub calls our house Land of Lavender. What about when she finds out I took her sweatshirt!

Then behind the man at the door I see a wash of darkly dressed bodies bending together like starlings on an overhead line and I think: has Mum dressed to fit in with the dress code of this party? No, probably not. Has Mum dressed up like a Christmas cracker because she wants to be pulled? Yes, probably.

Which means it's wrong for me to be there at all. Maybe I should call Dad.

Inside miserable women are roboting round with trays of drinks. I see no lads my age or older, though I can imagine one coming up to me and handing me a beer, and me just drinking it all down, wiping my wet mouth with the back of my wrist and throwing back the empty bottle, 'Cheers, innit.'

Mum is walking quickly, looking for someone, so I trail her sulkily wishing I'd nicked something smarter and older-looking off Cherub because this party is really deluxe and everyone is like Claire, neatly dressed and quiet and polite, and so I take a cocktail sausage and think while I eat it how disappointed

Claire would be to see me with such deadly poison. She is desperate for us all to go vegetarian, but Mum says there is 'no way on this earth!' If God had wanted me to be vegetarian, she says, he wouldn't have made me intolerant to dairy products as a baby, and Claire has no idea what I suffered as a baby because she wasn't there, and if Claire stops me eating meat Mum's definitely contacting a lawyer. So I'll probably have to be a humous-head at Claire's and a burger-babe at Mum's, though actually I might just go completely skeleton to punish the lot of them.

Then my eyes go blink blink as Mum sees a red-hot handsome man, and with a click I think, golly gosh, we really are here because of a man.

What if he is a killer, though? Claire says killers and paedophiles mainly target single mums with kids.

Why didn't I realise there'd be a man about when I first saw Mum's lousy slutty outfit? Cherub's right; women always dress up for men first, then for other girls second, and for themselves third. This is how it has to be, and if you do it the wrong way round, everyone hates you, men and women – not just murderers, everyone.

Then I suddenly recognise this man. It's the dick Mum abracadabraed into her kitchen one morning a week back. The one whose brother she knew, who was there when that Asian knocked on the door in the morning – in fact – it's all falling into place – that was probably the same Asian as she was going on about earlier, Mr Chutney. And this guy before us now is definitely the one who I hid from, and who I had to remember not to mention to Dad or Claire. The one I kept worrying about at night. The one Mum's looking at so deeply Arctic ice-caps melt. They kiss cheek to cheek, and her eye contact's superglue, and then as if magicked up by this kiss a woman appears and I feel that soft part of Mum's heart that is in me squeezed, as if in a fist. The man says something and Mum

54

mutters quietly, 'Your wife! Oh, I didn't know you were married, love. Oh, oh.'

I chew another sausage like a cowboy might a stick. When I was little I'd listen to her loud house parties between the banisters and see her, sparkled up, getting drunker and older and slurred and stoopy, falling over until finally she couldn't walk at all, and I'd often pretend to be sick myself so someone, hopefully her but usually Dad, had to keep tripping up the stairs to help me spit into a bucket.

Eating does stop you feeling nervous, but Caprice says even she knows that everyone hates fat people. I can't wait till I'm old enough to smoke; it's gonna so suit me. Plus I have heard of these headphones that cancel out absolutely all noise. They are what I am asking for for Christmas, to wear whenever I am out in public with Mum – or at home with the Steps.

But, hey, perhaps if my mother could die now she would too. Already the shock of the wife has sucked her out, she's the colour of an old mushroom and her white hair's limp. We make straight for the drinks tray and I hear her whisper, 'Didn't even know you existed, but if I am pregnant with your husband's fourth child I will be the first to let you know.'

I want another sausage. She takes a drink, though I am pulling on her wrist, so she has to transfer the tall thin glass to the other hand. And then another, before we hurry up to the bathroom and splash water on our hot faces. Side by side we look so alike, and I want her to say this, but she doesn't even seem to see me trembling there. 'I look like Gran,' Mum says quietly after several moments staring into the mirror with a look of dread; like she's expecting a decaying arm to reach out and grab her by the throat. 'Oh shit! Does that mean one day I'm going to look like you?' I say and she just leans down and hugs me, gazing with the tragic mother-look of huge meaning. 'Look like me by all means, Elle, just don't be like me, love.'

Like there's any danger there!

When we come down the stairs all the little party people in black appear like sharp type on a page. So Mum has another glass of wine and through her eyes I see the people all go wet and blurry. Because this is why people drink – to take the corners off, to hear and see less. Boozing is sulking for adults.

But I am refusing to speak a word to her now, though this means I unfortunately hear everything more. Soon I'm looking around checking for Security, but I can't see anyone capable of restraining her. So I give her a look I got from Dad; it's ninety per cent frown and says, *Whoa! Steady!* Then I knock back five lousy sausages in a row and chew them, scowling.

But then the red-hot man comes back to her and asks if there is a man in her life, and instantly I've evaporated, and she says her favourite three letters, y.e.s. Then she went on, because, she told me later, 'it seemed a shame to waste the chance to chat'. I stand by the wall like a sausage-scoffing pot plant and watch time pass in lines of golden glasses. Vikings, thousands of years ago, drank from leather tankards, and I try to think of every fact I know from my favourite subject, which is history and the old gone past. When I am older time will pass more quickly, Dad says, because I will have past memories more than present time. I will have memories like this: my mum getting lashed at a party where half the people are crying.

If I watch her without blinking I will protect her. *Steady*.

But soon she's doing the opposite of steady. She's drumming. She's banging those skins. She was the nectar and they were the bees, and I'm unable to move. 'Well, it's tricky having two guys at once,' she said.

I feel worried because I don't know what she means, but now Mum is dancing. Jesus. She is bumping into people who are looking afraid of her. She is chewing on the word 'wife'. Maybe her and Dad met like this; at a weepy party, where she was dancing, drinking, singing, and Dad had gone so blurry she didn't notice his crunchy frown. The old man who met us at the door comes over and he whispers to his son, the red-hot husband, and the husband comes over and asks how Mum is feeling. 'I'm feeling that two guys at once is tricky, but not impossible,' she says sharply. There is silence. Jesus. Mum lifts up the hem of her skirt, like she is stepping through deep water, and she's had so much booze now that if you put a match to her she'd blaze up like Claire's luxury Christmas pudding. All her limbs are oiled, moving high and smooth in lovely arcs. Then the man's wife was at Mum's side with a cup of black coffee, offering it to her like Claire did that day, like medicine. 'Perhaps she was a nurse, love,' Mum says later. 'A man likes a nursey, that's for sure.'

Then Mum jabbers on about her imaginary men, 'Yes, I do really like both of them. But it's the older guy that really does it for me. I really love him. Though I can see how some people might be surprised by that.'

I hoped she wouldn't mention her vagina. Or any words related to it.

Ashanti says she's seen loads of willies, but it's probably not true.

Listening makes your heart race, your palms sweat perfecto, and I hear Mum say, 'Well, actually one's a young guy, too young for me really but energetic, and the other man is older than me, by quite a bit really, sixty in fact.'

Dad says I can call home just to chat if I want. Of course I never do. Because when I'm with Mum it's like Dad can't exist, and same way when I'm at Claire's it's like I am another person, and my two stranger selves haven't even been introduced. 'One thing I love about older men,' Mum says, 'is how much attention they lavish on a woman.'

I see old people passing round photographs. I see women holding one another. I see shoulders being cried on. Everyone is slow and curled, becoming more like bending musical notes than sharp printed type. The husband was asking for a bucket.

Mum is laughing, weeping tears of neat vodka, and now I am hearing the music. I walk up to Mum and lead her away from her dancing self.

'Is this a funeral?' I say. She bites her lip, wipes her eyes, and then smiles drunkenly. 'And you think that's an appropriate day out for me?'

She sighs. 'It's not a day. It's an hour, honey,' she says. 'I used to know his brother. The one that's died. That's why they traced me through the internet. And I never intended you to come here today. I was going on my own until . . .'

'We've been here for three hours,' I say.

'Have we really? How time flies when you're having fun.'

She smiles at me sadly, and I want to scream because she never tells me the truth about anything. 'Is this to do with the lad you were talking to Marilyn about?'

Her brow is glistening, her cheeks are red and she's moving like she's on a jungle walkway. 'No!' she exclaims suddenly. 'Nothing at all to do with Mr Vindaloo. No, I promise. That dish is far too hot for me.'

'I'm your daughter, not your mother,' I say. 'You don't have to lie to me.'

She kisses me on the cheek and goes back to dance. I let her go and I stand watching her, wondering who died and if I'm ever going to shave my legs and wear lip gloss and have periods, then as soon as the dancing's begun it's over. 'I'll take questions from the audience,' she said, before she slid to the floor and sat there, sipping on her bleeding lip, with her legs spread wide.

But hey! Clock the knickers Mum has on, and how different her loose 'n' lacy is to Claire's tight beige thigh-huggers, which look intended for deep-sea diving. Caprice says her mum's big pants work like sausage skins; they keep the fat sucked in. Whereas my mum, dear Step, just goes for the warm meaty sizzle.

58

Remember that last Christmas Day and how I heard Caprice whisper to Cherub, 'I'm glad booze-breath isn't our mum, aren't you?'

'Yes, poor Ellie,' Cherub said excitedly. 'She'll probably end up just like that one day.' And I had to spend the whole Christmas Day pretending that my red weeping eyes were because I was allergic to pine needles.

Getting Mum out of the funeral and along the street was like walking a massive lame dog. She is reapplying her lipstick, laughing, baffling about, bending at the ankles, saying, 'Comeuppance, comeuppance, isn't that the funniest word? Comeuppance. Comeuppance see me some time.' When we finally had stumbled far enough away from the house I said, 'Is there someone we can call? A mate?' She thought for a while, swaying, then shook her head. 'Marilyn says I mustn't call Amir, not at all, no never.'

'Shall I call Dad?' I said.

'Do you think that's a good idea?' she said, smiling and stroking my hair away from my forehead. I didn't speak for ages, so she had to keep doing it. Her hand warm as bread.

'No,' I said eventually. 'Not at all.'

'Let's go home,' she says, putting her bare arm like a soft heavy scarf around my shoulders. 'Let's pull the steel shutters right down, turn the key, bolt the door, set the alarm and run upstairs to bed.'

And so we did, and when we were in bed in the dark she said, 'And anyway whatever Mr Vindaloo-breath thinks about me, before today the last time I sat on the floor drinking black coffee was that Christmas Day at Claire's. Oh God, do you remember that?'

'No,' I say.

'I came round and . . .'

'Look, Mum, I don't want to talk about anything sad.'

I can't think of any topic that is not sad and not related to Claire or the Steps, but then Mum breaks the curse of mentioning my other life and says, 'Well, have you got a snack for the plane? Sometimes they don't serve food nowadays, love. Your dad's bound to be economy. I don't want you going hungry on the flight.'

Somewhere lost in time was another girl, sometimes called Ellie, who felt lousy and looked like a lad and was a weekday Catholic and who might be turning vegetarian and who was soon going on holiday to an Italian villa with her father and his wife and the Steps. 'Mum, we've got dried fruit,' I sulk.

'Oh my God, Elle, no,' she exclaims and I laugh.

'Yes, Mum, instead of sweets. All of us.'

I go all tearful, because I know Mum feels more loved when something bad happens at Claire's. She used to ask me, 'Is everything OK at Claire's?' and sometimes I'd make up dreadful disasters just to please her. But if she said, 'Are Claire and Dad getting along OK?' I'd just swivel my eyeballs and go all pretendy, 'Er, yes, fine, thank you,' because I know enough from living with the Steps about nasty female competition, and I don't want anything to do with it – even if it was a sign that Mum maybe still loved Dad. But now she cuddles me in her arms and says that if Claire's got me on a diet she'll thump her. And once again I want to make up all kinds of deeply private things about Claire so that Mum will get the thrill of having her enemy punished.

'I'm serious, Mum, Claire has this thing about dried fruit. Which are actually two of the most horrible words in the English language.'

'Elle, I brought you up to like fruit, love.'

'Fruity fruit, Mum. Not dried.'

'That's true, love.'

60

'Hell, Mom, you've no idea how hard I've tried to like dried,' I say in the American accent that she finds very funny and we pretend to be in a comedy film until she falls asleep in her tiny dress, snoring like a man.

AMIR

Ashfaq and me were having this argumenty conversation about how wrong England has gone one morning, very early. I had gone over to slave over the Saturday papers, while Ashfaq raved about the cokeheads and the prossies and the 'stream of slags' who come every night to the park across the road from the shop, then the recycling aggro with the crisp boxes. Halima was a few weeks away from having the next in her cricket team of babies and was too tired to be up at five am, as she usually is – poor lass, I think, this can't be how she thought it'd be: up at five, then papers until seven when our Ashfaq the paperboy goes out to deliver them himself because he can't get any of the local lads to be reliable enough; they don't need the money, 'they'd rather mug old ladies, innit,' Ashfaq says regularly. 'They already making enough from them's drug deals,' Halima adds. I'd been keen to get out of the house as Ma was not sleeping, and she wandered down into the kitchen during the night, boiling empty kettles, making undrinkable drinks, until screeching steam woke me too, and when I go down Ma's in thick fog suddenly talking about a totally past event, like Wahida's evil husband slapping her in the face ten years ago, like it has just happened. At first I thought she'd just been dreaming, but soon realised Ma was always dreaming, and, like me nowadays, always of love, going right or wrong. And Ashfaq was right; I was becoming a pussy, and should change: become more like him.

My big bro goes out paperboying even when it's hailing and ice-rinky and slips for miles bent under his Santa-sized sack of lies. To provide for his wife and children and sick mother.

He couldn't think of his own eldest son doing the round; he don't think the area's safe for a Muslim kid to be out on his own, even early morning. Overnight there had been some lightning strikes of graffiti on the shutters of the shop. It's not unusual, though the area isn't generally hostile. Ashfaq don't bother much about the jibes or the spraying, he just thinks the whitey kids are jealous of us lot, for our harder working, our financial successes and our all-round better prospects. But then again, he thinks I'm jealous of him for the same reasons.

Yes, remember: in order to be less of a pussy become more like Ashfaq, more personally ambitious and money-hungry. And around this time I told our Jackie I was determined to be more than a fashion assistant. I was going to work my ass off and get rich. She shrugged and said, 'People with money just want more money.'

'And what's wrong with that?' I asked.

'It leaves no time for love, love,' she'd purred.

It's not talking between us, it's tickling.

At that time of the morning Ashfaq's shop was a cool inky cave, lit only by one dim overhead bulb, just the chug and hum of the fridges starting up, newsprint bruising bleary chins and thumbs. We were humped over the ice-cream freezer piling up the papers, trying not to talk about Ma's dangerous drink-making, so just slipping supplements in, over and over like a machine, and there is hardly room for our mechanical bodies to move because Ashfaq is so well mad for marketing that the shop has the Red Bull mega bin, the Walkers Crisps extra dumper, the Hula Hoops super-tall promotional board, all kinds of tacky ad shit that takes up all the floor space and falls over once the 'two at a time' school kids push in later.

Then Ashfaq was telling me not about the cricket or what to do about Ma, but about the supplement the council is thinking of levying on oversized cardboard, when the door edges open and the old bell pinged. 'Well hello, shop lads,' a very familiar voice said. In she oozed.

Dressed up and ready for work in a red mac, open to a tight sky-blue T-shirt, above spray-on jeans leaving nothing to imagine. Tits up and out, perky as morning daffodils. Ruby lipstick matched ruby toenails. Ashfaq traced her so curvy outline with his popping-out pervy eyes, like hers was an alien shape not of this planet, and when I, eventually, after a hundred years, said the introductions, Ashfaq just turned his head back to the papers and I thought, for the first time, that he was actually very shy with white lasses, and what might come across as hatred is really shock and gimpy fear, because from when we were real tiny they didn't go to our school and we didn't go to theirs. Jackie has told me all her horrors about her own daughter being sent to a Catholic school by the wicked stepmother. I've heard how there the kids call her daughter Elle-boy because she refuses to dress and act like the other lasses. Jackie says that she won't wear pretty smart clothes like her stepsisters. I've even remembered their names, Cherub and Caprice – though I struggle to remember the names of Ashfaq's five kids. I also know that Jackie's daughter just wants jeans and jumpers and has had her hair cut very short again. For her birthday she wants football boots. Some people meet her and think she's a pretty lad.

'Not seen you in here before,' Jackie says, taking a fiver from her achingly tight trouser pocket, so she had to wobble like a jelly to get the hand in deep, then asking Ashfaq, all huskyish, for the fags and the paper. Her hair was the colour of ice-cream, her lids gleaming flame orange, sparking like goldfish, and she must have had to totter on those sky-scraper wedges for a mile to get to our shop, for we're not the closest fag shop to her estate. Why had she come? Many of the shops on her patch have been torched, graffitied, ringed with mattresses and charred sofas, furniture ripped to wooden skeletons and heaped up, as if for a bonfire. So perhaps her fag shop has been boarded up, and we are the final fag frontier. I'm trying to imagine her journey; to think not stare. But really I am whirling. No handbag. Yes, yes, no handbag.

But no lust. I refused to act like a dog, again, so I looked away hard, because she provoked me, and she knew I knew it. When she'd asked my advice last month about what to wear for that funeral I told her to just wear the outfit she felt best in. 'Actually, I feel most comfortable in my birthday suit, Amir,' she'd replied and I'd blushed like a flaming virgin.

If she were a shop she'd be all tempting special offers, everything going cheap, mega marked-down deals, rock-bottom prices on the junkiest most-popular brands, discounts tilting over windows in super-sized fluorescent capitals.

'My brother here owns the shop,' I said, or something equally duh, though I know she knows this and this is why I'm confused. 'I'm helping out. Saturday papers take a long time. His wife's about to have a baby.' The fridges loud as rolling tanks and I was sudden sweaty hot, singeing under the grill of her gaze. And when she took her change she brushed Ashfaq's fingertips with her poppy-red nails so he flinched and frowned, like Stone Age man feeling fire for the first time. She jelly-wiggled again as she squeezed the money back into her pocket, on account of no handbag. I frowned as she shook herself before me like a creature coming up out of the ocean. That is why she don't carry one; for the extra hot wiggle handbaglessness affords.

I want to speak but can't, in case I cock it up: once again I'm an innocent bystander caught up in the disaster that is my own life.

Actually I thought her cheeks seemed a bit flushed too, but it was probably just make-up.

'See you later on, then, love,' she said, and stood there for a moment, hair caught in some unusual breeze, some new wind through our shop like she's blasted a hole in the wall to get in. Say what you like about the gori girls but they don't half make the air move. And then I was wondering, worrying, if I should be opening the door for her, or offering a light for her fag, or maybe just conversing about the English weather, the war, trends in the northern snack market.

What did I smell like? If I'd known she was coming I'd have soaped up extra-special.

But as she goes out the door I saw her forehead jewelled with sweat too, and in my chest I could feel the too-quick pound of her heart.

'You pussy,' Ashfaq said when she was gone, 'aint you ever seen a pair of ice-white morning melons before?'

'Me pussy!' I shouted, throwing packet after packet of crisps at him. 'You couldn't even get a word out, you were so totally stunned by those melons.'

'Stunned! I was so not stunned, I was bored by it actually, because I see melons every morning, these professional slags coming in. Probably not been home even, probably just come in from their night job as a hookcr, innit.'

I'd recently asked my middle sister, Yasmin, who is Ashfaq's greatest supporter, why our brother had gotten so hateful and hard and unforgiving. 'He just misses Pa,' Yasmin said. 'The world can seem a scary place when you suddenly become man of the family. He's trying to do the right thing. Uphold the traditions, not let people down.'

'She works with me,' I say now, throwing over a bag of ready salted. 'She's a mate. She's got a kid.'

'Exactly! Single-ma-slapper is everywhere. Ho's. Those vanilla tarts get big council houses and three hundred free quid a week to spend on booze if they have a kid. It's me paying for that house of hers! I'm practically her landlord. And it's so England, and England bores me, man.'

'No, not true,' I said. 'You is scared.' And for a short while a crisp-packet fight broke out like it used to when our dad ran a shop and my big brother would play cricket every night with me out in the street, and there we were, lobbing all kinds of packeted shit around the shop like we were ten years old, and well-excited mad brothers. Young, free, unmarried.

And when I walked out the shop minutes later I saw a sight I'd not seen for twenty years; bright sun-stars sparking over spring puddles.

It didn't end there. A few weeks later I had been seconded to Womenswear from Menswear as part of Orla's Sizzling Sexy Summer promotion. Orla insisted that male and female staff from different departments were moved around and paired up 'in exciting new combinations' to give 'an unexpected sexy zing' to till points.

'We're just commodities,' Danuta sighed, 'cans of sex, Amir, stacked up like baked beans.'

'Baked beans!' Jackie exclaimed curvily. 'Well, Amir, peel my lid off and heat me up.'

Very wrong. And just when, because of what she'd confided, vulnerably and honestly, about missing her daughter so bad, I'd decided to feel more sympathy for her. And less lust.

It was a breezy British day and we were all strumming through the perfectly conditioned air, wearing flipflops, sunglasses and beachwear – which Danuta said later had just increased Jackie's appetite for danger. It was certainly making me feel well dippy wearing swimming shorts, a T-shirt saying Lifeguard and a blue and white striped beach towel slung over my shoulder. While right next to me, for the whole four-hour shift, bad Jackie was wearing that very teeny red bikini top and a sheer sarong. My tosspot brother was well wrong; sometimes you couldn't 'ignore the slags'. So occasionally I risked it and looked at Jackie's arse and remembered a tale Leo had told me. 'Is this allowed?' she'd reportedly asked when he'd stroked her big curvy bottom in the storeroom in the middle of last year. 'It's not only allowed, gorgeous,' he'd smiled, 'it's required of all promoted members of staff. Think of it as your first ass-essment,' and she'd grinned and pushed her backside out further and said, 'Ass-essment, eh! Well, in that case.' And then turned and stuck her hand deep into Leo's trousers.

'Greetings.' Which was a word she'd say regularly around that time. Even to me: 'greetings, Amir' – as if welcoming an earthling to planet Jackie Jackson.

Leo and her: not good.

Me and her: very bad.

So I look away at an old lady in a wig, and a bald pensioner guy choosing a pair of sunglasses. Though this was meant to be a shop for cool good-looking young rich people only, ordinaries, poor, ugly oldies, kept breaching our defences. I was well tired really. Because of Ma's waking dreaming I was still not sleeping well, though around me all my colleagues were discussing if they were food what kind of food they would be. Marilyn goes, 'Amir'd be an organic apple. Wholesome, good for you, and recommended by doctors.'

'Hmm,' Danuta says huskily, winking at me, 'I'm not so sure about that at all.'

They were forever speculating about my sex life, about which I said nothing, ever. The truth was I'd had a few girlfriends, though I had never been out with a white woman before, English or Polish, though I'd – what do I call it, it certainly wasn't making love, and it shouldn't be described as what it probably was – so let's just say I'd *been with* a few, mostly white lasses I'd met at college, plus a couple of customers I'd met through the store. The real truth was that I was twenty-six years old and had never been in love, with one of their women or one of ours. I had stopped myself loving anyone in case I loved the wrong person and brought shame on myself and my family. Instead I had tried to love my career; this jackass job in retail.

Jackie's turn next. Sun on me, making me fainty. 'Perhaps more a kiwi,' Jackie says, 'roughish, dark and serious on the surface, but probably much more fun, bright and tasty when you get the outer layers off.'

'Stop it,' Marilyn says, 'you are sexually harassing him.'

'He likes it!' Danuta says. 'Don't you, Amir? Come on, admit it!'

I, of course, say nothing, just blink, then think of the last conversation I had with Uma, which makes me yawn very widely. I close my eyes and listen, because Danuta's right, I like this banter, the wild recklessness of these lasses, and maybe Jackie's right; deep down we're all aching for it.

No. I'm. Not.

It's just the store, which twists you, and this is deliberate, Jackie says, and we shouldn't be surprised, because wanting sex that you're not going to get makes you compensate by buying more stuff you don't need. Instead of getting what you want, you get more of what you don't need, until you are sunk and sexless, neck deep in expensive stuff. Which is almost the same as Ashfaq's analysis of why England is going down the toilet.

Jackie sighs: 'I've not had a decent shag for . . .'

'Oooh, at least a week,' Marilyn says.

'Five days,' Jackie says, giggling. 'Sorry, Amir. I know you disagree absolutely with everything I think and do.'

Instantly I understood the problem with Uma; she agreed with everything I said. And she followed me around like I was dragging a magnet beneath her feet.

'Amir would have me in full burka, wouldn't you, Amir?'

'Leave him alone!'

Ashfaq says this is what makes Uma a loyal and loving woman.

'Amir would only let me out if I was escorted by his mother and sisters, eh, Amir?'

So the fact that I have no desire for Uma is a good sign.

Danuta wandered across to where she was taking my place in Menswear. She was wearing a black swimsuit, a silver swimming cap and dark goggles – next to her posed Leo, who, on Orla's instruction, was wearing temporary tattoos, a tight vest top, Bermuda shorts, and holding a full-size surfboard. I remembered a cartoon Jackie had stuck to her till point, until Orla tore it down: *You have to be mad to work here but it doesn't help*. It doesn't help because it's not just our mind the job wants, it's our body too, and when you've lost your mind and your body to your crummy asshole job what is there left?

With Uma I will have a good and wholesome life.

The lasses are all nattering about outfits, and what Orla has planned for us, and I feel such a pansy. What kind of twenty-first-century half-head is the store-worker without freedom to think independently, and decide for themselves what to wear? Or who to marry? No, don't go there.

Light was hitting the white walls of the store in hard sparkles. Mobile phones gave out tinkling cries and babies reared from their million-dollar buggies and screamed. Not for the first time, it occurs to me that I'm in the wrong job. And when I am married this is another thing I will change.

Jackie and I had been standing together at the workstation for fifty minutes now, not mentioning the funeral, her morning visit to Fags 'n' Fings, her daughter, or my ma who was sleeping worse than Ashfaq's newborn. Hair was now the only thing Ma didn't lose – and so instead she squeezed it in her fists and ripped it out in clumps slowly, and when she wanted the toilet she'd pull at her clothes and some days she didn't even bother to pull at her clothes so my middle sister Yasmin had to come round each lunchbreak and clean her up, though she has four teenage lads of her own to care for at home. Yasmin said it really was like having a baby but in reverse; this baby got less and less capable every day, and soon she would be dependent on us for everything. Which was why I had to find a good patient stable wife soon; desire didn't come into it.

Yasmin was angry with me, and I knew she had been whispering in the kitchen about me with my other two sisters. Yasmin agreed with Ashfaq about most things, though Samirah said really she was worried about what future her own sons would have in an England that hates Muslims, especially Muslim lads, and when I told Wahida recently that I felt Yasmin disliked me, she said, 'Yasmin's made a lot of sacrifices to keep her marriage strong and bring up her lads. It's just hard for her to think of people in our family making different choices.'

'I didn't know I had choices,' I said.

'If we had no choices life wouldn't be hard,' she'd said and I wanted her to tell me more of what she believed, but she gave me a look that told me I had to work things out for myself. Just like she had maybe, when she decided to get divorced from her vicious Pakistani husband. Now she was bringing up her daughters alone and training as a social worker.

Thinking of Ma at home, without me, waved me over with sad, so I tried to watch the escalators smoothly spreading shoppers around the store, but I knew that if Ma could see me now, lifeguarding, she'd have something to shout to Allah about. But I only said to Jackie I'd been up in the night with my ma, and Jackie said that she too had been up watching the Ceefax, checking if there were any delays or adverse weather conditions or any suspect packages, and then we were trying not to stare at each other's flesh, and instead talking about Elle who was going on holiday soon with her father and stepmother. I'd heard all about how, the day before, Jackie had spent a fortune on her credit card getting her little lass everything she wanted for the trip. I'd had great detail about how Elle visited all the best stores in town, holding hands with her ma, choosing and touching, feeling fabrics, suggesting styles and colours. 'It's not right, you spending all this, Mum,' Elle had said. 'And I'm not really into girly clothes, am I, Mum?'

'It's not right but it feels nice,' Jackie had replied.

'Story of your life, Mum,' Elle had said sadly. 'That's the story of your life, isn't it?'

Jackie laughed, but us knowing how right the little lass was made me double-sad – and lonely, because there Jack was beside me still giggling about it.

I think of Samirah and how she is thirty-eight and not yet married either, and everyone says it is because she wants to concentrate on her teaching career, but really what if she is doing what I am doing: making sure she doesn't fall in love so that she doesn't cause any trouble or upset anyone?

I said she said I said she said I said she said – I was doing this in my head while Jackie talked, just to keep my eyes off – but after a while it's a tongue-twister, and you're left just like our Ashfaq, goggle-eyed and staring, and I knew that I really should go home and check on Ma. Call Uma.

Instead I just gazed at a black woman enthralled by a red shoe, and thought how Jackie was right; the store's constant thrum, its hard diamond sparkle, not only made you shag-mad, but it ruled out disloyalty in both customers and staff. For what did we have to be dissatisfied for, to long for, to complain about, amidst such glittering riches?

How would I ever get out of this place? I had loads of ideas of other jobs I could do, but I couldn't ever really imagine myself doing them. Though it was ironic how hard it was for everyone to leave the store, when practically every promotion we ever held was about self-transformation, about reminding folk of their constant longings to change their lives. Buy this and change; no this, no that, no these.

Then, as if by abracadabra, at our side an old bloke appeared. It was the senior citizen who would be both of our undoing, and he came, as perhaps jinns often do, in a hilarious disguise. 'Wow,' the old devil said first off. 'What a little stunner you've turned out to be,' and he stared directly at her – as if the bikini top was to him invisible, and then he grinned.

His perfect teeth looked about thirty years younger than the rest of him. He was practically sniffing her.

Was this Orla's much anticipated mystery shopper, for whom we had to be always ready, and very afraid? The bloke was short and fat and old, with a saggy stubbled chin and furry billy-goats' eyebrows, but right from the word go I could tell that Jackie, despite the dentures, liked it, appreciated this appreciation, then she mentioned his name and shivered slightly and he asked her if she was cold. 'Despite the fact that we are pretending to be in the middle of a sizzling sexy summer, they keep it pretty icy in here,' she said. 'To keep us moving, I think.' And she jogged a bit on the spot, so her tits . . . No. I remember Orla asking me later how could it just happen? How could a lad or a lass step out in front of you and hit you with their love as firmly as with an iron bar? Orla really didn't understand it, and months ago, neither did I – though I understood, from seeing what was happening to my ma, how madness comes over like weather.

He flashed his plastic teeth again and she giggled and a chill wind rustled my leaves. He was a sixty-year-old coach driver, bringing a party of senior citizens from Wakefield to the Sizzling Sexy Summer Barbecue Special that Orla had organised. I was twice his height, half his age, and if I had been that kind of man I could've had him with a single blow. I wondered if he lived on her estate too, because I pictured him CCTV grey, shuffling, baggy-trousered, through the trash streets, weaving between the lad-addicts on mini-bikes, with a fag and a can, a whippet on a rope, a flat cap, hobnail boots, stamping towards her grotty gori house. Where she stumbled over her words like a drunk groupie chatting to a movie star.

He was bald, and the sun came down through the transparent lid in our store's white roof, and spread silver light on his pink head, and to stop myself watching Jackie's joy I was thinking that in England now there is no point at which you stop flirting. Even marriage, fatherhood, old age, illness, nothing could stop the bouncy sex carousel that I and every other Englisher was spinning on. I should throw myself off the ride before I puked. Go home to Ma, marry Uma. Buy a shed.

But instead I was hearing how this dick was a former miner, who had taken to driving coaches when the pit closed. His coach party of OAPs were attending a barbecue beef promotion in the food hall and afterwards special fittings for 'red-hot swimwear'.

'The Large Cool Store?' the old coach driver said, dabbing at the warm pools of light on his head. His vinegary aftershave sharp in the air. 'Do you know it?'

Jackie bit her lip, squeezed her upper arms to her sides so her pink pups popped forwards. She looked fake-puzzled, nibbled on the tip of her forefinger, then said: 'I was at school with the guy who wrote that.' And George is going bananas and tells her all he knows about some poem, recited quite a bit of it, babbled on far too long because he was Everyman: nervous around her. 'Yes, I was definitely at school with a Larkin, him and another annoying git called Shakespeare.'

'I like his stuff. "Lemon, sapphire, moss-green, rose-lemon, sapphire, moss-green, rose," ' George continued timidly, his corned-beef brow moistened by her wet smile. He was even stuttering a little now too. 'He and I had the same t-t-t-taste in j-j-j-jazz. "Bri nylon, baby dolls and s-s-s-s-horties." I can't remember the rest. I'll have to look it up for you.'

'I so love reading,' she said with a pout.

I laugh loudly at this but she doesn't notice because the store, England, or maybe just the weather, something was making them both overjoyed and he was giving her a run for her money in the nattering stakes too and she liked it; this being listened to and responded to, and unlike me in Fags 'n' Fings last Saturday he was knowing exactly the right thing to say.

Uma: exactly how easy is it going to be to deceive her into thinking I love her?

'Everyone says I should read more. Apparently it'd calm me down. Though sometimes I just turn up the music and dance.' And she wiggled again so the pups practically jumped out barking. George would have wanted her back on the coach from that moment – and the way she'd honeyed out the ho words, 'I just turn up the music and dance.'

Later Jackie introduced George to me, and I nodded, shook his crinkly gora hand, then for a few minutes they discussed her father and her mother. 'I don't get round to Mam's much,' she said, 'if my mam's looking after Elle then she picks her up from mine.'

'You'd set cat amongst pigeons if you wandered round our estate dressed up like that,' George said, and we all laughed.

What a total hilarious comedian.

'I have to dress like this to bring home the bacon,' she says sweetly, and George nods appreciatively and smiles slowly. 'We have to look a little bit like prostitutes, I feel, though this is actually for a special promotion.'

75

'Well, where's the h-h-h-harm in that?' And he starts to talk about architecture and our Jackie's there and listening and smiling so he goes on about curves and buildings and symbols. Our building, he says, is a breast. Not abreast of top-end retail trends, as Orla insists, just a tit.

'The store is a breast,' she nods very seriously. She squeezes him on his naked forearm as she says it. She is always touching, hugging, stroking. And I took this, then, as a sign of the mother in her blooming up through the muck of her moral lack like a flowered weed.

Then with his arms wide he demonstrates how inside a modern building you can have great shafts for escalators like a big inner blood vessel, or you can have a circle and emptiness, like the womb.

Remember this particular false-toothed tosspot looks like he's pushing sixty.

'Like the very inside of a woman. Like the very mysterious dark and fundamental core of a woman.' He then used the sentence 'the walkway of the v-v-v-vagina'; I wasn't dreaming. I can't blame Ma, or the sleeplessness, because I definitely did hear Jackie Jackson reply: 'Well, my v-v-v-vagina's been a walkway, all right, love, but from now on anyone who wants to get in will have to put in a bit of effort and use the s-s-s-s-stairs.'

'Stairway to h-h-h-h-eaven,' he says, then apologises.

'I can do that on the guitar,' she says.

'You play the guitar?'

'Only "Stairway to Heaven".'

Then George said he did, badly, and mimed playing the guitar with an imbecile's expression on his face, then he mimed slitting his throat and the pair of them smiled at one another and sat for a while in silence just looking at each other's faces – wide-eyed as babies. She liked him for that little humbling joke, and because he was a natterer who played the guitar, because even if he didn't do it well she liked people who tried to add to the sum of human partying. And Ashfaq was right; lasses like her thought only of fun, of urgent entertainment, because she believed in nothing beyond herself, lived nowhere but the dying moment.

And, yes, as Ashfaq keeps reminding me: that's how life is if you live for lust. Even if you dress it up as love.

Then Jackie and George generally chatted, and she pointed out different departments, detailing people and brands, but, for a change, him doing most of the talking. 'You know, department stores started up because young women were thought not trustworthy enough to wander around a town centre unchaperoned,' he says, drool slapping out of his big wet gob. 'By putting all the shops under one roof, in departments, there was less chance of mischief.'

'Oh, for a bit of mischief,' she sighed, loosening her sarong. 'Whatever happened to mischief, Amir?'

Me? I just raised my eyebrows, and muttered, like I'd not been listening at all because I was a real lifeguard, utterly focused on gazing over the sea of the store, checking no one was drowning in designer handbags, going under in erotic underwear, no stripping sleepwalking old ma's who hadn't brushed their hair.

'They banned mischief,' the comedian says, 'along with curvy bananas and nobbly cucumbers.'

I couldn't stop glancing at them; it was like watching a bonfire blazing up your own living room.

'You can probably still get it,' she whispers, 'if you know the right people.'

No.

The weight of that kettle. Was probably too much. A smell around the sofa, too. Niggly crap like that, base irritating worries, that I thought of but didn't do anything about. Even dressed as a Hawaiian lifeguard, I was a dickless git.

Look away, go home, get another job.

'I could get you into some mischief,' he said, snorting down his nose like a bull.

Oh, what a cheeky entertainer!

'Oh, it's not getting into it,' she sighed, pulling up the red bikini strap that had slipped down her pink arm, and snapping it against her hard tight white shoulder, 'it's getting out of it that's my problem. Isn't it, Amir?'

Why was she prodding me? 'Sorry?' I say, but already the comedian is back going deep into her right away, emotions and everything, not pratting on about himself. No, he was connecting, asking, listening to the answers and generally giving the impression that he cares and can sort everything out. It sounded impressive but Jackie just said, 'It's just clothes, George, we have to wear something, don't we? I mean, until someone suggests that we take it all off.'

'Aye, wouldn't that be a right relief,' he says, wiping his brow, 'just take all our bloody clothes off now it's nearly summer.'

Oh, what an alpha male!

'I love it when things are nearly,' Jackie nodded. 'Don't you agree, Amir? Nearly is so better than is, eh?'

I smiled like an imbecile and gazed far away, thinking about the time last week when, according to Yasmin, my own mother had tried to take her clothes off in Somerfield because they had the heating on too high.

I had to get my mind off Ashfaq, Jackie and my ma. Over in Menswear I saw Danuta laying on top of the pay point and applying sun lotion to her legs. She was one of the staff Orla had recruited as 'living exhibits'. It meant they had to do a little act, applying lotion, for example, or laying in the middle of the floor sunbathing, or blowing up a rubber ring, every forty minutes and I wondered for a moment if Jackie was an undercover 'living exhibit' and she was not really flirting with this chat-happy gora pensioner, this excessively opinionated ex-miner, but just pretending to get it on with a crumbly half-head every forty minutes, as Orla had insisted. Maybe she was doing it for charity, or perhaps it was just all a dream, because Jackie could do that; make you imagine.

'Do you want a hot drink?' he asks.

'Hot. Drink,' she repeated slowly, letting her head hang back, whereupon she closed her eyes, sighed, wetted her lips with her tongue and then opened her mouth wide. 'Hot. Drink.' Then she returned her head to a normal position and she smiled. George gulped. 'Two of the nicest words in the whole language, love. Hot. Drink.'

He didn't know that the only word Jackie Jackson didn't have in her body language was no. And, against my will, I remembered a few months back hearing Danuta trying to fix Jackie up with another Pole. 'I can't, Danuta,' Jackie groaned, 'I have to stay in. I have to be a mam. A sober, clean, proper, smiley, staying at home kind of mam. I have to try and be like bloody Claire.' 'He's six foot, lots of hair, twenty-five,' Danuta said and Jackie put her hands over her head and screwed shut her eyes and repeated over and over, 'I don't care about such superficial things. I don't care about such superficial things. I don't care . . .' Until Danuta leant over and whispered something in Jackie's ear, causing Jackie to cover that plumpy-soft lipsticked gob and gasp, 'That is quite something, but I'm still not interested, love. I can't. I won't. I'm taking Elle shopping. All weekend.' 'How about Monday?' Danuta asked and Jackie sighed and said, 'Yes, Monday'll be fine.'

Ashfaq was right, she was an addict. And a landmine waiting for a foot, and on Tuesday she'd come in to work yawning and told Marilyn, 'I'm knackered. I've been up Pole-dancing all night.'

Now George wandered off to the coach, Jackie took one look behind and followed him. I was yanked, couldn't help it: a few minutes later I followed too.

The coach was parked on the street not far from the store. It was a cold May day and my Hawaiian outfit offered no protection against the wind-slapped English spring. It was late morning and the city traffic was blocked up and dragon-growling, and in the distance great cranes were building high-rise apartment blocks and more posh shops for lonely, money-rich, love-poor singletons – like me.

But I was just an insect drawn by a deep red perfume and I only had to drift along the pavement to see up into the coach and notice how George and Jackie were blowing cool air over one another's hot pink skin. I watched, like a bee trapped beneath the jar of my own inaction, fear and indecision, as George moved towards her and they were talking and laughing. She advanced more quickly and confidently than the lasses I knew. There was no fiddling with her hair, lip biting, gazing at the floor and then wham bam they were kissing, her reaching up from the seat, him standing over, one hand steadied on the overhead compartment, like he was a beast drinking from a pool.

Her eyes half-closed, her hands flopped down, her tongue licking in and out like a cat's. And her neck, arched in abandon like she was advertising lust. And the scene was framed by the coach window, so it seemed I was watching these unlikely lovers on a movie screen. They were in a different world to me. Clouds moved across the picture dappling the lovers with a moody shadow. And there at the back of the coach it soon seemed like he was taking photographs of her, as she made the curious movements of someone playing the cymbals. What was she doing?

I had had three dates with Uma and not touched her, not tried to kiss her once.

ELLE

I told Dad I was going swimming with Ashanti and I went round for an illegal Sunday lunch at Mum's. In preparation Mum had gone hygiene mad and washed the net curtains, hoovered the carpet, collected up the corks, scrubbed the shower cubicle and bought a daft new shower curtain. For a moment I thought she really loved me, but then soon as she served the roasties she told me about some latest charmer; and how he is kind and handsome, and all the many details of how she is in love with him, because, she says, she wants me to know this is serious, not just another hopeless fling. I can't believe it. She says before I have even taken a mouthful of chicken that she often thinks about having another baby now that she had met a great guy. I say, 'Mum, now slow down. Run that baby bit by me again.'

So she does and I think how me and Mum's new babe would be half-brother or -sister, truly blood-linked, not like me and Cherub or Caprice who everyone wants me to call 'sister' though the Steps are no more part of me than any other freaky kid on the street. Sometimes I tell them we are just cellmates; total strangers forced together by the law, not that they care, because they have each other.

'You know Claire calls me Ellie,' I say.

'But that's not your name, love,' Mum says, looking truly-troubled.com.

'I know,' I say, in a trembly voice.

'Well, why does she call you that?'

I shrug and carry on sliding my food around the plate, which is another major irritation, like sudden whistling, that I learned off of Caprice.

'Does she call you Ellie often?'

'Hmm.'

'How often? When? Please stop playing with your food, Elle.'

'Just sometimes.'

'Well,' she says and she is rubbing her fingers across her lips, and I let her feel useless and destroyed and certain that she has lost the only precious thing left in her lousy life.

To cheer herself up she tells me how the lorry-driving new boyfriend has such a masterful way with the wheel, spearing the blocked city traffic in two, even with one elbow relaxing on the windowsill, a fag between his fingers and thumb, a frowny scowl on his flinty face and his legs cowboyishly apart. Blue eyes set on twinkle. How his skin is rough, tough and browned like bark – and at the bar, he pays for everything. In the car, he checks her seatbelt is secure before he drives off. And her old knees feel exactly as they should, lemonadey.

'Sounds like you're dating your dad,' I say, and she smiles strangely. 'Mum, I don't like you more because you have a boyfriend.'

Some girls at my new school think they are more tasty once they are not virgins, but Cherub says the thing is to be famous, and then it doesn't matter if you're a virgin or not because everyone likes you anyway, and Ashanti says her mum is a bit famous but I've never heard of her, but then again I've never heard of loads of people Cherub says are famous.

'I like myself more when I have a boyfriend,' she says.

'I think that's rather sad, Mum.'

'You sound just like Amir,' she says. 'What's sad about liking being in love?'

And that night she told me that yesterday at work the Asian had jogged over to tell her that Orla was in the restaurant right then, complaining about Mum's hair not being hairstyley enough. He said their boss was planning to bring the entire management team, plus Human Resources, to see the outrageous bird's nest for themselves. Apparently the Asian manned the station while Mum went to the locker room and fluffed herself up. 'It was so nice of him to warn me,' Mum sighed.

'Do you think he's nice to you because he likes you?' I ask, quietly and not looking at her.

'You mean perhaps he gets extra points at the temple if he's nice to me?'

'Mum, they go to a mosque not a temple.'

'Same difference,' she says with a shrug.

'No, I mean hasn't it occurred to you that he's being nice to you because he wants to get to know you, so he can change you.'

She just laughs and says that she'd need subtitles to truly understand Amir and anyway she says that her luck in love seemed to have prompted Amir to get himself a bride. 'Mail order, of course,' she said.

'How'll you know she's not lying, pet?' Mum asked him when he tells her how his brother has written a list of good respectable women. He tells Mum that their women don't act in the way home-grown English girls do. 'Perhaps she'll get infected by our slutty local ways,' Mum tells him. 'In that case, Jackie, I won't let her out the house,' he says, 'I'll chain her up in the garden until she learns how to behave.'

Mum laughs when she tells me this.

'Mum, why do you find it funny the way they treat their women?'

'He was joking, love,' she says, like her miserable daughter is the biggest dim in town. 'Making fun of himself.'

'He wasn't. That's what they do to bad women. They don't allow them any freedom, Gran's told me. If they go with someone they're not allowed to, they get sent to Pakistan and have to marry old men and work on farms looking after goats.'

She just flashes out a cold hard look that I rarely see; it says, *that is exactly the kind of harsh, distrustful attitude that meant I couldn't stay living with your father; perhaps you're a horrible lousy little bastard just like him.* Then Mum's look softens to one that is more familiar and sad and she says, 'It's easy to think that, love, but I'm not sure it's true of everyone. I can't imagine Amir acting like that.'

'They have to do things the way their family do things,' I say. 'They have to think the same as their religion tells them to think.'

'We can all think differently to our family,' she says. 'I don't think the way Grandma does, do I? And you don't think just the same way your dad does.'

I don't say anything, because maybe I do think the way my dad does, or at least I probably do when I'm with him; I just don't say that I do because if you don't think the same way as at least some of your family you are probably gonna end up like Mum: with just one little part-time person left in the whole world who loves you.

I want to go home but can't 'cos she's got no one to talk to but me.

'Well, Mum, in the olden days if your dad was a blacksmith you were a blacksmith – and everyone was happy.'

'Unless you didn't want to be a blacksmith,' she says.

'Well, you had to be,' I say, 'for the good of the village.'

'What about progress? Some brave soul had to stop being the blacksmith and go forward and invent the motor car.'

I can't think what to say so just bury my head in my elbow and wish I'd nicked some underwear off Cherub, because that is one thing in my pimpy little life that makes me a bit happy. 'Elle, love, I'm moving forwards. Because actually, Elle, your mother is nothing like her mother. She gets on with life, and does not endlessly discuss her own emotions. She does not turn to self-help books like Marilyn, does not exhaust friends with her own impossible situations like Danuta, does not weep in public and demand pats and hugs like her mam, or bully like Orla, or moralise like Amir; no, Jackie Jackson tries to go forward with as much positivity and dignity as possible. Oh come on, love, please.'

I walk off. It takes me ages to think of it but eventually I come back into the kitchen and say, 'Well, actually I don't think the motor car is progress. What about global warming?'

And she hugs me and lifts me up off the ground and says, 'You know the greatest achievement in my hopeless mistake of a life is to have produced such a super smart intelligent little lass as you. Gifted and Talented! I'll give you Gifted and Talented.' And she starts to kill me with kisses so I squeal and kick her off and go and watch the ballroom dancing, but when she comes to cuddle up next to me, with a big bag of luxury handcrafted crisps, I let her.

But later that night, 'Wot u really fink of G?' she asked the Asian by text.

'That he's same height sitting down as standing up,' he replied. A second later Mum had sent back a text to confess that her last lover was very young and very tall, and Amir texted back instantly, 'Y u such extremist? Wot's wrong wi moderation?' Mum explained that she was the lass who, at fourteen, engraved Get Pissed, Destroy on her school satchel and Amir texts, 'So y can't u now grow up?'

I don't know why she's letting him treat her so bad. Then again Ashanti begs lads not to give her the bumps. Though she wants them to do it really. The begging not to just gives them the idea for it. So four catch her and hold her at each corner and jerk her high in the air and she squeals like an animal, and when her uniform's all stretched and ruined, she falls in my arms and sobs that her mum's gonna definitely kill her.

So it's probably something like that.

I don't mention these texts to Mum, or anything about the Asian. But she says while she is drying my hair that sometimes she thinks she would like to convert to Islam just to not have to blow-dry every day. I tell her she could get arrested for making jokes like that, but Mum says she's already made her joke, yesterday, with 'her friend' Amir. And so I tell her again what I know about Muslims and that she'd better be careful about offending him. 'Oh no, love,' she says, 'he wasn't offended.' And for a long time she keeps on rubbing in the leave-in conditioner and she is remembering and smiling. 'He just looked at me for a long time, with a very faint smile.'

'Well, Mum,' I say, 'that might be genuine or it might be pity or it might be the beginning of a plot. At best he probably feels really sorry for you.'

'Actually after a hundred hours of ogling, he said, "Jackie, love, if you wore the veil I wouldn't be able to see your lovely face." '

And I noticed she had changed her nail polish twice in one day.

Then later, she gets this text from him, 'U were partly right; the veil stops women being judged on what they look like.' And Mum texts back, 'Wot if we want 2 b judged on wot we look like? Is that allowed?' And I was chuffed that her text sounded like she was understanding about what Gran says about how they hate us and are trying to change us.

'Y wd any woman want 2 b judged on just her body n face?' he texts later that night.

'If wot u look like is better than wot u feel like,' Mum replies.

'If u r in love, u should feel happy?'

'Ach, Amir, wot's happy compared 2 scared shitless n excited?'

'Gee, get a grip, girl,' he replies instantly.

'I can't I'm in luv,' she texts back.

'It's lust.'

'Wot is wrong with lust? Neither of us wd b here without lust.'

And all that night she natters cheerfully on about how Mr Chutney doesn't drink and he doesn't even go for coffee unless he's got enough money in the bank. Which is not a lifestyle she can understand at all. She even asked him how many credit cards he's got and he said sternly that he'd got none, zero. She raised her hands and gave a look of utter amazement, like he'd said he'd got no shoes; not even one pair! I say, 'That's right, Mum, Muslims don't believe in borrowing money where interest is charged.'

She bit her fingertip, then her lip, then said, totally blonde and slow, and in the accent I use to cheer her up: 'Gee, honey, you're telling me dey charge intwest?'

And I couldn't help it, I laughed, because Dad says Mum is even worse with money than she is with men.

Then just when we were being proper mother and daughter, proper light and happy, she makes a sudden announcement. Great news! She's planning to invite the Asian round to Gran's for lunch.

'Elle, please, calm down! I just want her to meet a proper Asian person. A decent shy handsome lad.'

'Are you confusing Gran with a normal person, Mum? She wants to meet an Asian about as much as she wants to catch bird flu.'

'But he's a really *nice* person,' she whines.

'I get it now. You want Gran to be so shocked by him and his preachy Paki views that she will be desperate for you to meet anyone else. Even an old coach driver who was once a friend of her husband's.'

There is a long silence which means I am totallyright.com.

'Amir doesn't have any preachy Pakistani views, Elle.'

'If he's got a brown face she'll just assume.'

'Anyway George wasn't exactly a friend of Granddad's.'

I whistle slowly. 'Did you hear yourself say that, Mum? Repeat those words: *a friend of Granddad's*. You are dating a man you refer to as *a friend of Granddad's*.'

'He's a lovely man, Elle.'

'So what's the problem with just taking this lovely man round to Gran's for lunch?'

'True,' Mum says, 'I feel terrible now. You're right, it's a dreadful idea.'

'Well, dear mother, I'm sure that won't put you off.'

I go upstairs and call Dad and say I'm coming home early. He chuckles like Santa and says, 'Ho dear, ho dear, what's happened now, pet?'

But of course I can't tell him the truth.

The hardest thing is balancing being horrible about Dad to Mum with being horrible about Mum to Dad – get it wrong and you're in the care of social services.

AMIR

'**M**y mam is not Gordon Ramsay,' she said, 'it'll just be defrosted Aunt Bessie's, and an hour of complaining about my hair.'

'Why me?'

'Why not you?'

'That's the answer they give to people wondering why they got cancer, Jackie.'

'Oh, it won't be that bad, love,' she said, in that deep smoke-filled voice.

So I asked Wahida to make the meal for Ma that day and I agreed to be Jackie's faithful Muslim mate. I knew she wanted me at her family party so she could wear me like a badge against alcohol, sluttishness and general delinquency. She'd probably come up with this tactic after a total giggle with Marilyn and Danuta. Perhaps they'd all suggested me as an advert for restraint, moral righteousness and dogma, though I'd not been near the mosque since Ashfaq had told the imam that because of my job I was susceptible to wicked influences.

'Be careful,' was all Wahida said, and I think she is the most understanding of all my family because she is divorced, and she has two teenage daughters herself and so is concerned about freedom as well as responsibility. But maybe the reason is that they all know I'm losing my mind and if Jackie asked me to dash into a burning building through flying bullets I might.

I was chuffed to get out of the ash-heap they call my home. My ma was burning every meal she made. Fire-alarm pingers going off like police sirens in a war zone, grill pan tossed blazing into flower beds, all pots bubbled with a black crust, cinders crunched underfoot after every meal in our arsonist's kitchen. This was if Ma did manage to make a meal without forgetting half the ingredients or substituting sugar for salt, chocolate for chickpeas, or just not remembering that eating was a requirement of human life. My sisters and nieces and nephews came in afternoons to help but it was like cooking with a clown, flour in her hair, eggs down her cardigan, and they had families and jobs, and Halima had her newborn baby and the shop, and I was too late home from work to be much use, though I tried.

Each morning I left flasks of hot drinks and sandwiches for Ma's lunch. I turned off the cooker and put a plaster over the switch, to remind her not to turn it on while I was out. Then one day last week she tried to toast a frozen chicken fillet and in a state of total sad defeat I called Ashfaq and said, 'OK, you win, I accept I have to do it some day. You can choose a few. But I want to decide myself who I finally . . .'

I couldn't bring myself to say the word. M-m-m-m-m-. But I did not want to bring disrespect on my family, so I would do in public what I had to do, and in private I would find some other way of being my own man.

'Have you forgotten what I told you?' Ashfaq sighed, 'those posh vanilla tarts you work with are not interested in you, man. They might flirt with you and fancy you and lick you over with mucky promises but you don't belong with them.' I could hear the new baby mewling in the background and Halima shouting for him to get off the phone and come to help, and Yasmin had told me they'd had more BNP graffiti overnight which had all upset him. 'You need a good woman who will love you properly.'

'But what if I promise to, erm, hmm, fall in, er, hmm, love with your – I mean my . . . lass, and then find that I can't?'

'Mind over matter, mate,' Ashfaq says. 'Concentration and strength of character.' I knew he was right, though sometimes I brooded on how our Ashfaq went to the gym most nights after he'd shut the shop and how he had been known to lay in the extremely bikini Jacuzzi for hours, watching. And I knew how some of the other husbands – ours and theirs – managed their marriages; with the help of Hugs 'n' Kisses, the massage parlour a few streets away from Fags 'n' Fings, which was raided regularly by police looking for trafficked women.

What a life. But no, if that was the way, that was the way and who was I to judge? Then I pictured myself at forty: a muscly mute, a nasty newsagent, alternately online or asleep on a sofa. Sometimes banging wood in my shed. 'But at least if I choose someone myself then it's my mistake that I have to live with. I'm not sure we have the same taste. I mean, Halima's great but . . .'

'What's with you and the talking, anyway? I preferred you when you were silent.'

I'd tried only the night before to tell Ashfaq that I was worried about Ma. We were outside the shop pulling down the graffitied iron shutters, below a perfect tangerine moon. I must have been yellowed with fear and cowardice because he gave me his eyebrow-heavy madman stare so I had to say, 'I'm just trying to tell you how I feel about this shit.'

'Well, don't,' he roared, well worried too. 'You're a future executive of my company and it's called Fags 'n' Fings not Fags 'n' Fucky Feelings. What use are feelings?'

'It's my future I'm trying to talk about,' I said, as he snapped shut the shop in its steel case.

'No, wrong. It's the family. It's the future of the community. You've got to stop putting yourself at the top of the list, man. When did you get the idea that you are so important?' and he tore off in his big businessman's car, leaving me there kid-like: loitering, moonstruck and scared.

He was right. Moonstruck. Exact same way Jackie looked these days. Just the day before Jackie asked me to the party at her mother's, Orla had taken time in a stock-control meeting to point out that 'grooming' was included in the terms and conditions of employment. 'Staff who can't be bothered to take the time and effort to look good might as well work on a market stall,' Orla snapped. 'Do I need to remind you all that this is one of Europe's première stores? You are international fashion ambassadors.'

Dozy Jackie didn't even notice that Orla was referring solely to her – though everyone else in the meeting did. It was obvious to everyone on Fourth Floor that this latest freaky gora of Jackie's had twisted her further than her others. Squeezed her dry of sense and direction. Wrung her out, exhausted and screwed her up.

Ruined by an old-age pensioner.

On Jackie's suggestion we met outside the store and travelled to her neighbourhood on the zombie express: the fag-smoky estate bus. Though I'd been to her house on the occasion I requested a hard-boiled egg, and her ma lived real close, Jackie feared I'd get lost, though I wondered if she really feared I'd get attacked. By violent goreh thugs zigzagging mini-bikes down her stinky summer street. The whole place smoky, with backyard barbecues or furious weekend bonfires, with half-headed lads flashing diamonds off their sharp silver edge; whiteness. We could have lived in entirely different cities, her and me, though we were only a few miles apart.

When I told Ashfaq that I was going to a mate's house for a little party he said, 'That slag! I knew it!' and that I should remember my duty to my family, my sick mother, my community and my religion when I am tempted to do the things I know in my heart are evil. I told him he'd got it so wrong. It was just food, I said, just taking a few hours away from home to get to know a colleague better. Meet her people. Share. Secretly, though I was both frightened and excited by the invitation, I thought Ashfaq was maybe right, so I decided I'd go but just be party wallpaper, find some guys to talk to about the cricket, have a lemonade and leave.

Then when Shirley opened the door she said, 'Oooooh, Jackie, if this 'andsome 'unk's your squeeze, expect a visit from police!' and the ma leant to kiss me on each throbbing cheek, so close I could feel her warm stretchy breasts against my chest and the mystery of Jackie was seventy per cent explained.

'Mum! You've gone to town.'

'Give 'em the old razzle-dazzle, Jack, that's my motto.'

It was hard to look right at the cackling ma and so to calm myself I closed my eyes and inhaled. The house smelt like I always thought a whitey house would: of gravy. And onions. Or maybe it's tears. 'What is it about you and the young ones, Jackie?' Shirley asks, staring at my belt buckle like it is singing a tune. She's flicking at the same snow-white hair as her daughter, though styled into a more fluffed-up cloud, and the plaster-cracks on her sharp face are deeper and longer. Combined with her paler, but still significant, tangerine tan Shirley is ice-cream on top, crumbly wafer cone below, though part of me did want, to my horror and surprise, to lick her, taste her.

How bad is that! What coven had I entered that made such evil thoughts possible?

'Leave him alone, Mam,' Jackie shouts, ''e's the shy one.'

'Oooh, the shy ones are always the best,' Shirley cackles.

93

It's around the thin pinched mouth that she looks the oldest.

I hoped the other guests weren't peeping. The two mothers look at one another real fierce, as if having a conversation I can't hear. Daylight hits Shirley's hair, blonding her brighter, pulling her back, making her younger, and for a moment those two bitchy blondes are sisters, and I can hear an aeroplane overhead, see dust like old magic in the sunbeams, and this is an utterly unintentionally thrilling moment, me there – exactly as Ashfaq predicted – in their mysterious, dirty, off-white lives, where they are about to suggest some trash-hot magaziney shock to me.

When I should be missing Uma and Ashfaq and Ma.

Then Jackie comes in behind me and whispers, in the lofty manner of a royal reporter, 'And the once disgraced elder daughter crosses the sacred threshold once more, and all will be well.'

I knew Shirley had two sons, and other grandkids, but she rarely saw them, so Jackie and Elle were everything she had to love and hate. This seemed to be the way with families round here, not that I could make the complaint that Asian families often made about Englisher grandmothers being filed away in pissy old folks' homes and the selfish breakdown of the family unit – because the doctor had given us a leaflet about day care, which we had hidden from Ashfaq, but saved.

'I can't believe we've not met,' Shirley says flirtatiously, wiggling her perfect red fingernails to a swarm of ladybirds. 'Jackie should have invited you down the bingo with our lot.'

'You play bingo, Jackie?' I asked, with a smile. 'You never said.'

Ashfaq, there are things about our Jackie so regular and dull and homely that you'd never believe them in a million years.

'Lucky numbers, love,' she says, tapping her nose. 'And lightning skill.'

'You'll have to come with us one night, Tamir. It's a right good laugh.'

'He's called Amir, Mam, and he doesn't do bingo. He's not into gambling. He's a Muslim.'

We have barely stepped through the door and are still wedged in the narrow hallway with its curly flower wallpaper. 'No popping down the bookie's, Amir. And you don't have a lager either? No wonder your lot aren't settling in very well.'

'No bacon either, Mam,' Jackie laughs, so they are both staring at me like I'm in a cage before them. 'In fact he's the very opposite of my dad.'

'It's true! All her dad needed was a bacon buttie, a *Racing Post*, five pints of lager and, hey presto, his perfect day. God bless his mucky cotton socks.'

'Dad's why I like Amir, Mam.'

She rolls her eyes at me then smiles nervously, embarrassed about all this, and I think I have to get her out of this place, find somewhere new for both of us.

'Plus the way his bum looks in those jeans,' Shirley cackles and Jackie groans in mocking horror and pushes her mother forward into the living room.

Which is empty: no other guests are here yet.

Now they've stopped prodding me, the women turn to face one another, as if even I wasn't there. 'I can't tell if you need 'aircut, or if you've just 'ad one, Jackie,' Shirley says. Jackie had warned me that her mother was an authority on appearances.

'Afterwards, if she likes you, she'll remember your name; if not she'll just refer to you as "that funny-looking one".'

And I wonder if Shirley's drunk, because Jackie has told me she fears her ma is 'a bit alco'. Now we are in the small square empty living room, Shirley turns and continues, 'So how is your poor mam, Amin?' – her sudden, frosty, sober tone implying that my ma's decline was like Jackie's haircut: another mistake that could, with a little proper care, have been avoided.

Sighing, I look around, hoping the other guests will arrive soon. I didn't like to ask where everyone was, so I just stare at the tablecloth, which is like a big net curtain. 'We have to keep an eye on her all the time,' I say. 'When I'm at work one of my sisters comes to sit with her.'

'That's 'ow it were with our Jackie,' Shirley whispered loudly. 'If we left her alone she got out and caused all kinds of trouble.'

'I was possessed,' Jackie growls in the back of my head, so my neck melts a little with her hot breath. 'By that old devil called lust.'

And she licks my ear with the tip of her very wet tongue. As I tried to remind myself what was wrong with lust.

'Now, love, can I get you a drink?' and Shirley goes to lift the bottle of wine that is already half drunk on the living-room table. There were ornaments on the windowsill, plastic daffodils in glass vases, a huge shiny fireplace with a gas fire glowing though it was a well-warm day. The red-black carpet looked like a pit of burning coals.

'Mam!' Jackie groans quietly. She's tender and calm with her mother, though the old lady is certain trouble.

'Ooh sorry, love,' she says and dashes out of the room to slam cupboard doors and then comes back in and says, 'How about a Lemsip, Amil?'

'Water's fine,' I say.

'I should have thought,' Jackie says, hand over her mouth, looking genuinely upset.

'They'll have that on your gravestone,' her mam calls out from the kitchen. 'Here lies Jackie Jackson, *I Should Have Thought*,' and Jackie exhales and rolls her blue eyes again. There are babies drawn on plates on the wall, and wooden spoons wearing skirts, and I wonder if the house was like this when Jackie was a child, and the wallpaper was why she went off like a rocket. Shirley must hear me think this because when she comes in with a pint glass full of warm cloudy tap water she says, 'You know when she was six months old I found two batteries in her nappy.'

Shirley sits at the table, with her jeaned legs spread wide like a man. She leans towards me over the table, lacing her fingers together and rotating her thumbs.

No one else is coming to this party.

I am the party.

Then she was talking to me about being a young mum, and how her driver husband, Mike, had died earlier in the year and Shirley was just left alone, unstable like two legs of a table, trying to hold the whole thing up with not one word of thanks from her wild daughter. As she was talking I found myself looking round like my ma would once have done – to see how clean the place was. Ma was of the frequently vented opinion that Englisher homes were tummy-bug dirty and white house-wives sluts. She didn't even like me going round after school to local lads' houses to watch TV in case I caught an infection.

Shirley must sense I'm not listening keenly enough, because she suggests she show me around. She takes my damp palm and says, 'Oooh, you feel ever so hot, love. Do you want to take your jumper off?' But still Jackie doesn't dash through to save me. We go into the empty front dining room and I look through the window and notice a tattered flag out the window opposite, and that there are more CCTV cameras on the streets round this estate than there are round ours, and this must be either because the gorehs cause more trouble, or because the goreh police care more about protecting the goreh public from crime. Or perhaps it's a symbol of what Ashfaq believes; that these godless Englishers are all utterly lost and all they have to guard them are tall machines. In their world love and family and spiritual security have given way to spools of taped footage, where on the edge of town in Security Control, guards spy on their fellow men on television monitors, protecting their lives, witnessing their loves and deaths, with nothing but millions of square steel eyes.

And they have parties – to which no one comes, except one terrified stranger. Who should immediately make his excuses and leave.

I had no reason to be there; she had another man now, I had to let everything go.

'The fact that she's been going away for all these mucky weekends told me something was up,' Shirley whispered. The thought of Jackie away for romantic weekends made my breathing thicken and my spine slump.

Then Shirley spoke eyelash and told me that all those years of careful eating had paid off, and she exercised every week at aquarobics and at line dancing, so she had strong slim northern thighs and it was still possible for her to wear a short-sleeve T-shirt because her arms were teen firm. She came towards me through the snow-light of the white estate and we were together, alone, and I had to squeeze at her muscles, which felt like, and looked not unlike, big raw chicken legs. But with that oily roasting-tin tan of course: she had the kind of nutty upholstery that tans nicely and I kind of half-fancied her because it was humid out in magazine-land, a dusty warm June that was predicted to lead to a blazing hot July and August. And as we waited for our roast dinner Shirley did all the talking and I just watched as she told me how Jackie had always been a handful in the lead-up to the school holidays.

Why was Jackie leaving me alone like this?

Spider plants, that was the name for what I was looking at on the windowsill, dozens of them, an infestation.

'She just couldn't wait to be off out of control.' Even before the end of term Jackie'd be wandering off, lying about where she was going, drifting through the streets with a stick, always trying to get away from the house, unwilling to do any of the helping that Shirley herself had done as a child – had had to do.

'I bet you weren't like that,' Shirley said quietly to me and I laugh because there was lately something hugely inappropriate about our ma too. 'Your lot are far too fundamental for all that, aren't you?'

'If you mean we're more spiritual . . .'

'I mean you're all more held back. You've got something at stake. That's why you're all so serious.'

Me serious? I was the one who came here expecting a party! But I couldn't say this for it would be like drawing an ugly's attention to their crooked nose: they'd laid on a party for Jackie and no one had come. And anyway, Ma would lately look – no, leer – at the dustbin men, talking of 'needing a man'. Yasmin and Wahida had caught her taking her recycling out in her nightdress and teasing the bin men not to look through her 'mucky magazines'. Not that anyone but us would ever know this. If there was one reason we all had to stick together, it was to keep our secrets safe.

'There's good Muslims and bad Muslims. Just the same as round here,' I say.

'But when a Muslim's bad he's very, very bad, but when we're bad we're just naughty,' the ma says, all the time curling her ladybirds through her ice-white hair. Then reaching over to slowly pat my hand. 'Just a bit naughty, eh?'

I see Jackie busying about in the kitchen and think: don't judge the apple by the tree.

Then I think, yes do do that. Be warned! Do anything to stop yourself going further.

'Not true,' I say, taking my trembling hand away, and Shirley looks down at the garden and itches her chin as she tells me that she knows of some remedies for memory loss and if I give her my phone number she'll pass them on to me. I know it's not right, and that it's strange her asking even, but

I'm mouth-blocked, shocked by her daring, and can't think of an excuse, so, when she hands me her phone number, I give her my number and she writes it down in a small gold note-book she takes from, then quickly returns to, her silver handbag just as Jackie comes into the room with the roasting tin.

'He don't say much, does he?' Shirley says. 'I like a man with a bit of patter, a bit of charm.'

'Mam, that's just language,' Jackie says, her face flushed from the meal steam.

'Well, language is what makes us human, Jackie,' Shirley says.

'I prefer more animal instincts,' Jackie says and smiles at me, rather nervously, as she sets out the food on the table. I have no appetite.

'Yes,' I say, because I daren't disagree. Though maybe I did agree that touch, and what a person did with their body, was more important than what they said. And I'm thinking to be able to sit easily with a woman in silence and later make love to them noisily and wildly, that for me would be just . . .

No! Stop it.

But as she puts the food out I watch Jackie tricking her mum back into truthfulness by telling tales of Elle and the two women are laughing honestly together and Jackie tells a few cute lines and Shirley melts. 'Her teacher says she's top of the class. She's definitely going on that Gifted and Talented thingy again next year.'

'I should hope so. I've always said she's a bright spark. I knew as soon as she was born.'

But just when I think Jackie is going to reveal herself further to be a loving ordinary ma, she suddenly stared at a rubbery roast potato and confessed, 'And I've some news too. I've met the man of my dreams, Mam. That's why I was away last week. I wasn't on a training course at all.'

At work they'd been worried earlier that month about how much weight Jackie had lost. When Marilyn confronted her Jackie just said, 'That's love for ya!' Then confessed that now there was just herself to cook for, she often didn't bother. 'Oh, I just have a sandwich,' she'd sigh, 'and maybe a half glass of wine.' But Marilyn had told me Jackie didn't eat because she didn't go to the supermarket so she wouldn't have to walk down the drinks aisle. What a flaming disaster.

'I wouldn't like to imagine what the man of your dreams looks like,' her ma said and I carried on serving myself, ignoring that mother's look I once saw in my own ma: the fury of always having to listen and suppress herself. I didn't want to understand mothers but somehow I couldn't help it: I was the youngest son.

And it occurs to me for the first time that maybe I feel so comfortable and happy around Jackie, though she is thirteen years older than me, because I have such older sisters. Even Samirah, the youngest, is twelve years older than me.

'Are you happy for me? Why aren't you speaking to me, Mam?'

'What about my granddaughter?' Shirley cries out at last. 'She's already been brought up in a broken home, and seen things no child should have to see. She's living between two houses like a drifter. Whatever happened to stability for the children?'

As I carved the bird, feeling as if my every crumbling slice was being caught on camera and would be used by Ashfaq later as evidence, Shirley began to pick apart her daughter further. Jackie just listened, her face tight and pink. 'I'm trying to get my life back together so I can not be bitter and screw Elle up with my own unhappiness and loneliness. I've been so lonely, numb, since Dad, since Paul. Since it didn't work out with that guy at work. Since Elle. I don't want to pass that on to her. Which is what some women do. Don't cry, Mam. I feel so much happier than I have for years,' Jackie said. 'I wanted you to know. It matters that you are happy for me.'

'Well, I was telling Auntie Jean that you were behaving all secretive again. And that I suspected you were not with the right man. Again,' Shirley said.

Hell would freeze over before Shirley let her daughter triumph in love. Same with Ashfaq and me.

'Please will you stop telling everyone everything about me. I won't tell you anything in the future.'

'What, are you asking me to not speak to my friends? Are you suggesting I become like you – all dark and secretive.'

'I don't gossip about you to my friends, Mam. I respect you.'

I could hardly listen to this. There had always been a lot of gossip around our Samirah, since she was a teenager. Ashfaq policed her like it was his full-time job. There were rumours that she had been seeing that postman – a white lad. For several months a few years back our ma stopped her going out alone; either me or Ashfaq had to accompany her everywhere. Now she comes to visit when Ashfaq is out and she says little, though I know Ma loves her; she just doesn't trust her – which I know means Ma doesn't love her anyway near enough.

'Jackie, that's because you hardly ever remember you even have a mother.'

'No, Mam, it's because I respect your privacy.'

'I take it as a compliment if people want to talk about me, Amir. It shows they are interested in my wellbeing, it indicates that they are thinking about me and my situation.'

Jackie looks at me, and shakes her head. Even though she belongs to someone else now I want to hold her. But she just wants ordinary friendly help though I can't think of a single word to say. 'Well, some people are more sensitive than you, Mam. I don't want everyone to know my business.'

'Oh yes, secretive. Always have been since you were a child. And sulky. And I don't know where you got it from because the rest of the family are very sociable. We're a cheery bunch, Amil, everyone says. Except 'er.'

'OK, I'm happy to be the black sheep.' Jackie laughs and shakes her head and serves herself some food, and whispers, 'Sorry, Amir. I didn't think it'd be this bad.'

'Sulky, you are, and always have been.' Shirley began to bubble like a kettle coming to the boil, while outside the sun was ripening, black trees before a pinky blue sky, and a gang of lads and lasses passed by the window in a smoky shuffle.

Jackie frowned and held her chin heavy in her hand. 'I can't believe you're behaving like this in front of Amir,' Jackie said when there was a pause in the ranting. 'He shouldn't be having to listen to this. Sorry, Amir, I really didn't think it'd be like this.'

'You only brought that poor Paki so you wouldn't have to talk honestly to me,' Shirley sighed. 'What use is he to you if he don't drink and he don't shag around?'

Jackie looked at me and smiled; *ours is a magic only we two understand*.

Actually, if you focused on the positive, it was a luxury to be around a conversation of such rapid fire. My own ma could nowadays only take questions that came very slowly and which required yes-no answers and even to the most simple enquiries. To 'Shall I turn the fire on?' she would respond, 'Fire, what's on fire?' – though if the kitchen really was on fire she'd not notice. Or alternatively reply to a question about margarine with, 'The worst thing about your father, Amir . . .' And generally as a family we didn't ever say how we felt, so – if you again focused on the positive – it was a splash of shock to be around rude older women who said what they wanted, however crazy, who weren't held in by anything. So I sat between Shirley and Jackie and didn't get up from my chair, but watched the women across the table, from left and right like blazing tennis, and I felt as I always did around Jackie, sparking with life and warmed by the flame.

'I'm happy, Mam, honestly.'

'And that's how I know it's a mistake.' Outside even the raindrops froze still against Shirley's icy stare. 'Thirty-nine and about to be married for the third time, it's a huge humiliation for a mother to have to send out three lots of invitations, even insisting from the second time onwards that the guests don't bring gifts. Still greedy and wrong. Like demanding to have triple the number of birthday parties.' I winked at Jackie. 'And you'll 'ave to do summat with your 'air before the big day.'

A wedding? Was it true? My mouth was dust-dry. But no, it was good news. It was for the best – for everyone.

Or perhaps it was just that all mothers thought about weddings constantly. My own ma, increasingly unable to sustain any conversation, could still say important words about weddings. It didn't mean there was to be one. 'So we are down to the last two girls, Amir. Tell me when are you getting wed, Amir? I beg you, son,' she'd asked me the previous day, like none of the recent madnesses had ever happened.

'Mum, I'm twenty-six. When I'm thirty I will have a think about it.'

'And what kind of women will be left then? All the shop-soiled returned goods, that's who! Your childless, divorced, washed up, boozing their way through the menopause.' I kept my head down and said nothing. 'You all think you can be having it all, you lot do, and you are wrong. Wrong!'

'No one gets married in their twenties any more, Mum.'

'No one you know in that place, the so-called store, seems to get married at all. Or stay married.'

'I'm undercover, Mum,' I said, 'I'm pretending to be a regular Western guy.'

And for the zillionth time, there between Jackie and Shirley, I wonder what would be worse: honouring my mother by marrying a woman I didn't love, or waiting and one day maybe finding a true soulmate – and losing the respect of my family.

Not that there was any chance of anything with Jackie now. Now she was getting married to someone else.

'Of course I'm not getting married, Mam,' Jackie laughed. 'You think I'd be stupid enough to do that again?'

Invisibly I punch the air, skip a victory dance round the dining table.

'So why is that interesting? You're always seeing someone,' Shirley said with a snort, intended to be nasty, but just seeming sorrowful. 'You should fit a revolving door to get them in and out faster.'

'And I thought you would want to hear it from me, before there was gossip.'

Shirley's scowl was tightening. I think I should stand up and leave, but don't because that would remind them that I was there at all. 'It's George. I'm seeing George. You know George, one of the drivers who used to work with Dad. He left a couple of years ago. Now he works for Graysons doing European trips. The handsome bloke, with the cowboyish looks – those dazzling eyes and long crooked legs. That guy. We're in love.'

There was no one at this party because she hadn't invited anyone; she didn't need anyone because she has George.

It was like her whole life had been whittled down to the sharp point of George.

She'd probably barely even noticed that I had agreed to come, so jammed was her brain with George, and Jackie was pressing now, forcing her mother to accept it, and Shirley closes her eyes. When an old woman closes her eyes like that and goes quiet I know that they are racing inside with memories – old conversations, records, items from yesterday's news. Theirs is a history of love, bad and good. They couldn't tell you later what they are hearing because they are lost beneath pictures and sounds from their own long, sad, loving life. Then Shirley opened her wet eyes and listened for years through all the details of the last few weeks of the daughter's romance: the gifts, trips, jokes, even the old romantic tunes he'd played on the guitar. How he can do a three-point turn in a thin country lane, and push the ten-ton vehicle out of a ditch with one finger. How he knows not only about Elvis but reggae and bhangra and poetry too.

So we listen for hours, for days, until eventually Shirley looks at me, yawns and says sleepily, 'And now it's your turn, Amir. You tell us about your fantasy romance.'

ELLE

Because she had a new boyfriend, and because despite all my warnings she had still taken the Asian round to meet my gran, I was working super-hard to not need my mum, or anyone, and to become my own person, apart from the Steps or the British law system. But some lousy days I was unable to pull back, as if I was just a teeny iron filing and Mum was the powerful magnet. One hot day in June I just suddenly slipped, couldn't hold independence any longer, and so told Claire I was off to Ashanti's and I let myself in at Mum's with the secret key. I knew Mum would not be home from work so I could be in her warm space without her ever knowing.

The house was lemony light and quiet, and I saw bright empty shapes on the walls from where my photos had hung, and on the shelves dustless sections where some other memory of me had been. On the back of a chair was the Kiss Me Quick hat she'd brought back from a trip to Brighton. While there she had texted me with details of the wonderful time she was having, and the gorgeousness of her man. I texted back: 'My mum: handsome man. George Best: glass o wine.' Which was a bit disappointing because it was something else I'd gotten off Claire.

There was nothing in the fridge except half a block of cheese and a pint of milk. Just her brand-new laptop computer on the table, her coffee cup, a pile of ripped-open letters from the bank. One was addressed to Mum from Lucy Dixon, Head of Marketing Communications at MBNA Europe. The letter contained a list of boxes to tick: *Do you, Jackie Jackson, want:*

Someone you can have fun with	YES
Someone who understands you	YES
Someone who appreciates you	YES
Someone who's always there for you	YES
Someone who will look after you	YES
Someone who treats you right	YES
Someone you can rely on	YES
Someone you can trust	YES

Mum had filled in all the yes's in heavy blue biro, and Lucy had continued: '*If you're looking for a trusting and understanding relationship with someone who can provide you with all the financial support and freedom you need, then you've found your perfect match – with the Platinum Plus Credit Card from MBNA. A GOOD START TO A LONG-LASTING RELATIONSHIP –*'

Then I started up the new laptop and correctly guessed that her password is my name and date of birth, and then I read an email she's sent to Big Marilyn. 'Are you here to see me?' the man had asked her, when, no longer happy with just waving to him going by, Mum'd actually stepped off the pavement and right into the path of the coach. It was rush hour and the traffic was heavy, and he needed totally expert breaking to stop before he hit Mum. This caused beeping and swerving and a few minutes of sheer traffic chaos. 'You say it like you're addressing the grim reaper,' Mum replied, as she settled down beside him in the cab, because he did look alarmed to see her, apparently. There was a charred smell of rubber where he'd had to skid the coach on the tarmac to avoid killing her.

It reminds me of those too-sad little pots of food I'd discovered she makes for the man to have when he gets home from work. 'It's like you're feeding a stray pet,' I'd said, poking at the cold casserole.

'He's been looking very pasty lately,' she said.

Already he doesn't want her any more, I know that much. Part of me leaps, *yes, yippee, another dick bites the dust!* Part of me sinks to think that once again she's got so much crazy lonely ahead.

Without her it is like the house is sleeping, and I walk round carefully so as not to wake the table and kettle, the corkscrew and cup. And another thing to miss so bad it makes you cry: her high glossy shoes, cast off around the house like bright boats, and I crawl round and collect them back into pairs, and line them up in a sparkling harbour and put my head beside them on the carpet. I lay like that for ages, smelling her bare feet. On her bedside table she has George's address and several phone numbers. I comb two fingers through my hair and stare out the window, then give in and go sniff at the pillow but I can't smell any sour man scent, just her lovely flowery shampoo. But I know she is crying more because last weekend I heard her telling Big Marilyn that Amir had started bringing her a tissue when he brought the cappuccinos, and sometimes he added a croissant without saying a word. In one recent text he'd just written, 'Re: wot u sed earlier. I fink love is forgiveness.' He said he needed to find a bride who he loved so much that he could forgive them anything. And Mum texted back, 'Amir, u might get taken for a ride, luv,' and he immediately replied, 'No, if I loved em, I'd trust em.' And according to one text to Big Marilyn the Asian had touched Mum somehow, suddenly on the hand, so it shocked Mum a little and he had to apologise.

Some days even the tiniest thing makes me cry.

I had intended to go home before she got back from work, but somehow I'm still there on the sofa as the whole soft-pink disaster appears. Her tight face falls apart in joy because I am waiting there, scowling. Then just moments later she says, 'Elle, have you ever been frightened of me?'

'No, Mum,' I say, 'I've never been frightened of you, but I've spent a big part of my life being frightened for you. Why do you ask?'

'Oh, just something George said.'

'Who's George?' I say and she just snaps her lips shut, breathes out of her nose sharply and shakes her head.

Later, when we've had our takeaway and she is stroking my forehead with her silky warm hand, I think she is going to talk to me truthfully about love and leaving. But instead Mum tells me that she is worried about George's coach-trip guide called Babs.

'Guide as in dog or girl?' I say and Mum smiles sadly.

'Girl.'

'Perhaps she's his wife, Mum.'

'I asked him that,' Mum says quietly.

'Oh wow,' I say.

'But he just said no, that they had to work together very closely. He said it can get really hot on board. And I said it made them sound like a couple of old porn stars.'

'Er, stop right there. Consider, is this a good conversation for us to be having? Remember how old I am, Mum.'

But really, I don't know what porn is, though I keep hearing it everywhere and it's gotten so embarrassing and gone too far to admit and now there's no one to ask. Even Caprice, who is only ten, knows because I've heard her saying it. I'm so shamed. It was even ages before I proper knew about periods, despite supposedly having two mothers. Though I do know porn's nothing to do with shellfish, not *prawn*, or chess, not *pawn*, I know it's sex – so what sex *exactly*?

'OK. Now what did he say about that porn thing, Mum?'

'Well, he said yes in a way they were like porn stars, really. Him and Babs. But without the sex. And I said it sounded like they were an old married couple. Then he said he couldn't imagine me as a married woman. So I asked him if he could imagine me as a porn star and he started laughing and said that yes he could imagine that.'

I just comb my fingers through my hair, then tut in the disappointed way that Dad does. 'It wasn't an insult, love,' Mum says. 'He was laughing.'

'Yes, Mum,' I say. 'He was laughing. At you.'

'Well, darling, someone has to be the joke.'

'But why does it always have to be you?' I say and straight away wish I hadn't because I'm meant not to be getting involved at all.

'You sound exactly like Amir,' she says sadly and I want to cuddle her and ask if we can go to the cinema but she's got that faraway gaze on. 'Now I'm older, Elle, I'm not too bothered, I'd rather like to be a housewife. I'd like to have another baby and stay at home and cook, and look after people and have you back at home. Make a family. It'd be a challenge.'

'Er, if you're gonna cry about the life you've chosen to live, then I need to go,' I say and go straight upstairs because more than anything I hate it when she implies that she'd like to be Claire, because that means the Steps have won.

When I come downstairs she is washing up, but still looks like she's poked herself hard in the eye. 'Oh Mum, you're not pregnant, are you?' I say. I can almost smell the sweet little babe and see Cherub's green complexion as she gazes longingly at my new little blood relative.

'Afraid not, love,' she blubs.

'But when you do get pregnant, Mum, you could always say it was mine, to save you all the embarrassment.'

'It's meant to work the other way round. You get pregnant and I pass it off as mine.'

'Why would I want to get pregnant! I'm not like you, Mum. I'm not stupid for a start.'

'I honestly don't want you to be like me,' she said and gave me that familiar movie moment – which is just another way of telling me nothing at all. I shrug her off. 'You're right,' she says. 'I need to change. I need to forget about men completely. That's what Amir said, and that's exactly what I'm gonna do.'

I go upstairs and pack my bags.

Trying to understand a parent who you see for two days every other weekend is like trying to follow the plot of a book by reading every tenth page.

AMIR

I slept with Jackie a month later. On the nineteenth of July. It was bound to happen but immediately after I sort of wished it hadn't. Out of nowhere it came that first time. I was just there in Fags 'n' Fings helping out after work because Halima was still at her ma's house, when the door pops, the ping goes off and our Jackie's there again, handbagless, filling the place, asking me if I want to come for a half, then saying that I don't have to actually booze, of course, I just have to watch her booze and she'll buy me a coffee to thank me for coming to her mam's with her. Though that top entertainment were ages ago.

'You just have to be my sober eye, love,' she says, and then adds the explanation for everything, 'because my little one's just gone back to her dad's.'

I give her a puzzled look, though really I know it's all because she's missing her daughter. That's why she's crushing all her sober resolutions underfoot like grapes.

Jackie seemed just stepped down from a billboard: every bright thing she was wearing was fresh off a hanger, and there were a few fresh summer freckles on her nose; I knew she was telling me the truth because she looked so damp-eyed and vulnerable. But just for a moment. Then Jackie is covering her honesty up, blathering on, gone total motormouth, telling us how she and her ex can't get on at all and so she has to leave her little girl in the house alone and go out, just stand round the street corner, and then he has to come round and collect the kid fifteen minutes later. He was a handsome guy, her age, but a bad wrong choice, she tells Ashfaq, mistaking my brother for a regular person who's interested in another human's life. Jackie and her ex-husband can't even share the same doorstep any more, she tells Ashfaq. 'That's a shame,' Ashfaq says. And Jackie nods and sighs and tells him more stuff about her ex. She even tells Ashfaq she wishes she hadn't had so much choice when choosing her husbands; 'I was like a hungry kid in a sweet shop,' she says, laughing as she looks at the sweets in our shop, and then from them to me. 'Hey! You are the kid in the sweet shop, Amir! No wonder you can't choose a wife.'

'It's not like choosing a chocolate bar,' Ashfaq growls.

'Well, exactly! And that's been my mistake!' Jackie says. 'I've always just gone for what I fancied at the time.'

There is a long silence. She's lit Ashfaq's touchpaper. I look away. She coughs awkwardly, and I'm thinking how she didn't just come in casually, she thought this through, and how short life is, though she is fingering a Flake. 'Are you coming then, love?' she says to me, when I am just standing there staring at her.

'Are you going then?' Ashfaq asks, and then turns to me and hisses, 'Don't go!'

I tell him in a low whisper that Samirah and Wahida are both at home with Ma, but daren't look him in the eye as I say this. She has no handbag. No handbag, I'm thinking, like another lad might notice a lass not wearing knickers, or tit-swingingly without a bra, and so I tell Ashfaq I won't be long. 'You should ring Ma first, and ask her permission,' he says.

This is a deliberately crazy suggestion, not only because I am not seven years old, but because Ma could no longer answer questions. I might as well ask permission from the cat.

So goodbye paradise.

I turn away from my brother, walk right past him, head down, ears shut, and go to the pub with Jackie Jackson and listen to her ranting on about the gorgeous old gora, her sulky genius daughter, her miserable ma, and when I come out of the pub two hours later we share a taxi together and one minute I'm leaning over her to get out at my house and the next she has a hand on my hard cock.

Still bright evening, heat softening the air, light floating over pale skin in shimmering coins. She is the drunk one, but both of us have lost the power to reason why this is so wrong. She follows me out of the cab. It's been a week of sticky sleep-lessnesses, and this night has the fragrance of spices cooking, of mustardy weeds tickly between paving stones, and thicken-ing in the wild old gardens, brambles and strong nettles and tall flowers from other generations all pushing against the fally-downy wooden fences and making eyes hazy-itchy and hearts punch at chests and the whole terrace cough and sneeze, lose their minds with exhaustion and lust.

Though looking at her now I'm unable to remember what there is to be ashamed of.

'You can't. I mean not come in,' I mutter. 'My family . . .' They are so close by I am sure I can smell the dinner Yasmin cooked and hear TV, mad loud in the dust-warm living room. Reason and righteousness are just a few steps away and I remember all the family conversations we have had recently about what to do, about Ashfaq telling us all about Islam and the elderly and quoting passages from the Qur'an, and all of my sisters agreeing to move back in with us and take it in turns to look after Ma. Everyone reasoning it out, putting them-selves second except me; and the anxiety of my own self-interest means I can smell burning, that might be summer garden bonfires but is probably our living room – torched by Ma's evening meal.

Go right home. Get forgiven. Jackie presses her sharp red nails into my waist as she holds herself up against me. 'Seriously, you can't. I mean, come in.'

'S'OK,' she says, 'I'm a northern girl, I can do it anywhere.' And a moment later we are down the alley where the nettles reach right across and the curly thorns hang over from once tended gardens, wire twisting with weed-flowers. We are right behind my ma's house and the air is peppered black with midges and Jackie is turning her face to the old stone wall of the next end terrace and pulling up her tiny skirt from behind. Like a dog bending over, I think.

That's well wrong. I stop all that, turn her round to face me, her chest to my chest, and put one paw on her creamy cheek, the other in her silky hair. Then I stroke her slowly, firmly, swallow with my fingers that cool bolt of flesh, like she is a statue and I am a blind lad. 'This is all wrong,' I say.

'Isn't it just,' she says.

'Dreadful.'

'Dreadful.'

Holding her hair like a rope, I climb up with kisses, while I screw her right there in the sneezy green summer alley, hard and fast as it gets, until she is moaning like a wild cat and I have to put a hand hard over her ruby mouth, until neither of us can breathe or speak, and she holds me, her white hand on my brown arm, to stop herself hitting the ground, then whispers in my ear, 'Thanks, Amir,' and pulls her skirt round, tucks her blouse in and, smiling, leaves.

And I notice, for the first time ever, though this has been our back alley all my forever life, that the entire stretch is fringed with tall, strong, yellow poppies.

*   *   *

A week later I am walking through the train station with Orla, and I'm all fizzed up to a sizzling anxiety. I'm nibbling at thoughts I've been chewing all week, about how I should not have let Jackie walk away. I should have gone after her, called a cab, taken her home, made her a coffee, settled her into bed. I am deeply ashamed that I made love to her and then just let her wander away – though it's hardly the first time I've treated a white lass like that.

'Just look at that,' Orla said very quietly, widening her eyes as if the sight before her was delicious. 'Modern motherhood.'

Jackiejacksonjackiejacksonjackiejacksonjackiejacksonjack-iejackson – even the name repeats like a runaway train, and indeed here she was, red-cheeked, flat on a bench like she'd been tied to the tracks. My lover. I have tried so hard to think it just a laugh – every sleepless night – and I can see that Jackie has tried too. Thinking our bodies almost naked in the open air meant nothing has left her there like that. It is my fault. Though really, still, whenever I see her and think of those poppies, they were fitted with bright bulbs, blazing up the entire alley with the yellowiest most electric light.

A surge of passengers are spreading through the concourse, some glancing at Jackie, most not noticing, pressing on, hurrying away to work. Orla walks up and gives our Jackie a now narrow-eyed look that says, 'you are my enemy and I am yours,' and then Orla bends down to listen, and she can surely smell Jackie's slight sweat and salty creaminess: the mermaid perfume. I can hear the words she's crooning. 'There are worse things I could do. Than go with a lad or two. You try being misunderstood. Feeling flashy and no good. Just suppose it could be you. But there are worse things to be true.'

'What the hell are you doing?' Orla says, shaking Jack's arm to stop her singing. Around us announcements for trains boom out and the escalators crawl upwards, grey-thick with office bodies.

'Sssh, love,' I say.

'I thought he was the love of my life,' she says, only half opening her eyes.

'Unfortunately I think he was also the love of someone else's life,' Orla says, and I am determined not to stare at Jackie but to consider if Ma has left the kettle on with no water, or is crawling round the sofa on her knees looking for her glasses. Five minutes ago Orla and I had been discussing the sales figures from January to June, though I'd realised for the zillionth time that I had zero interest in retail. Orla said that she had something else she wanted to talk to me about and I was deadly sure I was about to get promoted, and I felt rotten deep in my gut.

There was a tag on Jackie's suitcase from the airport. And the store bag with its distinctive colour and shape screwed round her wrist, like it was from a cheap Yorkshire butcher's. 'I just fell out with that guy, nothing more,' she sighs. 'Same old gory story.' I felt breathless and dizzy. August, the coming month, was partly to blame. The heat and the holidays and the children just off school, the old feeling of being freed from rules and the bell, it still affected – and the feeling of who might like you after the break and who you might not. How you held on to dreams, job, professionalism, through this heat, how you maintained yourself, and what others thought, against the certainty that by September you wanted to be different – maybe more of a bloke, or a different lass entirely.

There are cancellations and platform changes and warnings about leaving bags unattended. I felt sticky hot now, and reckless, perhaps because I was carrying a child's school-style blackboard, which I'd just helped Orla lift down off the train, which was why I was there at the station at all, to help Orla with all the props for the Schools Out! promotion. Could you blame me for feeling like a gimp? 'I think her and her bloke might have had a row.'

'Well, Amir, even without consulting the staff handbook,' Orla whispered mock-sweet, 'I can tell you that's not our problem. Though I understand that you must be appalled by this, Amir,' Orla says. 'No wonder your lot keep yourselves away from us lot.'

Was this true? Had I done to Jackie what every other guy had done; taken what I wanted and then let her go? And was this guilt just a way of pretending I was really a better man? I knew that every minute of the day I was trying not to want her, not to think of her, and as I looked at her, there before me, I was trying to see what Orla saw, all the bad and none of the good.

In addition to the blackboard under my arm I was holding a rucksack full of school ties. Later that week the store's entire staff would dress up in uniform as school girls and school lads and the store signage would be written in chalk on these dinky blackboards. 'So what latest sales ideas you picking up there that can make Fags 'n' Fings an international retail power-house?' Ashfaq would ask me a few times every month and I'd tell him about the chalk boards, the fairy lights, the 'happenings', the costumes, the experimental music, the celebrity appearances, the theatrical events, the glittery artworks, the free samples. All our fun and laughter. 'That's not a shop, it's a circus,' he frowned. He'd only just stopped yelling at me for going out for the drink with Jackie.

'Yep, bro, we're putting ping back into shopping,' I say. 'It's the future of retail.'

'You're putting your spiritual reputation on the line, just to shock the Englishers into buying more slaggy tat they can't afford,' Halima says with a shrug. 'That's why he won't get married. He hasn't got the stamina no more because that batty-lad shop has given him too short an attention span. He's like a school kid who just wants gimmick after gimmick, and that's no good for adult life.' Though I'd not told them Orla was designing our special uniforms in conjunction with a London fashion designer, and of course they were to be 'more sexy than school'.

I place a hand on Jackie's arm and say to Orla, 'Just checking her heart.'

'I know they all insist motherhood is tiring, but surely this is taking it a bit far,' Orla sighed, upturning both palms and shaking her head. 'You're right, we shouldn't let them out alone.'

'We can't leave her here.'

'Why? Do you think they'll carry out a controlled explosion? That might be no bad thing, Amir.' Jackie's palms were pink and damp and I pressed her little left hand into mine and held it firmly.

Despite everything she looked absolutely gorgeous.

'I thought she was away sick,' Orla said to Leo on her mobile, as I stroked her fingers, 'isn't that why she wasn't here over the last week?'

'Yes, she's been ill,' I heard a tinny, faraway Leo gabble. I'd not told Leo anything about me and Jackie, though I knew everything about him and Jackie. Some guys needed to tell you about it, not exactly boasting but more like because with lasses like Jackie, those half-heads couldn't believe it themselves. Or forget it.

I move a forelock of white hair from over her closed eyes. She has one high shoe hanging off, and she looks lamed like a horse and hungry, and I suddenly wanted to ask her round to ours for a meal. Like ours were the kind of cheery Bollywoody Asians who had a ding-dong of chatty shiny visitors all day long. Witty chit-chat and the spice of good food always warm in the sweet air. And even the thought of her appearing through the black smoke of a burnt meal, or of Ma wild-haired, half-dressed, opening the door to greet Jackie with a growl, didn't stop me imagining it.

'Women's problems, no doubt,' Orla snorts, turning to me and raising her eyebrows, closing her eyes, drawing her lips in so tight they look pulled by a string. 'Like being too drunk to stand up.' Orla flashes me a smile and there is a moment before Leo replies. I can picture him on the other end of the phone, the thumb and forefinger of his left hand pressed hard into his screwed-up eyes.

Jackie groans into life, just as Orla is ringing Human Resources – 'just to check' because if Jackie is already on medication she cannot be disciplined too harshly. For if she slit her wrists in response to some action Orla has taken – well, that would not be good. There had been suicides in the other branches, Orla told me. In the past. And confidentially it is thought that because the store recruits beautiful young slender people, it has a workforce full of the lonely, starving and vulnerable. The less they eat, the more they hate their bodies, the more predatory sexual attention they have, and the less love. They die. But Jackie begins to rise, to sit up and stretch. Wounded but walking. 'Stay there,' Orla calls out, but Jackie just keeps on reaching upwards, back into perfect life.

'I'm going to check she gets home OK,' I say, dropping my sack of plimsolls and school ties. Dumped there the bag looks forlorn and ridiculous.

'The thing is, Amir, I'm going to make you an offer,' Orla said as she folded herself in, tight as a penknife. 'I think you would make a great senior fashion specialist.'

'You do?' I say and three miles away I can hear Ashfaq and Halima screeching like gulls with laughter.

'And I know you are going to be getting married this year and will need extra cash for that.'

'It's not definite,' I mumble.

Jackie's walking now, looking backwards and forwards down the line of cabs, not seeming to realise there is a queue already waiting.

I should just let her go, same way I let her walk away from yellow poppy alley. It would be best for everyone. Think of Ashfaq, Wahida, Yasmin and Samirah, and my mother.

'Do you want a rung on the management ladder or not?' Orla snaps. 'Doesn't have to be in Menswear. If Jackie Jackson continues like this, we will have a vacancy pretty soon in her department.'

'I'd be a fashion specialist in Womenswear,' I say, as Halima and Ashfaq roll off the counter and on to the floor and thump their fists on the tiles weeping tears of primetime-comedy joy.

'Well, you could be,' Orla says. 'If you don't screw up and that nasty slapper does screw up.'

'She's a good woman,' I say, still watching as Jackie weaves her way to the end of the long cab queue and sways there.

'Oh God, you're far too innocent for her,' Orla says suddenly. Her cheeks flushed, as if some of Jackie's reckless- ness has burnt Orla too. 'She just sees an innocent guy like you, Amir, and thinks yippee let me corrupt this lad before someone else does.'

'I'm going to put her in a cab,' I say, and a few metres away I see my friend stumble, and the line splatters apart to avoid her.

'Leave her,' Orla says, but I run and reach her just before she dips to the ground and I lift her and she is light and giddy like a body caught from the high-wire or the flying-trapeze.

'You won't get anywhere in management if you carry on like this,' Orla shouts in the distance, as I carry that warm near-naked body, that pale velvet face sequined with tears.

'Excuse me, sorry, excuse me, sorry,' I say loudly, as I march my bundle of curves to the front of the queue, 'let me through, this woman's sick.' And sweet-scented, eyes closed, head hung, mouth shut, she giggle-smiles and rests softly in my arms.

ELLE

Mum sighs and stretches like a cat and says it's too warm to stay indoors all day.

She's been off work for a week, because she's been 'a bit run down' though this is nuts because the air stinks of nail varnish and she's wearing pimpy styled-up clothes and her armpits are freshly dotted with tiny red berries. Cherub has started shaving and sugaring and waxing now too, and she explains body hair in great detail to Caprice, but never to me, and so I still don't know where and when you're meant to do it. Though I did hear her say some *girls* shave their *face*. How sick is that!

'Mum, if you're ill surely you're not meant to go out!'

She bites her lip and puts her head on one side. She never tells me about her illnesses, and they can't all be hangovers. This secrecy is terrible because there could be something really wrong with her, and I'd never know, though there's no one else to help her but me.

'A walk would help,' she whines. 'Oh come on, love, loosen up a bit.'

So I agree to go for a walk, and then, before I know it, there we are, hurrying down the brown part of town, where the mango and aubergine, lemon and lime stalls push out over the pavements, past the smoky internet cafés and dodgy turbaned money lenders and seedy travel agents, past coriander and cardamom and green bananas and the gruesome blood-soaked butchers offering 'whole sheep, baby chickens', and through the unspeakable languages, and there's an Islamy hustle even early evening and an old beardy stares me out and sucks his teeth when we pass, so I pull my bare arms in tighter and hurry past the old-style traders in full overalls or bow-tied aprons eyeing up what Mum is not wearing, the stink of spices, and tomatoes on trays out the back of a mucky white lorry, plotters everywhere. Satellite dishes cupped to every house beaming in news from Arabia. Definitely the smell of, maybe the sight of, a goat, or an elephant!

The fact that I am twelve years old won't matter to them one bit. In fact it just means I am old enough to be wrapped up in a black sack and married to an uncle. Claire has a friend whose daughter goes to a school where the Asians won't allow lads and girls, even in Year One, to go swimming together at all. Which is another reason I went to the Catholic school.

Crowds of black-shrouded mothers pushed past us, snipping at Mum's high heels with their double buggies, shooting bitchy looks through their eye slots – as though us two were the intruders not them. 'Where are we going?'

'I'm going to go round and see Amir, Elle. I need to thank . . .'

'Don't.'

'I am.'

'Please don't, Jackie.'

'Why are you calling me Jackie?'

'Because if you go to this Asian's house you won't be my mum any more.'

'You really are turning into your father.'

'No. I'm scared. They don't like us round here. And anyway aren't you ill?'

'How do we know they don't like us until we try? Come on, there's nothing to be scared of.'

Mum is talking to herself now. She is muttering about how she only has a vague idea of where he lives, because the last time she was down the alley she was lashed, and had arrived by taxi. We have to try out several terraces before Mum sees the door that has haunted her waking dreams. Then, ding-dong, Mad Lady Calling. A friendly older lady opens the door, smiles, grasps Mum's hand and holds it, warmly, before she's even explained who she is and this woman leads Mum into the house like she is the one guest they have been waiting for.

I should text this address to Ashanti in case we are never seen again.

But I have no choice but to follow like a little kid, staring at my horrid flat shoes, with my hands sunk deep into my freaky pockets. Just the thought of being in the Asian's house rolls a feeling that goes right up into my throat and parches it, leaves me scorched out, tingles my skin surface to a net of nerves.

Inside there are lots of people and I'm probably looking like such a total Catholic from Freaksville and suddenly I'm heart-racing and the only calm I can get is by thinking if there are any lads my age, strangers who look so chuffed and excited to see me, and then I'm imagining someone whispering, 'Hey, white girl, you wanna get away from these oldsters, innit, and come up and see my room, man.' 'Sure,' I'll say, combing two fingers through my hair, 'whatever, innit.'

But already I was seated slumped down in an old armchair and all around me was a warmly scented family party with food and sparkles, and the guests are all women who turn to me and smile; some women touch my hand and welcome me. In the distance I see Mum with her hands pressed over her mouth, saying, 'I'm sorry, really. I didn't know it was a party. I wouldn't have come.'

125

My clothes and hair are wrong. I am in the wrong house on the wrong day and I can't put my big, manly, stubbly, grubby finger on it, but there's something odd about this party. The Asian sees me, but he does not approach. His brown eyes are the shape of almonds. Instead he looks at an elderly woman, there in the corner of the room, in the chair with her TV mags and a cushion. She's grinning for a moment and then frowning in confusion, and this must be her, the sick mother. The one he cares for so tenderly. Then he turns and leaves, so it's just women in the room now, and I feel edgy again, scared for Mum. The men can be seen through the kitchen door, eating and chatting, but there don't seem to be any lads my age, though if there were I'd probably just go 'Huh' and turn away, like I weren't even bothered.

But Mum feels more comfortable when there are men around watching her. At school when girls ogle I feel kind of criticised, which is why I stopped even trying, and cause Claire such despair by wearing the black hoodie day and night. A bloke glances round the door and catches my gaze and I go cross-eyed, and think all the daddies in the kitchen are talking about me and Mum, about why we are there, and who we are, and if only I'd had the chance to steal something proper off Cherub to wear then maybe a friendly lad would have appeared and come to talk to me.

The women are still laughing and talking too, perhaps not noticing or worrying about the men. For a while I tell one of the women about school. And then, because she asks, I tell her about the Steps and Claire, making it very clear I am not related to them by blood in any way. 'I'm one of three sisters, and we have a little brother, and we used to adore him, we all treated him like a baby for years.'

I wonder if the lady thought I was a lad. I try to sit different so I look more like a girl, but I really don't know how. Maybe I'm in the wrong body too. Over there Mum is trying hard. She is looking at the woman she's talking to, not seeming the least bit ill. She is not lifting her hem, or dancing, or looking around, or making jokes, though it must be hard to give up all the tricks of making men want you. Clock Ashanti doing cartwheels through the football.

A young girl zooms by on roller-skates. A baby cries. On the television dancing twinkles out. When a lock of hair falls from the mother's headscarf, a woman gently tucks it back in. By the old mother's side is a plastic baby beaker of tea, and I watch as the Asian is touching the sides of the cup, checking its heat, then lifting it towards the mother, who frowns then sucks like a baby lamb. Another woman hands her a plate of food, which she picks at and examines with a grim look, exactly the same as Caprice uses when she's about to refuse to eat anything at all.

The Asian is wearing a loose sandy-coloured suit, very different to what he wore when he came round to Mum's house. He has long, curved, lozenge-shaped fingernails, clean and pink as inside shells. He is the tallest man in his family, but still he doesn't come to talk to Mum, but stays with the men – like me and Mum are of no interest to him at all. Instead the aunt appears with a glass of Coke and tells us that Amir's mother has eleven grandchildren, and that she sees them every week. 'I see my gran one week, and my nana the other week,' I say and she smiles and says, 'That's good, that's very important nowadays for a boy to learn from his grandmother.' And I go quiet and then croak, 'I'm a girl,' and she says, 'Oh, of course, I meant girl, silly me.'

Now I realise why Claire insisted that my next school is the Catholic girls only: it's the only way anyone will actually know I am a girl.

I want to call Dad but he's miles away on the other side of the city. In the kitchen the Asian makes jokes, and around his family he seems the funniest man in the room, and when he speaks, even distantly in another room, all the women in this room go quiet, like his low voice is a teacher's whistle that means *sssh, stop and listen*. Into this quiet he suddenly appears and says Mum's full name, 'Jackie Jackson.' Then repeats this full name to his mother, 'Jackie Jackson, Ma,' who stretches out a large curled brown hand to touch Mum, then looks back to the TV screen and studies the show like she is one of the judges.

There's a display case stuffed with school photographs, just like Claire has at home, but this one is more messy because there are more kids to display. Amir tells them all again that Mum is Jackie Jackson, and Mum turns and tells them all that I, Elle, am her daughter.

Clock the sharp gasp of surprise throughout the party as my surprising sex is revealed. I scowl and pick at my jeans, and want Mum to say about how I won a prize at school and how I'm going in Gifted and Talented again, but I know she won't because she's gazing like a special-needs at Amir.

Then I know she's not lying, she really is sick; lovesick. But this time the lovebug's making her dopey and calm, rather than hyper and weepy.

But then again all the women smile at every little word he says – even these words: *Jackie is a friend of mine, Ma*. They adore him, even when he is saying about Mum and her job. Particularly one lass, who is tinselled with gold chains, hung with hoops, and who gives a tiny smile at the floor whenever Amir glances at her, and when he speaks she opens her mouth – like she's one of those voice-recognition baby dolls. She is about old enough to be my pretty big sister, and when I think this Mum must think it too because she glances at me sadly: *poor little lonely only who looks like a lad*. Amir is asking Mum questions about her day, how hungry she is, but she is finding it hard to speak, so he leads her to a table with a patchwork-bright buffet spreading a warm fug over the dining room. I follow as her dark shadow. An older guy in a suit comes in from the kitchen and is chatting loudly in another language, blowing the words in Mum's direction, smiling, and the skating girl wheels round us in circles. We are the only white people in the room. When Claire was explaining why I couldn't go to the big school nearest Mum's house, and why I had to go to the Catholic girls', she said that it would be horrible for me to be the only white in a school. Mum had reluctantly agreed though she didn't want me going to the Catholic school, or a girls only, because Mum says we're not Catholics and the world isn't made up of only girls, but Dad and Claire said this wasn't the point, the point was getting me the best education around.

Because, obviously, I'm not going to be able to rely on my looks or my body to make my fortune.

But now Mum loads up her plate, like she's completely well and never has needed a rest in her life, and comes to stand near to me and goes on about how wonderful the food is, so I decline to have anything from the buffet though I am starving. OK, I know I am doing what Caprice does, punishing my mother by refusing to eat, though unlike Claire, who weeps and rages about it, my dear mother doesn't even care to notice.

'Sorry, love,' Mum says to Amir when her big pink gob eventually stops chewing, 'I didn't know you were entertaining.' For some reason Mum can't stop smiling, though I've refused three invitations now to get something from the buffet.

'Neither did we! He's definitely not entertaining me,' says a thin-lipped woman with a baby on each hip, giggling at Amir.

'That's my sister-in-law,' Amir says, still smiling at Mum. 'She loves me, really, don't you, Halima?'

'I do not!' she says. 'I think you are a disgrace!'

'Shall we go?' Mum asks, and everyone says no, we should both stay. Amir agrees, yes we should definitely stay. He is looking at Mum like she has a secret message written on her forehead and I am wondering why everything seems to be going OK, when I remember that there is no booze at this party. This is the first adult do I have ever been to where there is no booze, and the first party where Mum hasn't been the centre of attention within minutes. Though it would be horrible to think, like Claire and Cherub and Caprice, that there was no more mystery to Mum than alcohol. And anyway why shouldn't she be the centre of attention if she wants to be? So I'm chuffed when a little lad comes over and strokes Mum's shimmering skirt, and he says it's like she's stepped down from the TV screen, and a little girl comes over and gives Mum a warm sweet straight from her gob. A pretty woman who looks a bit like Amir comes over and says that it's nice to meet Amir's friends. I don't say anything; just look round at the pile of videos in a rack, the CDs, the vases of fresh flowers, and the horse brasses by the gas fire. Another aunt appears and gives me another plate and says I should help myself to some food, but before I have a chance to make a point about the fact that I am not eating, Mum stretches over and introduces herself to the aunt. 'I'm a friend of Amir's from the store,' she says, like she is Alice reminding herself who she is and how she got to Wonderland. The aunt offers Mum a drink, though Amir gives Mum a look that says he hopes Mum knows this drink will be non-intoxicating. Though you could suggest they throw a bucket of it over a big letchy bloke who's been gazing at Mum non-stop. He's got that agonising strain, like he's down the gym and lifting an impossibly heavy weight. He calls Amir's name and Amir tells Mum that he has to go and talk to his brother about cartons of milk.

A likely story, as Dad would say.

When the glass of lemonade arrives, delivered by the skating girl, Mum tries to make a joke with me and two other women about wondering how half the world gets through family parties without alcohol, but no one laughs, perhaps because they don't understand it.

A little girl comes up to Mum and says, 'Do you dress like that so everyone will look at you?' But before Mum can answer the thin-lipped mother pulls her away and slaps her legs and at the other side of the room I see Amir watching Mum and laughing. 'Remember Marcel,' I warn. 'Your love is poison, Mum.'

'Are you cold?' the Asian asks when he comes back from talking to his brother.

I understand his cheerful busying about. This is what you have to do when you are trying to keep everyone happy. One minute he's joking with his men-mates, the next he's speaking quietly to Mum. He looks cheery but I bet inside he's like me on last Christmas Day; edgy and totallyfreaked.com. And even when Mum tells him she is fine and not too cold at all, he disappears and comes back with a cardigan, which he puts round Mum's bare shoulders. The family look at her more closely now, but I say, quietly, 'Gee, great, he's covering you up.'

'I was just . . . popping round to say sorry,' Mum says.

'Sorry?' the aunt frowns. 'What've you done now, Amir?'

But before Amir can reply, the aunt is explaining the buffet again and starting to put food on to a plate, rice and curry and breads and then a bowl of trifle, and ice-cream. The old lady just glances up from her TV magazine and smiles at Mum kindly – one sick mother to another.

Eventually, because no one notices anyway, I nibble at the onion bhaji. Kids come thundering down the stairs and gather round the television and the channel is changed into *Robin Hood*, which some of the children watch, while others break off and play a game of jacks, and I want to say that once upon a time I was a master of that game. Mum is smiling and laughing and I suddenly realise one unusual thing about her –

she likes change, whereas most grown-ups hate it and try to avoid it, and are fond of what's past and gone, and are afraid of the future and what is to come.

Amir is dashed off again, to be a different person elsewhere. Mum says we should go but we stay. So I get more buffet and watch *Robin Hood* with the little kids and a small lad tells me how this is his favourite ever programme, and I tell him that I love it too. I hear Mum over with the women and they are talking about their husbands and children and relatives and I bet Mum hasn't felt like such a single mother in ages.

Ashanti says her mum chose to be a single mother, but she's probably lying.

The old woman is looking itchy and Amir whispers to his sister who leads her away. A group of women are talking in English about driving lessons, and my foaming stomach tightens and my forehead moistens as I hear Mum tell them about the instructor from Quick Pass who tried to touch her up. *Whoa! Steady!* They just laugh, though, and say she should have asked for a female instructor, and Mum admits that it had never occurred to her, and they look at her like she is perhaps a little stupid. And they ask if she is too hot, or too cold, and if she would like a window opening, or the fire putting on, and Mum says that we are just fine and their eyes make eye-sized question marks: *why on earth are you here?*

Then they are talking about school league tables and class-room discipline and the best ways to get a baby to sleep through the night. Mum says, 'I don't think I slept at all for the first year Elle was born, which actually explains a lot.' Then they are sharing stories of sleepless babies, and someone else is discussing the advantages of giving a baby antihistamines before flying to Pakistan and I am full up with buffet now and just listen to the gabble, feeling a little sleepy, like I am that happily drugged baby on the long-haul flight.

Caprice is right about one thing: it's terrible the way eating makes you feel so damn good.

Then Amir comes over and introduces Mum to his uncle, who nods at Mum shyly. 'We work together at the store,' Amir says.

'It's a crazy job but someone has to do it,' Mum says, wiggling her shoulders so her udders bob up and down.

'We used to love *Are You Being Served?*' the uncle says and I don't know what he's on about.

'That's why I took the job at the store.'

'Are you serious, Amir?' Mum asks.

'Why else would I have ended up there?'

'So do you enjoy the work, Jackie?' the uncle asks.

'Well, I love the people,' Mum says and Amir blushes, and both me and Mum and the uncle notice how Amir looks down at his feet as he agrees, smiling, 'Yes, it's all about the people, the people are fantastic.'

Amir hurries away and I see a little girl playing with her father, and I think how I never ever have any time with my dad alone.

'Are you all right, love?' Aunt asks, coming over to me and Mum and exchanging blinks with the uncle. It reminds Mum of what trouble she can be.

'Not really. But am I getting better? I've been heartbroken,' Mum says. *Whoa! Steady on!* But Mum's talking now about what's happened to her over the last year and it's like a sudden emergency and they should be dialling 999, rushing out into the street waving their arms. There is an uneasy bubble of quiet. The beautiful gold-dripping girl looks around over her shoulder at Amir, and smiles. Mum gives me a comedy eyeball roll which I understand: *I've seen more brains in a Barbie.*

'Which means we should leave, Mum,' I say, putting my plate down and standing up quickly.

Mum nods sadly. 'This was lovely food. Thanks so much for having us. It's been like being at a wedding,' she says. 'But we'll get off now.'

The tufty old mother comes back into the room, led by the sister, and hearing this she suddenly laughs long and loud, itching her hair and stabbing at her TV remote, trying to turn Mum off. She is not speaking English, but I know, from that mouth-curl that I recognise on Gran's face, what she means, when she turns to Amir and gabbles: *Weddings! Don't talk to me about weddings!*

We have said our goodbyes now and are about to leave. Uncle has led Amir away, back to his proper place, then suddenly there is a snapple of shuffling at the other end of the room as the beautiful doll-girl bounces to her silver-strapped feet and throws her napkin on the floor – remember in Disney the way young princes throw down a leather glove before a duel? Then men stop talking, Amir puts his head to one side, I pull on Mum's wrist. 'What's a woman meant to do, Jackie?' the beautiful girl says. 'Have you any idea how many idiots I've met since I started looking for a husband? I'm on the verge of giving up.'

'Come on, Mum, let's go,' I say. 'Hurry.'

The woman is speaking with a broad accent, and throws Mum a sharp smile. Like Mum is the sequined assistant spinning on the wheel, and this lass has a belt full of daggers. Amir's sisters frown-blink at one another. Even sober, even wearing a woolly cardigan, my mum ends up eventually causing grief. The old mother has gone flappy again, and she scrabbles in her hair as if she's lost something in there. Amir's face is crumpling like mine does when you feel your two huge metal worlds meeting in midair.

'I'm sorry, I didn't know,' Mum says to the girl.

'Would jacking it all in be the right proper thing to do, eh? Just giving up and going out for a laugh on my own?'

Beauty snaps her clickety heels then throws this knife in precisely, so everyone is watching Mum, her clothes, hair, her too-much make-up. *Whoa! Steady!* Amir slides his glares between Mum and the bride and I know exactly how he feels inside; he wishes he was invisible, or didn't even exist at all, because then his family's life would be a lot easier.

'Well, love,' Mum says, though I'm pulling on her sleeve to just go, 'I'm no expert, but I think you just have to weigh up what hurts more, the ache of looking and trying and longing, or the emptiness of no longer bothering.'

And Mum had probably meant it as a joke but there was a stretched bubble of quiet until the thistly old mother came over, put her arms round Mum, held her firmly like a sad child, and cried, 'Poor you. Poor you.' And she hugs us both and I feel my hot forehead fall into her soft warm neck and my wet eyes close as she strokes our clothes.

It stayed like that until her handsome son came over and gently led her away from us.

AMIR

'Now u r officially off sick u shd consider getting over lttle old bloke, clearing ur debts n giving up drinking n smoking,' I text, and she texts back excitedly – 'U r a genius, luv!!!!!!!! Tell me more!!!!!!!' and suggests we meet. I could still smell her in our living room, though Jackie had left quickly and without me saying goodbye, and shortly after Uma had left too and I'd not seen her since. So there was nothing stopping us. Jackie was signed off with stress and exhaustion – officially free from both her dickass man and her silly job – and I had no future wife either.

When we get to our coffee bar I repeat what I've said in my text, but in more daddish detail, then add, 'If you just use this doctor's note to calm down and rest, and definitely forget romance for a while, you might notice a difference.'

'There'd be a difference all right,' she says, applying her lipstick while looking at me, like I am her mirror, 'there'd be nothing left to live for, love.'

I study the menu, knowing she is smiling right into me, frying my brain like some powerful laser beam. To stop me wanting her I am wondering hard if I am really in love with her, or if like a bad kid I just want to annoy my brother. I thought of Samirah, who each night now has to bath Ma. Ma who was newly afraid of water, and most days unable to remember how to dress herself. Everyone agreed that I needed a kind, strong, fit bride, with good genes and a straightforward practical mind, and a knowledge of basic hygiene issues.

This woman was not Jackie.

This dirty fox, with her soft pink chin resting in her warm white palm, who is softly saying, 'I love it when I make you blush, Amir.'

'And why's that, Jackie?' I say seriously, trying not to encourage this too-familiar empty flirting.

'I guess I just like making a man's body do things it thinks it shouldn't do.'

If I don't encourage her comic routine, then she might speak truthfully to me and we might move on.

I need to think straight because everyone was panicked that I had rejected Uma and yet I had still not chosen the next meeting, though my aunt had come with new news of more women. Seeing Jackie round ours had put the international matchmakers on overtime. The desperate, the lonely, the baby-crazed, the young, old, fat, bearded, beautiful but mad; they were seeping out of the cracks in our extended family in a steady desperate drip now. Anyone but Jackie.

And I'd stalled for time, by saying I'd marry anyone as long as they were smart and kind. But this was proving a mistake. Because I'd said I'd rather have a pleasant clever plump-pot than bitchy beauty the doors had now swung open to frumpy second cousins, friends of cousins, the girl who knew the man who'd been engaged to the girl who'd worked at the dental hospital. I'd said I couldn't think about it now but would decide definitely by the new year. 'How old will you be then?' my poor ma cried. 'He's already an embarrassment. He goes around with women as their friend. Yes, Halima's right – it's just like he's a gay. My son the gay gooseberry.'

'I didn't think she knew the word,' Yasmin said later.

'She knows more than the word,' Wahida said wearily, and I knew it was harder for them. Wahida was thinking of postponing the last year of her training and Samirah was talking of going part time at work to help care for Ma.

Jackie keeps staring at me, smiling, and I suddenly, madly, imagine her caring for Ma. She's looking at me as if she's imagining something crazy too. Perhaps she knew that I'd had girlfriends, but the ones I trusted I didn't fancy and the ones I fancied I didn't trust. Perhaps Ashfaq was right; you certainly couldn't find both in one English bird. Perhaps there really was something corrupt in them, an irreparable moral kink.

I'd certainly felt a strange nervousness first seeing Jackie there with my ma in our living room. Like she was highlighted with a fluorescent marker and the whole world could see her there. Her mad ways putting ours in danger. And I felt ashamed of something. Not Ma, I'd not think of her like that. But maybe it was Jackie with her keen grin and her purple, revealingly low, T-shirt. I felt embarrassed by her flesh but excited too and a bit annoyed. As if she was trying to control my world with that body I so helplessly desired.

Yesterday lunchtime I had come home to find Wahida and Samirah both there in the kitchen feeding Ma, who had had to be bathed after soiling her clothes. Wahida had called Samirah for help when Ma got angry and upset. Samirah had had to leave work. I was on an early shift and I got home just in time to see Wahida brushing then plaiting Ma's hair while Samirah wiped Ma's mouth gently with a wet face-cloth. I watched them for a moment, and inhaled the women's faintly soapy scent, there in our kitchen. 'Why didn't you call me?' I asked. I stroked Ma's face with my hand and she purred. She liked me to hold her old head between my palms like a heavy fruit.

'You were at work.'

'You were at work,' I say. 'And my job's the most useless of us all, I should be the one coming home to help.' This was true. Samirah was a teacher and Wahida was training to be a social worker. I sold shirts to wannabe celebrities that cost more than my sisters earned in a week.

For a while we spoke wearily of Ma and what we should do about the doctor's suggestion of day care, and then hesitantly, because we were all alone without Yasmin or Ashfaq, Wahida glanced at Samirah, bit her bottom lip and began, 'We were just saying it was good to meet your friend the other day.'

'Yes, you never introduce us to anyone you know from work,' Samirah said, too quickly, perhaps fearful of the coming conversation. But there was no danger because there was no conversation; I just stood there, like a kid who's been caught with condoms in his coat pocket.

'It seems to be causing you such problems, being friends with Jackie,' Wahida says gently, spreading Vaseline on to Ma's mouth, so Ma giggles and pouts. I open my own dry mouth but no sound comes out. Ma looks at me and grins, then with just the shift of one muscle Ma's giving me the total evils.

'Let's have a cup of tea,' Samirah says, and we all laugh because this has always been her solution to every family crisis.

When the tea is served, and Mum has hers milky in the baby cup, I croak it out, 'I suppose I fear perhaps Ashfaq's right; I might be disrespecting my family and my religion by being friends with Jackie.'

'Your family have coped with worse things,' Samirah says, and I wonder if she is referring to Ma, or to Wahida's unspoken-about divorce. Ma sucks on her baby spout noisily and Samirah strokes her back as the old baby sups.

'And it depends how deeply you go into your religion,' Wahida says, and looks at me with a smile that I know means, *after all you don't want to end up like Ashfaq.*

'But our religion is more than religion, it's our inheritance,' Samirah adds, with what I think might be a little warning glance at her big sister, the daring divorcee. 'All our history and experience and tradition is caught up in our religion.'

We all nod.

No one says anything for a while. Instead we listen to our mother suckling and then sighing. 'But you have to balance what you take from the past with what you build for the future,' Wahida says, not looking at the unmarried childless 38-year-old, but at poor old Ma.

'How?' I plead jokingly.

'How on earth do I know!' Samirah exclaimed. 'If I knew that, Amir, my life would be a whole lot easier.' And we knew she was referring to the mysterious white postman who we'd all heard whispers about but knew nothing for certain.

'Don't ask me either,' Wahida said with a sigh. 'I'm the one getting tempted by internet dating.'

So I put my arm around Wahida and hug her and Samirah says, 'Like that, I guess. That's how you balance the past and the future, by just caring for people.'

'Yes,' Wahida says as she begins to rinse out the teapot, and refill Mum's plastic baby beaker with warm milk, and check the temperature, and then fold Ma's stiff fingers round it, 'that's the main thing, I guess, just caring for people.'

'Yes, that should be the basis of any religion,' Samirah says. 'So if you're doing that, Amir, you can't be going too wrong.'

And that was it, we moved on to talking about day care again. Which, we all simply suddenly agreed, seemed like a good idea.

Now, I drink coffee and Jackie drinks tea and eventually when we've stared at each other for a century I say, 'Anyway, what do you mean by having nothing to live for? What about your career? What about the store?' I hope my deep wide-eyed stare adds, '*What about us?*'

'Would you really want to marry me, Amir love, if I was the kind of woman who lived for her work? Hell, I'd be bloody Orla!'

'I don't want to marry you,' I have to say, because her hard teasing makes you lie, and anyway it seems that I am too much of a dickass coward to speak honestly to her when both of us are free and single, and there's just the two of us alone together, staring at one another in an empty coffee shop on a grey Yorkshire afternoon.

'Just checking, love,' she says, blows me a kiss, and trots out.

PART THREE

ASHFAQ

'Jackie?' I say to Amir, curling my lip like I've never heard of her. 'Who the hell's Jackie?'

Halima says that if we mention this woman too much it will encourage Amir, but he is already encouraged, and now the little prick just ignores my question and pansies around putting on his tight leather jacket, tying the white laces of his expensive polished shoes, and combing his girly rock-star hair. No surprises. I've seen all this coming. 'I'll be back late. Don't wait up,' he says now. Like I am his spluttery old father and he is some international fucking playboy.

I stand up. 'Just turn to Allah, no one can shoulder this shit alone,' I say.

'I'm going to meet my friends,' he says like a little girl, so for a moment I smile at him.

'Don't go,' I say. 'To that tart.'

He frowns and, as he does so, for a second he reminds me of our pa. That picture in my wallet of Pa beside the net of red and blue footballs he hung up outside the front of AP News. Blokes round here remember those footballs, it's part of their childhood memories, just like they have recollections of our pa wearing that bran-brown cotton overall, same every day.

145

A blue biro in the top left-hand pocket – which he'd use to write down every sale, always on a small, lined pad of paper – the amount paid carefully detailed next to the item, even when it might be only one Kit-Kat and a roll of bog paper. There was nothing you couldn't get at AP News. Pa took great pride in stacking the shop right up along every wall, tight to the ceiling. That old wooden stepladder to get up to the top shelves. That long-handled pole, with the brass hook for poking high boxes down. Remember how he'd whack you with that pole if you were going bad, or spoke to him rude. That original mahogany counter, glass-topped, polished each morning with a soft yellow cloth. In there, in a wooden drawer, the finest chocolate bars and the boxed sweets. Tinkly silver foil, glossy paper wrappers, proper firm cardboard boxes. Pa slides out the chocolates drawer carefully, like a top jeweller, lifting it up on to the counter so the customer could consider the selection close-up.

All gone that. Nowadays our local kids are so big and fat, both theirs and ours, lads and lasses, they stuff their hands in the chocolate mega dumpers and are buying five bars at a time. Eat most stuff while they are still waiting to pay. Drop the litter before they are even out the door and now Amir is standing before me nattering to Wahida about where they are meeting and who's coming along and how they might go for a meal, or might just stay in the bars because it all depends if Jackie has a babysitter arranged or not, because this is one of the weekends Jackie has access to her daughter.

'You'd think if she had access to her daughter, she'd want to actually be with her daughter,' Yasmin says, but Amir just ignores her.

'Amir, do you need a thump?' I say, staring at the carpet.

For years I thought all Pa's carefulness, his quiet detail, was unique to our pa, but later when I travelled through Pakistan myself I saw blokes like him all over in the shops and markets. Proud, serious, authoritative men. And back when Ma could answer questions she told me all about my grandfather, Pa's pa, and how he had sacks of lentils and peas and peppercorns out the front of his shop. Scooping spices into brown paper bags with a silver cup, and the boy on the big black bicycle delivering groceries all day long in the blistering heat to grateful customers, and on through the warm evening until everyone was served.

These days Ma thinks I am Pa, and she don't even remember my grandfather and his shops, and I'm the only one who's properly been to Pakistan and Amir don't want to go, says he's not bothered about going at all, and now Amir's kissing Ma on the cheek and stroking her hair, like he's her distant relative come on a quick charity visit. He even said to me the other day, 'And what shall we do about Ma? We've got to make a decision soon,' like she's some troublesome pet we should take to the vet.

'Amir, if you carry on like this you will definitely soon be going into town. In an ambulance.'

Now in our warm living room Yasmin appears, frowning, arms folded, and for a moment I even think she is Ma, years back when she was firm and strong, as she says, 'Listen to your brother, Amir!'

Wahida says, 'He's old enough to make his own decisions, Yasmin.'

Samirah says, 'Wahida, let's calmly talk this through.'

'I'm off,' the little bum-boy says. 'See ya later.'

'Those gori slags are not your friends and they are too much for any normal man to handle,' I say calmly, though I can smell him, stinking up like some goddamned girl, but I don't mention that.

'He's not normal,' Halima says. 'He's a fashion freak.' And Amir nods and blows my wife a camp kiss, and Halima gives him the finger. 'Batty lad,' she says. 'Gay lad. Bum lad.' She was right that on a Friday night in our town all the white lasses went out to get lashed with their mates, and then the following night they went out to get lashed again with their blokes. Today was Friday, so it meant Amir was out as one of the lasses. But he didn't care; if it meant he could declare his love at last, he'd go out with the hen parties, wearing devil horns and L-plates.

'Perhaps you're right,' Amir sighs. 'Who knows.'

I stare at my brother very calmly. I assumed that, like Pa, every day I would work hard for my family, and when I had built the business up then Amir and his wife could take the shop over, and Halima and me would open another branch elsewhere. When Samirah married, she could have that shop, and I would open another one to give to Wahida and her daughters. Amir would learn about the business from me, and then he'd teach his sons what he knew, and our pa and his pa before would see all this continuing and be glad and one day we even might all go back to Pakistan and live in a beautiful mansion we'd built, and help our poor neighbours and Pa's old friends, and so honour our pa and his people, and all they had given us.

We would be good.

Amir is back to explaining how he's got a text from his friend at the store, called Marilyn, explaining where they are meeting. 'Yeh, I'm still so worried about Jackie, I need to go. I hope she's gonna be all right,' he says as he checks the money in his gimpy zip-up wallet. Ma is concentrating real hard on a grain of rice that is fallen on the carpet, and her old fingers are furiously padding away on her knees like she's typing at an invisible laptop, and I think if he really loves a lass like that Jackie, how can he also love and care for any of the women in our family, which means they will have no protection in the future and will all be in danger.

148

'You see, she's had such a hard year, and now she's been dumped by her bloke and she's still not over him, and her daughter . . .'

They are all looking at me. Waiting to know how I will take charge and bring us back to the path of respect and calm. It's like I actually am Pa, as Ma thinks, and I'm standing a metre above this family, looking down. I try to advise the Muslim lads and lasses that come into our shop about their manners and their dress and their responsibilities, but they just smile and say, 'Yeh, Ash, man, yeh.' Even the Muslim girls are proudly having their bras busting out of their school cardigans nowadays and huge bruising eyeshadows like they are starring on MTV.

'Amir, I command you to stay here with us. You're not leaving this house.'

'I am,' he shouts like a gimpy little kid. 'I'm off to meet my mates.'

I repeat that line, in the same whining way, then laugh because I can see a tiny tear in his baby eye and it makes me proper chuckle. Halima leaps forward and grabs my shoulder. 'We know you mean that blonde bint who came here, to our house. When Ma was there watching! And ruined another perfect match. That fat old slag with her hair all messed up,' Halima says, holding on to me hard.

'Make-up like a circus clown . . .' Yasmin says. 'Dressed like a prostitute.'

'Drunk as a fish.'

'She wasn't drunk,' Amir says, and I admit that, surprisingly, that was the truth. 'That's why you were disappointed. You wanted everyone to hate her and they didn't.'

'Upsetting Ma. Bringing shame and dishonour on us all. What kind of woman will want to marry into a family like this now?' Yasmin says then starts crying.

'If you go out that door to meet that vanilla tart you can

forget coming back here tonight,' I say very gently with a little smile.

'It's my house,' he shouts, and I think he's coming over to hit me in the face, and I want him to, because at least it would mean that he was listening and caring about what we were telling him. And then I'd flatten the cocky little bastard. 'I live here. I have a key.'

'Correction: you used to live here,' I say calmly, smiling. 'You used to have a key. But if you go out tonight with that slaggy lass from your slaggy shop then you don't live here any more. Sorry.'

My sisters are shouting and crying, but Amir's is the only voice I hear clearly, the only face I see. Suddenly somehow we're wrestling on the floor like we did when he was the little kid and I was his big brother and it's such a shock, and it's like he's gonna tickle me, while still kicking and jerking around. Halima and Yasmin screeching for us to stop. Ma standing up, scrubbing at her hair like she's rubbing in some invisible shampoo.

Finished, I throw Amir down for dead and hold the keys up above his head. He looks nine years old and I have to smile. Which makes him try to kick me, which makes me proper kick him in the ribs.

'She's not a slag, she's my friend. I like her,' he says quietly, curled there like a sad little girl.

'Say you'll never see her again.'

'No.'

'Say it.'

'No.'

'I command you to say you will never see her again.'

'No.'

'You're in love with her, aren't you?' I say.

When I say that word, Amir looks at me deeply and his bleeding mouth opens a little wider. Then I am looking out the window at our moonglowing street, the normal people going about their ordinary lives with dignity and restraint, and there is a long period of quiet – just crying. 'Then get out,' I say calmly. 'And never come back.'

In the distance I can hear Wahida sobbing about caring for people and I say to the room, 'Calm down, and go and put the bloody kettle on.' But behind me no one moves, and when I turn round all the women are down on the floor, crouched, as if round a little fire.

ELLE

When Mum curls out into the starlit night holding a huge goblet of wine I shout out, 'You drink too much, Mum.'

'I'm drinking for two,' she replied and kept a very serious and sombre face on as she settled back down on the rickety wooden bench and lit up a cigarette. Mum watched while my jaw hit the table and Marilyn gasped, and Danuta shrieked until Mum added, 'Don't be silly! I mean I'm drinking for both of us, you and me, Elle. You're not old enough to drink, darling.' I giggle and a smile springs on to her lips, and I know she wants a baby for me as much as for her.

I go back to pretending to read my book about the Romans, while staring at the golden spike heels which have appeared on her feet like magical hooves. The women all talk about babies and when is best to have them and I carry on reading because I know I'm not there at the pub with her for my cheerful company, I'm there because Claire found out that Mum once hired a babysitter during my access visit and sent a long letter about it, which ended with the line, 'I really don't know why people have children if they don't want to spend time with them.' But that's not the only reason; I'm also there so Mum can't get totally lashed, or cop off with anyone, so I do have a proper purpose and I'm delighted to be out with her, no men, just her best girl mates. Clock Cherub's face when she hears I spend Saturday evening boozing outside the pub!

Happily I pretend to read and listen to them talking about all that has gone wrong and what Mum should do about it. 'I guess you're not surprised, neither of you,' Mum says, lighting another cigarette. Mum is smoking hard like she does it for medical reasons and it's true it does make her look rough and gorgeous, the headlamps behind beaming sudden sparkles round her soft hair.

'He was an old man,' Marilyn says quietly.

'But he was my old man!' Mum says and sings and sups her way through the whole song. ' "Lost me way and don't know where to roam." '

'So you dillied and dallied, dallied and dillied,' Marilyn sings.

'And I can't find my way hoooooooooooome.'

Then there is a pause while we all wonder what will happen next. 'I don't want you feeling sorry for me. I mean, it was nothing. Just a fling. I'll be fine. I'm going to take some time to sort myself out.'

'I don't feel sorry for you,' Danuta said and it was obvious from the way she coughed that she just meant she was glad that she was not Mum.

'At least Orla can't say anything now you're under the doctor,' Marilyn says, sipping her ice-cubey drink, and gazing up at Mum like what she'll say next will be very interesting.

On and off all day I've been feeling nervy about what illness she really has and why she doesn't tell me nothing about it, but I don't want to mention it in case it worries her.

'Dear Teacher, Tommy can't come to school today; I'm under the doctor. Boom boom.'

'You know, there's someone out there for everyone, Jackie,' Danuta said.

'But that's what worries me, love. I have to make sure I don't meet anyone else.' And everyone hooted again, like Mum has her own popular sketch show. 'Actually the worst thing is I keep remembering him undressing me for bed,' Mum says, in a whisper when she thinks I'm not listening – and again everyone does huge porny laughs. Except me, because I haven't heard about anyone undressing her recently.

'I thought he'd be here by now,' Mum says and stands up and looks left and right down the dark empty road. Danuta and Marilyn glance at one another and jiggle their ice-cubes, and I look up and round but no one catches my eye. To our right a gang of boozed-up girls are shrieking and standing on the bench and the wobbly table next to us is rocking and the daft big umbrella's swaying dangerously and I want to go home.

'What?' says Mum, grinning and lifting her palms to the sky, but her mates don't reply and I don't know what's going on and want to ask who else is coming to the pub, and if it's the man who saw her naked.

So I tell her that Claire has bought the new school uniform already, though my new term at the all-girls school is ages away. 'Er, well, that's very efficient of Claire,' Mum said, calmly, turning to smile at her fans, 'there's another month before you start your new school.' Boom boom!

'Claire likes to be prepared well in advance, Mum,' I said. 'Remember she's totally the opposite of you.'

'I'm prepared for the things that matter, Elle,' she said and there was a long pause while I pretended to carefully consider this, and then put a finger on my chin, narrowed my eye, turned to the live studio audience and said, 'Er, no, you're not, Mom.'

And everyone laughed, which made me feel a bit better, and the chatting and drinking goes on and the air comes smudgy with night and zoom and swishing headlamps and the boozy girls have gone, and if I look hard up at the stars then I just hear little dark snips of conversations that shoot around the night air like midges. 'You mean you're still wondering about that girl, the one you called a crazy bitch?' Marilyn says.

'She called me a crazy bitch. I was the crazy bitch not her,' Mum says, looking hurt.

'Oh sorry, I'm getting all confused,' Marilyn said. 'But surely there's room enough here for two crazy bitches.'

'No, that's the point, this story ain't big enough for both of us bitches.'

Mum keeps checking the time on her mobile as she talks, and I keep looking backwards and forwards up and down the road too, because I like to be very alert when I'm with her. All Mum's mates are getting drunk and they are talking about anything that comes into their heads. 'I really used to think when I was a teenager that I'd end up famous and on television,' Mum says and they all laugh.

'And now what? You're nearly forty and work in a shop, so *Crimewatch* is your best bet?' Marilyn said, giggling, though I thought it was a really horrible thing to say.

'I'm not going to commit a crime,' Mum laughs, 'I'm just going to try and find out who he's seeing.'

I wonder if she means the Asian, or the oldster, or some other lousy pea brain.

I can tell they are all waiting for something else to happen and are just filling in the time with chat. 'Is it a crime to fall in love?' Mum sighed, and Danuta whinnied like a horse, so Mum looked at her hard. 'Surely you know what I mean, Danuta? I'm serious. It might be a joke to you but to me it's the meaning of life. Is it a crime?'

'Only when you do it,' Marilyn says.

'I don't think he's coming,' Mum says. 'I thought you said he was.'

'Perhaps he's changed his mind,' Danuta says.

'Or maybe he wasn't allowed out with us,' Mum says, standing up again and looking round, worried.

'Probably for the best,' Marilyn says, staring into her drink.

'Yeh,' Danuta nods. 'I think so.'

'But . . .' Mum says, and then looks at me and stops, and I think if a silver car comes round the corner next Mum won't get lonesome and upset.

'Look, can I ask you one thing? Don't do anything stupid,' Marilyn says, stiffly.

'Shall we go, Mum?' I say.

'Stupid, as in wha' exactly?'

'Getting drunk and going off with unsuitable men.'

Mum looks around the busy noisy tables outside the pub and says, 'I can't see any unsuitable men to go with.'

'Let's go home,' I say and fold my arms hard and rub at my shoulders and go, 'Brrrrrrrrrrrr,' and tap my feet on the concrete loudly.

'They're different. They don't act like us,' Marilyn says, getting up to go to the bar again, and when she comes back with the drinks one of the blonde hen-night lasses, now at the next table, was opening her big white handbag and letting small square packets slip out over the table.

'Here, for you,' the drunk woman said to Marilyn as she passed with the drinks, 'help yourself, party girl, it's Friday, it's party time.' I watched as Marilyn collected a few of the dinky packets and came back over to our table.

'There you go,' Marilyn said to Mum, 'more use to you than a packet of peanuts.' And threw the little red squares in a shower over the table towards Mum.

'How generous,' Mum said, sitting up and collecting them, 'are you sure you don't need them yourself, Marilyn?'

'And what's that meant to mean?'

'Well, you never say anything about what you want, do you?' Mum said. 'You just criticise what other people want.

You just take the easy way out, judging others and never getting stuck in yourself.'

I don't know what the cute, shiny packets are, or why Mum's getting all meany with her mates. Maybe it's her mystery illness, like I once heard Dad saying to Claire that after I was born Mum once chucked all the bed sheets out the window into the street. Why? No idea.

'Why you getting at me?' Marilyn said, getting annoyed. 'It's not my fault that he's not turned up. Don't take it out on me. You know what I think about it anyway. You know what happened last time you got your claws into a young one.'

'Now you're making me sound like a . . .' Mum said, looking at me and stopping.

'Well, what are you implying about me!' Marilyn snapped back.

'That you want to do stuff, but don't so you won't fail, and so that you can come over all superior about being above normal behaviour,' Mum said, checking the time again.

'And just because I don't broadcast my desires doesn't mean I don't have any – fun,' Marilyn goes on, looking upset.

Mum sighed then threw the daft square packet that she was fiddling with back on to the table, which was now full with bottles and glasses and fag ends, and said, 'Don't need them anyway. I've told you I'm wanting to have another.'

'At your age,' Marilyn sighs and shakes her head and Mum looks sad and I feel like a dog that's been tied to the table leg and forgotten.

'And single and lonely and depressed and probably soon to be unemployed,' Mum says.

'And the men round here will be riddled with diseases, anyway,' Marilyn said.

'Well, not if you get them young enough,' Mum said, and laughed to herself and I knew she really had forgotten I was there.

157

'Actually Amir told me his mother had him when she was forty-four,' Danuta says. 'He's twenty years younger than his brother.'

'See!' Mum cries out, slapping down her palms so the whole table rocks. 'A baby's a blessing whenever it comes.'

'Sometimes you disgust me, Jackie Jackson. I mean that,' Marilyn says, and she means it nasty, so I stare at her through slit eyes and tight-in lips.

'Good. I disgust everyone. I try to,' Mum says, and Marilyn looks at me and laughs.

'Well, go and do as you like, love. But I do think it's the most appalling thing that a lass can do, debase herself. Especially when she's meant to be off flaming sick!'

'Well, I don't,' Mum said, collecting her fags and money and keys and still not even looking at me. 'I think the worst thing a woman – not just a lass, a bloke too – can do is not take the chance of loving, and being loved.'

'Promise me you'll not get involved with him,' Marilyn says.

Mum eyeballs her mate for ages, then shakes her head.

Then she looked down and oh, what a surprise to find you have a daughter. It looked like blue tears were about to spill over her red eyes as she said, 'Come on, love. I'm sorry. Let's go. He's not coming.'

'They all like you really,' I say as we walk home through the thumping city, past snakes of drunk lasses queuing to get into clubs, bouncers like bears at the doors. She's hardly talking at all and I know if I'd not been there she'd just have slipped into a bar and got completely plastered. 'And I can tell Danuta really admires you.'

'Danuta admires Buffy the Vampire Slayer,' Mum says, ruffling my horrible hair.

'Shall we watch a DVD when we get in, Mum. Shall we?'

'Oh, well,' she sighs, and then looks at me and says, 'Great idea, love,' though I knew from her tired smile that no entertainment I could suggest was any match for him who didn't turn up. And later Mum watched the funny love comedy like she was viewing the world's most depressing disaster movie. 'They're right,' she sighs, talking to herself. 'It'd be terrible. It's good he didn't come tonight.'

'Yeh,' I say, like I'm her wise mate and understand every-thing about her life. 'You're right.'

'I should have tried harder with George,' she says.

'It's not schoolwork, Mum, it's love and if it's hard work then perhaps you should just give up.'

'I'm sick of giving up, I want to keep going. Why is it with relationships that you are always meant to give up if you start to fail? That's what I did with Leo and Marcel and your dad. I don't want to do that any more.'

There is a long silence when even the TV feels too hopeless to speak. 'Because, Mum, if someone doesn't want you then you can't force them to want you.'

'Oh, Elle,' she says. 'Oh, darling. Come here.'

AMIR

The sign on my yellow cardboard door says Peese be Quite, Warkmen Sneeping. But otherwise Primrose Lodge is just a seedy B&B where the damp patch on the ceiling and the crispbread mattress accurately reflects how I feel. There's *tost* or *grayfruit (tinned)* and cockroaches served in the oily windowless basement from six to seven-thirty am, a mushroomy odour, and the rattly front door locked at eleven pm. My neighbours are asylum seekers and Euro workmen – though I hardly see anyone as I'm there only to sneep. To dream of Jackie, or Ma, who, now that I am gone, is at long last having her three days a week respite care at Cosy Retreat, so that Samirah and Wahida can continue their jobs part time. Ashfaq would rather agree to this than go back on his banishment of me.

For a few days I expected my family to come and find me. I had received one handwritten long letter from Yasmin, speaking of her sorrow and fury at my departure. She thought me mean and immature and irresponsible. If any of her own four sons acted as I had done she would be devastated and would disown them. I was a good example of all that was bad in England and Allah would punish me for my great selfishness and vanity. Finally she wrote that I should remember my father who came to England after Partition and how he had struggled, working twenty-hour days, to build his business but had never forgotten his family. 'There was a man able to not just live, but love, deeply and dutifully, Amir.' She enclosed three black and white photographs of my father in her letter. They are taken fifty years ago and he is wearing a suit and spectacles and staring, unsmiling, with thoughtful seriousness towards his English future. I prop them up on my stained carpet, against my dusty skirting board. The photos and Yasmin's letter made me feel sad and lonely, which was how I wanted to feel, and I read the letter over and over, till it played in the room like a tune, even when I had hidden it away in a book.

The photos were meant to make me think of the past, but in fact the more I stared at them I thought of my father as staring into the unknown, taking a chance on England though he'd not known what it would bring.

And this would lead back to thinking of Jackie.

Sometimes at Primrose Lodge there were mysterious knocks on the cardboard door late at night, which, when I answered, revealed no caller in the sour hallway, and so I decided the knock was a code for some bad-ass riot I didn't want to understand. Or perhaps it was all a bad dream born of my restless mind, because at the knock I still expected it to be Ma, come home with a complaint about the catering and the dirtiness of the gorehs. Come to Primrose Lodge to find me, slap me and take me home.

I'd not seen Jackie for ages, and so she didn't learn about my beating. I'd have to tell her I'd fallen down some steps. I didn't want her to know any of it. She was ill and heartbroken and needed to rest and I didn't want to tell anyone where I was living and why, so I'd deliberately not contacted Jackie since – though the willpower required was, I imagined, like giving up heroin. Instead of scheming of ways to meet Jackie I'd tried to take my job more seriously, to not resist the way that shopping was leisure nowadays, and instead accept that the store provided entertainment first and goods second. So I went to meetings and guffawed, and gave Orla madly fun ideas for events and promotions and in-store innovations till my face ached.

Without Jackie work had finally sent me bananas.

Wahida says I can go to live with her and my two teenage nieces. But the thought of being around happy cheerful people is depressing. I want to be alone to think gloomy thoughts, because this seems more faithful to Jackie, and though Ashfaq has forbidden me to see Ma, Samirah lets me in when he has gone to work and if Ma is not at Cosy Retreat I spend an hour helping with her, feeding, combing her hair, talking about what I'll be doing at school that day.

Wahida worries that we shouldn't pretend to be the people Ma wrongly thinks we are, me her school-kid son, Ashfaq her husband, Samirah her younger sister. Wahida worries that this is unacceptable deception but I think it would hurt Ma more to constantly correct her, to tell her her husband and sister are dead and her youngest son is just another unhappy and corrupt grown man. And I think, so what's the big deal about pretending? Adults all agree to be the people others want us to be: Ashfaq the great macho provider, Yasmin the dutiful housewife, me the useless little brother. We are all of us acting, every day, and with just a few turns of the dial we could all change and be different people entirely.

So when possible I play schoolboy for Mum between seven and eight, then I leave for work exhausted and guiltily relieved to be gone. If Ashfaq is definitely going to be elsewhere I come round in the evening too and meddle with the cooking and cleaning, as I tell my two sisters jokes I've learned at school. My sisters look at me like I am crying not joking, and they tell me to sit down and rest and they will bring me a cup of tea. 'You can't pretend this situation with Ashfaq isn't happening,' Samirah says, spreading a blanket over me like I am old and sick. 'You have to decide what you are going to do,' Wahida says, and I pretend I don't understand what they mean. Though I know my vanishing has unsettled Ma, though Ashfaq insists she's not noticed, though she had on one terrible night been found by moonlight by the police, wandering in her nightdress in the park, skipping and singing and making daisy chains for her long grey hair. She told the cop that when she was at school she had hair she could sit on. It was all she would discuss, for the first two days she went along to Cosy Retreat, the length of her girlish hair.

'We have to accept this illness is happening,' Wahida said recently, 'and we have to go with the flow of it. Everything I have read about this disease says that in order not to be angry or constantly irritated or appalled by Ma and her situation, we have to just roll with it. It's not Ma's fault and we can't stop it so we have to accept it and deal with it gently, day by day.' We all nodded, and perhaps it wasn't just me, perhaps all of us thought of Wahida's evil husband ten years ago, slapping her around for months before any of our family mentioned her sadness, then her depression and finally her bruises. I was only a lad then, but I agreed with Pa and Ashfaq that to mention it would make it shameful and worse. So Ashfaq and Pa confronted Musa privately, man to man, while I stayed sulky and secretly upset. Now we don't know where Musa is, or ever even mention him, and Ashfaq and I just pretend he never existed. 'So are we all agreed? That the true test of how much we love Ma,' Wahida continued, 'is how willing and able we are to help her without being angry with her? There is no point wasting our time trying to forcibly control her or try to bend her back into who she used to be.'

'She's changed, she's a different person now,' Samirah agreed. 'That's the hardest thing to accept. But how do we tell Ashfaq?'

'It's happening whether we tell him or not,' Wahida says. 'Just because he doesn't like it won't stop it.'

And for some reason they all seemed to glance at me then, and I just nodded and Samirah said, 'You're right, we all have to loosen up if we are to survive this.'

'Then we'll be able to get to know this new mother with as much patience and generosity as we can,' Wahida said.

The problem was I couldn't even talk about how to handle Ma without seeking a secret message about how to handle Jackie. That's how lost I was.

I turned up at Cosy Retreat on Wednesday 13 September and Ma was sitting chatting keenly to a pretty young nurse. It was my third visit to Cosy Retreat; on the previous two occasions, Ma was sitting in the same chair, in the same position in the room, looking out over a scratch of clumpy grass before a parade of shops – that she would never buy anything from, where she would never live to see a mega branch of Fags 'n' Fings rise up. Now I was pleased that this visit wouldn't just be me and her. On the table by Ma's chair I saw the heartbreaking plastic beaker with the baby's spout. Opposite her was a big white bloke curled over a Zimmer frame, frozen there like a big old snowman with his trouser bottoms gaping open, sitting down or standing up I couldn't tell, rather just bent, fists claws, skin grey and blue cheesed with veins. I watched as Ma went over to the man and helped him into a chair. Though the wards are single-sex, it seems the men and women mix freely during the day. This made me unsure, and Ashfaq would have a seizure. I thought of Jackie's old coal miner and how Marilyn had told me how recently Jackie had been in a car crash. Just nudged gently,

Marilyn said, into the back of a woman's car when she stopped at traffic lights.

'Amir, you've come,' my ma called out in English, like she'd not seen me for a month, and sprang up energetically from her tall-backed chair. 'I have someone I want you to meet.' At first I thought she meant the bloke, but when I turn to look I see a big blonde beauty beaming as if leaning up from her holiday lounger.

I felt I'd been hit by a moving vehicle.

And the impact had left me crazed with joy. 'I rang work and they said you'd gone to visit your mam.' She lifted both palms helplessly to the ceiling as if everything that happened to her was the sudden act of a cheeky God. 'And now that I'm no longer working . . .' Then she was nibbling on her lip and saying how when she came round to ours Ma was so kind to her that she wanted to find out how she was doing.

'What are you doing here?' I say, like all my reactions were delayed.

'Visiting your mam, love.'

'Yes, at least your sister here thinks to come and see me regularly.'

'I didn't say I was your sister,' she says. Then she apologises for being there but says, 'I also thought it would be easier to talk here than going to yours. I don't think your brother liked having me round.'

'I've been both times this week,' I say, replying to Ma but staring at Jackie. 'I heard you crashed the car?'

'Ach, nothing, just a little scratch, nothing serious.'

'You crashed!' my ma laughs. 'You were that keen to get here to see me?'

'I only did it so the lass would have to get out the car and I could take a look at her to see if there were definite family resemblances,' she says. She glances at me, and quickly I look away.

'Amir, Jackie thinks this other woman is either her lover's lover, or his daughter!'

And Jackie confesses that the nudge had been more of a proper bump, actually cracking one of the brake lights. And causing 'a big jolty feeling'. She was pretending to joke about it but I could tell she was shocked. 'Now both of you kids sit down and I'll get you a cup of tea,' and my mother clicks her fingers and a tea trolley rolls towards her. I've not seen her so nearly-normal in months. There was no surprise in Ma about meeting Jackie, at least no more surprise than there was that there were chocolate biscuits on the trolley that day, a fact she discussed with unusual detail, all the time Jackie chatting along and offering her own wisdom about tea and biscuits. 'So what is going on?' my ma asks. Politely. 'Who's got some gossip for me?'

'You start, sis,' I say to Jackie. I've not told Ma anything about Primrose Lodge. She still thought I was doing my homework upstairs, and the ease with which she could be deceived was total heartbreak.

'No, you,' Jackie smiles, 'you'll be quicker, bro.'

'Come on,' Ma says, grinning and itching at her wild grey hair, 'tell me some love stories.' And then she looks all worried and says, 'And where's your father? He came yesterday, but I haven't seen him yet today.'

I look up at the trees, and the leaves laughing down on us. 'I'm afraid there's not long enough for our Jackie's love stories, Ma, visiting's only an hour.'

'Well, at least she's trying,' Ma says, 'not like you, turning down every girl I offer you. Not letting me help you out of this lonely pit you've fallen into. Jackie might be a funny one but she is not lonely. I don't know, Jackie, he spends so much time in his bedroom. I hardly see him nowadays.'

Jackie looks at me and smiles sadly, then she tells Ma more about her gorgeous handsome coach-driving man, and all the funny things he does and says, even what fillings he likes in his sandwiches, as Ma happily nods. I am going mad and the trees and grass are going mad because she is going mad. And we're not the only ones. 'There are some people whose role in life is protection,' Marilyn had told me that morning, 'and I am one of them. That's why I'm not reckless myself. But it is very hard to protect people who won't tell you truthfully what they are doing. Jackie is up to something but I've no idea what it is.' Marilyn had looked sore-eyed and desperate, and now despite the laughter for my ma, Jackie looked the same. What was happening to us all? Really I knew; we were all desperate for love and trust – we didn't know how important it was until we'd all started trying to live without it.

'Numb': that was the word Jackie had once used to describe the beginning of the year, after a Christmas without Elle, and the dumping by Leo. Neither happy nor sad, she said, neither drunk, nor sober. Just like I felt nowadays. Couldn't sleep in my bed in case I dreamt of her, but couldn't risk keeping my eyes open in case I saw that sexy ghost there in Primrose Lodge, writhing on the worn pink slippery sheet.

Now Ma seemed calm and cheerful – maybe because Jackie treated everyone as though they were sane and the world was mad. 'It's so important to know the truth, isn't it, in life?' Jackie said. 'That's all I want in life, to know the truth. That's why I came to talk to Amir. I need his help.'

I shake my head. If she knew the proper truth – how I'd agreed to leave home, leave everyone and everything rather than deny her – it would seem creepy and too much. Women have to choose you before you can choose them, or it looks total weird and pushy. So I did what I always did, and said nothing.

'It is the most important thing,' my ma agrees. 'That's why it's horrible when you are being lied to by your own children.'

'What do you mean, Ma?' I say.

'You didn't tell me,' she says sadly.

'I was going to, Ma,' I gabble. 'When I'd decided what I was going to do next.'

'You should have told me you were in love, son.'

'That's my sister you're talking about!' I say. 'Aren't I meant to love my own sister?'

Then I look away, try to think of what's-her-name, with the blue-black hair and flawless baby-soft cheeks.

'You what!' my mother laughs. 'This isn't your sister. This is that wild gori you told me all about before, that single mum. The one who had to go to court to get to see her own kid, had that business with your African boss.'

Jackie looks at me and says, 'And that's only half of it, love!'

'Ma! He's not African.'

'You know, the one your pa thought was a you-know-what when she came round to our house.'

'Now there's an idea,' Jackie says sadly. 'I do have a few debts to pay. I could do with some extra cash.'

Here she goes again – dirtying herself to push me away.

Meanwhile Ma is inviting the big old Zimmer guy to take a look at mad Jackie and her schoolboy son. Jackie tells the old guy about her handsome lover, like she truly believes she's dating a movie star.

'Why are you here?' I say to Jackie, while my ma explains Jackie's history to her friend.

'I came because you're right, I'm a screwball and I need your help.'

'Help to stop?' I ask. 'Or help to make things worse?' It was true she had no one else to turn to: Leo kept his distance, Danuta binged on tales of Jackie's decline, Orla only needed another incident and Jackie would be gone – not that Orla could sack her when she was off sick. But in a few weeks, perhaps. Sacked, like several mothers before her.

We look at the crumbly patients wheeling and stumbling

through their last days, as if they are only there to prove to us how little time is left to love. But no! There I go again, thinking this is the only world, believing there is nothing more than what we see before us with our two eyes. Before I know it Ashfaq'll be right and I'll be a proper Englisher: godless, obese, addicted, depressed, in debt, alone, living only for the shimmering visible world of today, this exact minute.

We say goodbye to Ma together, like we are truly related, and this really is our joint ma, and then Jackie says she doesn't want to go home yet. Instead she links her warm bare arm through mine, like we are long-time pensioner mates. 'It's not possible to make things worse,' she says, when we are walking away through the grassy grounds of Cosy Retreat towards a heavy willow, a total private place.

'What do I have to do? And will I get arrested?' I say to cover my pounding heart. It's kind of funny that we don't mention how we made love in the alley, but a total relief too, for to talk about it would make it shoddy, for we would find only the words of our age; that it was nothing, meaningless, a mistake, a laugh, a joke, a drunken fuck-up, a lusty moment of nothingness that we were going to put behind us and forget.

And now Jackie is nattering on about George. 'I just want you to watch him for me, just to see once and for all if he is telling me the truth about that woman, if she really is his daughter. It's the not knowing that's screwing me up,' Jackie said, biting her sore lip. 'I've seen him going into her house. I was hidden behind a bush, on the other side of the road, but I was so afraid he'd . . .'

'What?'

'. . . notice me.'

'I thought it was over,' I say.

'It's not over until I know.'

If I say no I won't see her for a long time. If I say yes I risk disgracing myself and my family yet further.

'And did she look like him? Like her dad?' I say and I see there is a new panic in Jackie's eyes, hope and panic, and our ma says, or used to say when she could think, that those who love most deeply hurt most deeply.

'It's like she's half his daughter and half his lover.'

'Perhaps she's his secret love child.'

'Amir, you should write for a soap.'

'Write for one! Knowing you, Jackie, I live in one,' I say, and it's true, and not because of her tacky adventures, but because of the secrets and lies loving her has given me.

She looks down at the ground as I think of the day Ashfaq thrashed me, of Yasmin standing up to stop him, Samirah spreading her hands like she was directing traffic. How we were all suspended there in a sudden soap moment. And perhaps because Ma views endless TV at such a cinematic volume, we had all been zapped by lurid plot lines, and will soon be screaming our secrets in the street. 'He should be on the stage,' Halima had roared. 'With the other gaylords.'

'He is on the stage,' Yasmin shouted. 'The childish stage!' Then Yasmin told me to sit down and more calmly she said, 'Amir, think what kind of example you are setting to your young nephews.'

Now I am looking at Jackie and wondering.

'You're right, it's mad, I shouldn't involve you. I'll do it myself. It's not as if I'm busy with other things.'

But already she is rubbing at her forehead with her fingers and I can't stop myself, but I have to. I have to, and maybe the best way to stop myself getting her is to go all out to help her get someone else.

And whoosh, it all happened so fast; there I was in Jackie's love-mad world and it was like living in thick fog, and the phantom mist was your desires, which clouded everything so you were forever falling over and into things and hurting yourself and causing accidents. Just as if you'd stumbled into a dark room, only to discover there was no light and the only way out was by feeling along the walls. So far only small accidents – losing custody of a daughter, getting a verbal warning, a spot of depression, a string of disastrous affairs – but big catastrophes were never far away surely.

But I was driving a brand-new Ford Fiesta, that Jackie had presented to me for the assignment, one just off the track, a transparent sheet covering the passenger seat and the interior mirror still protected by a sticky film. 'How's she affording this?' Marilyn cried when I told her. I hadn't asked. Once I made a decision I stopped questioning, and just stuck to it. You might call it naiveté, I call it trust.

Those October days had hazy autumn dawns, leaves tumbling auburn from tawny trees, a honeyed pile each morning thickening like fairytale money on the pavement. I'd got to like the drifting smouldery rhythm of it: the arriving, the exhaust smoke burning the leafy air, the leaning back and the gentle recline of the bar beneath the seat so I was half sitting and half lying there, legs spread wide, all the better to look up, through the baring branches to see the pretty gori's top-floor flat. And even if part of me felt like what Ashfaq said I was, a Bollywoody prick, I loved the delicious warm plasticky tang of the new car.

Could even taste it, so heady-sweet was that adventurous aroma.

It all added to the sensation that this was the start of a new me.

Loving her had changed me. Being away from home had freed me. Soon, after I'd saved her, I'd move on.

By the second day I was loving it. Two great words: private and eye. Go together like open and closed. An eye on Jackie's world, her eye on the world, keeping an eye on her, keeping an eye out for her, giving her the eye, eyeing her up, catching her eye, being her own dark confidant. Her Private Eye. And the role suits me because I am a private man by nature. While Jackie Jackson is open as an eye, sensual, all-seeing, feeling and tasting. Helpless to resist, occasionally I still allow myself to think we'd have been the perfect pair. We'd have been a wink. Not that I have any illusions in that direction any more. No, her sanity and safety is my only concern. Jackie was ill and because of Ma, or Ashfaq, I knew this life required you shield those you love from embarrassment, damage, humiliation, neglect, disrespect and misunderstanding. Go along with things. Don't draw attention to a person's screw-ups, don't mention the smells they give off, or the state of their hair; just help others, friends, strangers, to go on with as much dignity as possible.

I was only much later informed, by Marilyn, of the statistics; how many stalkers are aided and abetted by family and friends.

'Marilyn says you wander away for a while and don't come back,' Jackie says very seriously, but digging her sharp nails into her fists with excitement, as she gave me advice at the end of my third unremarkable day. 'You make sure that you conceal your identity above everything. You are undercover, Amir, and Marilyn says there are three stages to getting rumbled: warm, toasty and burnt. If you feel warm, get cautious, but if you feel toasty you get out, because you don't want to get burnt.'

'Burnt is like noticed, right?'

'Burnt is like arrested, love. And don't just stay in one place is another thing to remember. Marilyn says if you watch from a static position you stand a much greater chance of being revealed, whereas if you keep on the move then you will be better equipped to zoom in or zoom out as the case demands.

Which is why you are in the car, and you must drive off occasionally, come back, come and go.'

By then none of this seemed bonkers, it seemed a completely sensible thing to do.

The next morning, my fourth, it was raining and I didn't catch the lass's exact expression, or her mood. 'Regular,' I'd say to Jackie later, 'nothing unusual and no visitors.'

'Did she seem happy?'

'How do I know when a lass's happy?'

'Simple stuff, Amir, like was she weeping or smiling?'

'You mean it's really that easy?'

'Gazing, quiet, still, moist of eye. You're right, Amir, bored, suicidal or in love, it's hard to tell.'

Jackie's eyes were pinky damp with sleeplessness, or pills, or all-night steamy sex sessions, or crying. I'd been in her bedroom, when I took her home from the station, and there was a vapour of steamy nothingness there, that I now knew from the atmosphere in Primrose Lodge was watery loneliness heated by red-hot desire.

'Perhaps it would be different with the right guy,' I say, 'maybe then there'll be no confusion.' Hell, there I went again! I couldn't help myself. I'd have to start wearing masking tape across my gob twenty-four seven.

'Hmm, good point, professor. I've experimented with many things in the sexual arena,' Jackie nodded solemnly, tapping her finger against her chin, and looking out over the streets, then up at a hardening sky, 'but I don't think I've ever tried it long-term with the right guy.'

I should have walked. I tried.

'Surely you've had a few memorable romantic occasions,' I say instead, looking away.

'Oh yes,' she says, 'actually this summer I had the best time I've ever had with a man. It was just a shame it was only the once. We were outdoors. Can you believe he wouldn't invite me in?'

'He sounds like a bit of a bastard.'

'Oh, he's not, Amir,' she smiles. 'He's the least bastard I've ever met.'

Every time.

Three mornings later, on my seventh day of spying, we were in our coffee bar at nine-fifteen am. Jackie liked to meet as soon as possible before work to get a debrief. She said she hardly slept anyway, for missing Elle or dreaming about George.

I'd explained to Jackie several times that it was Ramadan but each time she went to the counter for a coffee and another muffin, she asked me what I wanted to drink. 'You could probably get me arrested for being so clueless,' she said, and apologised.

'If I wanted to get you arrested it wouldn't be because you keep forgetting it's Ramadan,' I said, and she bit her lip and asked a cappuccino if what we were doing was illegal.

The cappuccino said no, what we were doing was entirely legal and sensible and we should carry on as long as we wanted.

Anyway, I didn't care, because I'd never been happier, though it was a grainy northern morning, soft seal-skin sky, pensioners lurching by, gangs of lads shooting past without aim, balloon faces on jelly bodies panting up the hill, knots of long-limbed fashion mothers with their heavy hand-bags rushing towards our store, which, to differentiate it from a normal shop, didn't open until ten am.

Later I would wonder why I didn't ever consider telling Jackie that this – surveillance, private-eying, spying – well, it was not only probably a serious crime, it was also not a sane thing for her to do. She was only just back at work, after all; she should be resting, getting over the dick. She should not be prolonging the agony, the love, with crazy plans. My excuse? Several: firstly I didn't say anything to dissuade her out of sheer selfishness; this was my chance to busy myself outside of Primrose Lodge and not think of Ashfaq or my ma. Also it was Ramadan and I was happy to be busy after sunrise. Plus, I'm ashamed to say, perhaps because of the way Ashfaq had humiliated me, I longed for any adventure that transformed me from a dickass shop boy to a macho spy.

But most of all, as I detailed for Jackie what I had seen that morning outside George's flat, I felt fatherly. I was being dutiful and careful and protective of my friend. A corner of me felt like the hard-working, honest, reliable adult my mother had loved for forty years, and the better man Ashfaq and Yasmin wanted me to be.

ELLE

Mum's last day at work started innocently enough. Though I was worried about the free champagne the shop staff were sipping, and the way Mum's dress showed her milky udders, and the flower displays which were strange and enormous, petals like parrot plumes, all plucked that morning, Mum said, from a tropical hothouse. SUMMER WEDDINGS, it said on the banner now spread across the whole of the store, LET US RING YOUR BELLS.

Still, I was so excited to be there with my proper very own mum at this special celebrity event, and I'd told the Steps every lush detail of the fun they would be missing. It was not even Mum's weekend to have me and Dad said he and Claire needed more notice, but I begged and shouted and said, 'It's like I have to apply for a fucking visa to see my own mother.'

How silly I was to think I could make things right by wanting them to be right, when everything that had ever happened to me should have taught me that this was not how the world worked. How many hours had I wasted praying for Dad and Mum to get back together? And had that happened? No it had not.

That day of the store promotion I had even agreed to wear a skirt and a proper pair of shoes and had stolen Cherub's silver necklace and Mum kept stroking at my hair and she was introducing me to everyone who came by, though no one else seemed to have brought their kid along. I wanted Mum to suggest that now I was twelve I wear some lipstick, but I knew she wouldn't and even if she did I'd refuse. Still, for once in my life I felt totallyloved.com.

Clock that twelve-year-old fool!

All around was the buzz of the press, who'd been invited along to comment upon, and photograph, this 'landmark event'. I want Mum to say that now I was twelve we look alike but she doesn't and the lighting was making everyone woozy. Tipsily Mum told me it was 'designed' by a contemporary artist to re-create the eerie stillness and 'the transforming hallucinogenic power' of stained glass. I remember everything she told me so I could tell it later back to the weeping, sobbing, uninvited Steps.

Though in fact by the end of that day they'd have read much more than I knew in the papers.

Mum said the lighting and music was meant to work because the store was 'a church and a nightclub and a shrine', and 'a family'. Mum had been told this at the last staff meeting. She had found it hilarious.

I think if I see a bride in a black dress Mum won't ever be unhappy again and she won't get plastered here, at work. I realised then that Mum was recounting everything about her job as irony – which our Year Seven teacher said means saying one thing and meaning another. Like that's not just everyday life!

Still, I should have seen Mum's non-stop irony as a sign that she had finally had enough and wanted to leave her job. Perhaps I understood nothing about her, really. I looked at each one of the brides, but none were wearing black wedding dresses, and Mum was well along to getting plastered. But we were all standing together in Menswear and Mum was rather cheerful and I wasn't too worried yet because everyone was speaking to me and asking questions about my life, and laughing when I made jokes. I wanted them to offer me champagne but no one did even though I was twelve. Still, it's hard not to be stroked into thinking life is good when everyone is acting like they are your best friend. Particularly the kind of handsome unshaven half-dressed men and stick-thin boobied women that Cherub now has pictures of pinned up on her wall.

Away in the distance I could see the Asian who was dressed as a traditional best man in top hat and tails, Danuta as his lacy and lovely chief maid.

The Asian was keeping his distance because bad Mum was starring as the sexed-up, red-eyed, contemporary bride. 'Why did I have to be the "modern"?' she moaned to her mates. 'Everyone else looks dreamy and romantic and I look like a bloody slut.' And they all turned to Mum and raised their eyebrows until she attacked them with her white patent-leather rucksack and her silver hobnail boots.

Actually, I found it a bit funny that they thought she was a slut because I was really muchhappier.com since the police-woman had been round and finally ended everything with George though I was surprised that the police could get involved in making you split up with someone. I thought it was good to know for the future: 999. *Hello, police? My mum's just met a man!*

The policewoman was younger than Mum and seemed to understand something that I didn't, and she spoke slow and firm like a teacher, 'George wants you to leave him and his family alone, Mrs Jackson. He doesn't know what impression he must have given you about what he wanted, but it's not this.' The woman took out a notebook and asked if Mum had been round to see George one evening. Had she stationed herself across the road from his house and watched? 'Jackie, what are you doing out at this time?' he'd allegedly asked her, when he hurried down the path past her. 'I was popping out for milk,' Mum allegedly said as he panicked with his key, scratching at his own lock, 'but it's a long way to the supermarket. Could you lend me some?' 'No,' he allegedly said and was gone indoors, just a gust of slam behind him. 'A saucer of milk for your old pussycat,' she allegedly shouted at the house. More than once.

Allegedly is what you say to imply someone's lying, like, 'Cherub's a nice person, allegedly.'

Still, that was a week ago. Forget it, let it go, I thought as I watched the brides. Because the only bruise on this glittering day was that here was no lads my age, because this day was for Brides, Maids and Mums exclusively and there were to be no male customers present (if this day was a success Mum says her boss had planned another, similar do for Grooms, Stags and Dads in the spring), but male assistants were thought to be a good idea. They had been told they were there to smile and grin at the birds all day, Mum said. Ironically. 'That's probably Orla's idea of feminism,' Danuta said to Mum when she slid over, and Mum smiled and congratulated her on starting to see the world as it was. Big Marilyn looked around and said, 'It's kind of Sleeping Beauty meets Ann Summers,' and I laughed though I didn't know who Ann Summers was, though I'd heard of her, of course, but didn't want to ask in case it was someone really famous and obvious like the prime minister. Then everyone was pointing at the tightly bodiced wedding dress a lass near us was trying on. 'They'll all be crooning into their vibrators by lunchtime,' Danuta says, though giggly Mum tells them to sssh because I am listening, though actually even though I'm twelve I only have a very shaky idea of what a vibrator is, and again there's no one to ask. But I know it's probably nothing to do with what it sounds like, some antique bicycle, and like most funny things it probably has to do with sex, so I roll my eyes and say, 'Right! Like I've been raised on pure innocence, Mum!' and to my relief I must be on the right lines because they all laugh.

Under my breath I said the word vibrator three times so I remembered to Google it – though it's really hard to do any proper private computering because back in Land of Lavender Claire has put the computer in the kitchen so she can check up on exactly what we are all seeing. Not that I cared about home. I wished Mum would ask someone to take a photo of us two together, but she never did.

Then we saw Gran. It's like Gran is Mum's bad-luck charm and seeing her should have warned us all that it really was toogoodtobetrue.com and the true date was in fact, really really, Friday the thirteenth of October. 'What you doing here, Mam?' Mum cried out, shocked, when Gran floated over in her lilac mother-of-the-bride garb, high heels, tall glass of bubbly, pink make-up seemingly applied by a five-year-old. 'I told you, Mam, I'm not getting married. Never again. I want you to shoot me if I ever say I'm getting married again.'

Mum takes a big glug from her glass and I think, *Whoa!* As her udders judder I think: don't get plastered and ruin everything. Though later I'll think that's exactly what she intended – to end it all.

'Don't tempt me, Jackie,' Gran says, kissing me on the cheek and saying how great I look. 'At least little Elle gives our poor family hope for the future.'

'But why are you here looking at wedding outfits when I am never getting married again, Mam?'

'Who said I'm looking for you, Jackie? What about me?' Gran said with a champagney giggle and a strangulation cuddle for me.

'You only came for the free booze, Mam,' Mum says, sipping on her own bronzy bubbles.

'See, we do have things in common, Jackie,' Gran says and sways a little and I know she is lonely, and that is what Mum and her share. Gran would like to hang around with Mum and her mates, be introduced to everyone. That's what I want too. And maybe all the pain in the world is because all we lousy well want is to be loved and admired by our blood families, though that's totally the hardest love to get. And as usual Mum has work to do, so she can't chat and so she gives Gran a bottle of bubbly from under her counter and Gran curls away like she's crossing the deck of a big ship, during a storm.

I wish I'd gone with her.

Music was everywhere now; a new creation by the student winner of a prize to compose 'a romantic experimental piece'. Imagine the moment in a horror movie when the half-dressed heroine's just taken her soapy shower and is now creeping around the mansion, opening doors, peering round corners. It sounded in places like rapid sneezing, and in others like a handful of forks falling quickly, then slowly, on to a hard floor. I must have sensed something coming because I felt miserable as I looked at the brides, maybe because Mum's drinking fast, or because I've been thinking about family, and it is like being surrounded by swans; hard to tell, just by looking, which bride is better than the next. Hours pass as women wander, tall, smooth and white as candles, and I wonder sadly if love and family will do to them what it's done to Gran and me and Mum: burn them down, melt them all away.

'You had a white wedding like this, Jackie?' Danuta asks, just when I want to cry.

'More beige,' Mum says. 'But I looked just as flammable. And my second was grey, but by then I'd learnt my lesson. If I ever say I'm getting married again my mother's agreed to shoot me.'

'I'm never getting married either,' Danuta said with a sigh. 'If I ever need a bread-maker I'll buy it myself.'

And I laugh at that because at home we say Claire loves her bread-maker more than Dad.

One of the men assistants asks me my name, and I say it and he smiles, though I still felt lousy because I knew that now I was twelve I should be trying the kind of wide-eyed fluttering Mum does, though whenever I'd done it before I felt ill and scared, and then Mum was behind me laughing and this set me off giggling and worrying. To me, being near a man was like being in a scary play, but to Mum performing for men was her entire life – so she'd gotten used to living with this stage fright.

Shortly before the arrival of the 'fairytale parade of gorgeous brides-to-be', the confetti was spread throughout the store, on every floor. Sprinkles were also left on the counters, in the hair of the shop girls, in shoes, in pockets, like snow, or icing sugar. It was 'a dusting of sweetness and romance'. At the time I thought: *yeeees, and the Steps have missed it all!*

Then the fairytale parade begins. There are brides big and small, tall and short, black and white, many rocking with giggles, tiara'd heads hung low, holding their embarrassed grins in the girly palms of their diamond-heavy hands. I could see Gran having her glass refilled by the handsome guy from the Food Hall. I could see the Asian chatting to some customers. I could see Mum sipping and swallowing, posing and pouting, and when someone asks if they can take her picture she winks and says her old photography joke, 'Oooh go on then, take me, I'm yours.'

I don't like her being photographed ever. Because it's like they want to own a bit of evidence, then use it to betray her. Meanwhile the other mums and daughters wander around the parade route, which is marked out by a line of lilies on the floor, to a brilliant song that goes: *oh you pretty thing.* The brides are bending at the waist with giggles, and slapping their knees in piss-takery of themselves, when they are told to pause in the parade for a press photo shoot, and all around us there is a storm of silver and the flashing of a thousand bridal teeth.

I wished the Steps could see me, there, with my pretty mum.

What a fool. As though little me and poor Mum were a match for the power of Claire and her perfect family.

I start whistling.

And then because it's a magical day and I wished it, I actually do see them all standing there in the crowd. Really! Claire is wearing her warm beige fleece, and Cherub and Caprice are standing at her side watching in amazement at the glittering fun they are not part of. I frowned and waved to get their attention as we all watched the brides-to-be moving around with more samples of champagne and nibbles, gliding up and down on escalators, smooth as angels.

Then Danuta hurried over and said a journalist had tried to ask her some questions. She was scared because she'd answered. Mum told me the worst thing that a member of staff could do was to speak to the press without authorisation, for that meant instant dismissal. Mum said that they'd all signed an agreement to say that, like frightened children, they wouldn't speak even if they were spoken to. I think it was irony, and Mum was swaying about and laughing.

Danuta told Mum that she had panicked in the middle of the interview and vanished.

At that moment the freaky churchy singing started, and soon there was a choir echoed around the whole space – it could, I imagined, be heard around the whole city, even underground. There was nowhere to hide. A radio station was there to broadcast the sound live. My drunken gran and my horrible Steps were there watching. My mum was just getting her life back on track. The Asian was far away over the other side of the store.

'Here she comes,' Danuta said.

'Oh my God, it's you,' the young journalist cried, stepping backwards and pressing her fingertips to her lips. Slowly I realised she was talking to Mum. 'I've been waiting for you to appear again. It's like a horror film. Why can't you leave us alone?'

'Is there a problem?' a bouncy woman said, appearing at our side, revealing too much gum. She was from the press office, she said. Now, things weren't looking so romantic, but still my blurry mum had not made the link between herself and the coming disaster.

'It's him, too,' the woman said, pointing wildly across the store. Nearby brides were shifting, starting to hear. The choir tried to sing louder. Still Mum said not a word. 'He's outside my house every morning.'

Then I heard Mum say, 'It's me you need to talk to, love.'

I felt like I did in the big corridors of the Bitch Academy, a very tiny thimble-sized girl, who, though pulling on her slutty mother's bridal dress, has no more force than a ladybird trying to topple the flower. I saw Claire and Cherub and Caprice staring at us keenly and I could hear their quick breathing. I could hear the nearby munching click of a hungry camera. The woman was shouting now, 'She's been spying on all of us, outside our house day and night, following me to work. And then she rammed into me, caused a car crash.' I was thinking, *oh, no, whoa, steady on*, but it was useless as usual, and too late, and the woman stepped forward and touched Mum with the tip of a pointed finger. It was like her finger had a bullet in it.

I'll later think that Mum dived like a stuntman because it made the whole episode more thrilling and it hurried us more quickly towards the end. She knew the game was up. She wanted to leave that crazy silly shop. Remember my mother likes what most people try and avoid: change, big sudden dangerous events that alter everything for ever. If the music had been playing or the hymns had been louder then no one might have noticed but in fact it was churchily quiet in the store and the shouts of the woman and the sound of Mum crashing back against a steel display cabinet rang out like total gunshot. I tried to hold her as she fell but I was too small and weak against the power of the bullet finger and the weight of the lump Mum'd become, soaked like a sponge with heavy champagne. Mum said later to Big Marilyn that it was painful but pleasant too, for it was not the deep constant bleeding ache of guilt or shame or loneliness, and the pain did not oil through her like wine. In fact it did the very opposite; it seemed to thump the pain out of her, she said, sober her up instantly. So by the time her boss Orla, then Gran, then Marilyn, then a dozen dozy others from Security Control arrived, Mum was totally aware of what and who had hit her.

At least Mum's suspension from work was quick. Boss Orla immediately said Mum had to leave the premises there and then, collecting belongings from her locker on the way out. But when I call Dad to say I will be home late because I have to stay and help Mum, he completely freaks. He says he's been told everything and that there is my home, etcetera, and how they are all waiting for me, and how they are getting a DVD and how Claire saw it all and is terribly worried and she has made a special comfort tea. And Dad says he has finished hanging the family photo above the fireplace and that it looks lovely.

Actually, without even a touch of irony, I'd say it was totally true that Dad had made my other house very nice. Though it was hard to imagine how Dad could have made such an amazing effort with a daft house, and have made no effort with Mum. He worked so hard to get the tiles polished and the plaster smooth and the paintwork glossy, and yet with Mum he just gave up and let her go.

And that day as I made her food, and cleared away the dishes, and washed up and wiped her kitchen table, I felt absolutely nothing. If you have two separate parents, two different homes, it is possible to do this; you can just decide to live in the empty space between him and her, here and there, now and then: that cool ironic gap where nothing matters.

AMIR

The headline in one paper read: WHACK! IT'S THE REAL BRIDAL BASH. And in the other: SLAPS IN STORE. In each the report was short and the picture large: 'Fighting broke out this afternoon during a lavish promotional event at the city's flagship store. Police had to be called when two women, one of whom was thought to be a bride at the event, threw punches at one another and tussled wildly on the floor. The store's general manager Orla McMahon said, "We are looking into the incident."' It was not headline news, not even page one or two, but there was a blurry mobile-phone photo of Jackie, in her contemporary bride outfit, falling backwards into the white silk mayhem all around. Then a clearer proper photograph of bemused bridal faces and a smashed display cabinet. 'Fisticuffs spoil perfect day,' said the caption.

Then there are the pictures of a very concerned old man standing by his nineteen-year-old daughter. We learn that she is studying journalism at university and living with her dad while she gets her degree.

Of course Ashfaq and Halima saw the reports. 'And they call us the violent ones,' Ashfaq said when he called me. 'They call us the threat to national security.' We hadn't spoken for two weeks but now he was delighted to hear my voice, just annoyed by two things: that he had missed the fight, and that I wasn't incriminated in any way. 'We know it's her. That tart you were . . . with. The one who came to our house. Now look what's happened. Why do you think I ordered you to stay away from her?'

'Englisher women is just total minging wrestlers,' Halima said, coming on the line suddenly. She said she had been staring hard at the picture trying to work out if they could see me in the shot. 'I so wish we'd been there, Amir. I told Ashfaq we should have gone to laugh at you.'

'It's not funny,' Ashfaq said darkly. 'I mean, if you had been pictured. Imagine the disgrace. Imagine how it would reflect on the family, on me, on my business.'

'No one would know I'm related to you,' I said.

'They would if I told them,' he said.

I tell him that I have resigned from the store. This is the truth. Orla had surprised me when I went into her office at the end of the day: 'Amir, sit down. Don't look so worried either, you're fashion specialist Womenswear as from today.'

'Don't you have to advertise?'

'Not if I decide that we don't have to. Start later today, Amir.'

'No thanks,' I say. 'I don't want to work here any more.'

I hadn't planned it; I just knew: if Jackie was never going to be there ever again I had to leave before I found myself knowing the names of all the Saturday girls, despite being three times their age.

'I could call the police,' Orla said.

My family took news of my resignation joyously. All evening excited relatives called my mobile with thoughts, questions and speculations. Ashfaq even rang relatives in Pakistan to pass on the news of the fight, the press coverage and my subsequent repentance. Relatives there then spread the news throughout the Middle East. Al Jazeera carried exclusive pictures of me on rolling news, and at nine pm that night, so desperate was he for more bad headline news from my day, and still eager to gaze over the smoky ruins of my professional life, Ashfaq invited me round to the house for the breaking of the fast. He said that it was a time for a family to be together, and my ma wanted to see me. But really he wanted to point at me and laugh, though he said everyone needed to come together to decide where I went next.

'I'm sorry we fell out, bro,' he said when he greeted me on the doorstep. He clasped my shoulder in his fat fist and squeezed.

'No you're not,' I said.

'Now you won't be seeing that slapper again, it's all in the past. Everything is over. Ma needs you here. I realise that now. You were good with her. Come in and we'll talk.'

I went in. They all laughed at me and hugged me and held up the newspaper reports and Ashfaq said that I'd been taught a lesson and now Ma could stop going to day care at Cosy Retreat and instead I could look after her half the time and work in Fags 'n' Fings the rest of the time. Ashfaq would pay me. I would work for him; he would check my housework, give me housekeeping and pay me extra if all was well. 'It's going to be like being married to you,' I say.

'Well, you should have taken the options open to you before,' Halima sighs, and, like a dodgy salesman, Ashfaq grins and pulls his wallet from his slimy pocket. He shows me a photograph of a truly beautiful young woman.

'When was this taken?' I say. 'And is this her or is this her sister?'

'It's her now! You won't be disappointed. That's her for real.'

'What's the catch?'

Ashfaq grins and shakes his head. 'I've just saved the best till last, bro.'

But really it wasn't because of gorgeous Anaya that I returned home, more because Ma really was pleased to see me, and really did seem to know that I'd been gone. And because I had nothing good to offer Jackie. So when I looked out of my bedroom window late that night and saw my disgraced friend standing there in the dark street, her bare shoulders honeyed in a pool of lamplight, I didn't go out to her. Though it was lashing a drizzle and she was half-dressed. I decided she was just a naughty vision caught in golden static, because I was a useless dick and I'd let her down, by not protecting her and by agreeing to the madness in the first place, and then not leaving with her the instant she was dismissed.

I should have took sulky little Elle in one hand and big naughty Jackie in the other and, stripping off my dickass fancy dress, strode out of there like a Bollywood cowboy.

But I didn't. And if you'd done something wrong and couldn't make it right, best leave well alone till you knew what to do. Withdraw like a defeated army. Leave room for rebuilding, which, after a period of intense and violent chaos, will happen.

So I just went online for hours, but later, though it was the first night back in my own bed, I didn't sleep for thinking and in the middle of the night my phone rings. It's her, texting me to say that nothing was my fault. 'U shd never hv lost ur job, luv.'

'I chose 2 go,' I write by starlight. 'No want 2 work there without u.'

'Warned u I was bad luk,' she texts back, almost before I've pressed send.

'U r best bad luk a man cd hav,' I reply, and turn my phone off, and lay there for the rest of the night waiting for a scarlet nail tap-tapping on my window.

Howling at the moon.

*　　*　　*

But just the next day, Sunday, I weakened. I could hold firm no longer and I agreed to meet her one last time in our café. I see her sitting at a table outside in the rain. She is wearing an enormous pair of black sunglasses and dragging hard on a fag. 'I'm being hounded by the press, honey,' she says when I go over and kiss her on the cheek, and so totally married to the mob does she look that I fully expect she has a revolver nestled in her lap. Danuta was at her side like the mafia moll's assistant, looking as excited as Ashfaq by the headline events, and she says she is accompanying Jackie everywhere. 'If the press want interviews they are going to have to pay,' Danuta says.

'It's OK,' I lie to Jackie who is holding my hand and saying over and over how wrong it was that I lost my job. 'I'm a partner in my brother's business now.'

'Well, howdy pardner,' Jackie says and tips her hair like a hat and cowboys around for a while, until Danuta asks: 'So, what do you do, the fags or the fings?'

'We are about to expand our fings into Europe,' I say and the women laugh because somehow I can do this now that I work for Ashfaq; I make women laugh all the time.

Just like that gimpy coach-driving comedian all those months ago and I wonder if maybe she loved him as women will soon love me, because I am the safe option; the blameless, home-loving, risking-nothing, looking-back, family man. Will all the damaged, nervous, exhausted women soon choose me carefully and cautiously, so as to safely protect them from other, better, wilder, more dangerous, exciting men?

And I know then that if I'd loved Jackie truly and boldly and passionately from the beginning, as soon as we knew we wanted each other, then she'd never have got involved with that little coach-driving dick. And if I'd turned up at the bar that night to meet her as planned she'd never have pressed on with her mad plan to force him to want her.

191

This is all my fault.

'We can't let that mad bitch win,' Danuta sighs. 'She nearly killed you. I thought you were going to fall down the escalator. Or at least get a piece of glass in your scalp. She could be facing a murder charge!'

'But, love, I keep telling you: I'm the mad bitch and she's the family,' Jackie says, adjusting her dark glasses. 'That's what it said in the paper. That she's his daughter from his second marriage. I want to explain it all to George, though,' she says. 'Tell him how I didn't mean his daughter no harm. Now that I know it definitely is his daughter I feel I can finally let him go.'

Danuta looks at me and shrugs. I tell Jackie that she should not contact George again, and I'd have said more if I'd not been trying to hold myself in hard, pull back on a tight rein, so as not to trot off as soon as she flicked me a smile. Because it was all gone and over now. Think of the pretty Anaya arriving for a visit later that day. Think of how I've agreed to that perfect honey coming over all the way from Birmingham. Think of my community and family and my old ma dying before the Bollywood ending. Staying out of trouble, keeping Jackie out of trouble, moving on, getting Ma out of Cosy Retreat and keeping me out of Primrose Lodge.

'You're right, Amir. I'm going to keep a low profile for a while,' Jackie says, as she straightens her huge sunglasses, wobbles up foal-like on her sky-high black patent heels. She appears to be wearing a tiny bin liner as a dress and because of the glasses I can't tell if she is crying or not. No handbag. 'I have Elle coming to stay for a week. I need to make sure that goes OK. I'll be in touch.'

So I watched her slink away again, and then I go back to do my housework before completing the extra chores Ashfaq has told me to do that day; defrosting the ice-cream freezer and vacuuming behind the mega bins for mouse droppings.

ASHFAQ

Anaya was so way more beautiful than I had expected. She actually looked like her people said she looked – which is totally unheard of. In fact she looked better in the flesh than she did in the photograph. She was young and intelligent, and she laughed easily and her hair slipped around her perfect shoulders like a slick of black gold. It was well strange to think of this proper Brummie honey marrying my dickass little brother, but if that is what I had to accept to reunite the family and protect my mother and sisters, then I would banish all other thoughts.

So that teatime, Halima was in the kitchen making the meal, and I was watching TV in the living room, and my aunt and sisters were showing Anaya and her people around the garden, when I heard the front door open and very quietly Amir begins to speak. I turned the volume down and inched, super-quiet, close to the living-room door, from where I could hear the little prick clearly.

'Elle's gone back to her dad's,' the devil says. I look through the gap between the door and the frame and I see her there, high-heel-tall on our doorstep. Exact same vanilla slut who came round last time we had a visit from a prospective bride.

It's like she comes here on purpose to screw things up – or perhaps the little gimp invites her.

'So I'm free,' she says.

'Right,' Amir says. 'I'd invite you in but I think both of us might not get out alive.'

'Ach, what's living anyway?' she says. But I can tell in her eyes, her smile, her hands on hips, her fingers through her hair, her smell, her quick breathing that she is trying to ruin him – and that she's going to succeed. 'Come out,' Jackie whispers. 'Please, Amir.'

Remember we are about to have our feast and Ma is calmly settled in her chair. Remember I've already given him a good hiding about his association with this very slag.

'It's not a good time,' Amir says.

'It won't ever be a good time, will it?'

'No,' Amir says. 'Inside is my entire family and my aunt and a total stranger I might be marrying.'

'Is she very beautiful?'

'Yep.'

'I'll go,' she says, but doesn't move.

I go through to the kitchen where the women are now working on the food and I say to Auntie that she should bring Anaya and her mother into the front room so they can look out at our street. They look at me for a moment well puzzled. 'Our street?' Samirah asks, not wanting to imply to the visitors that I am completely mad.

'Just so she can get a feel for the area,' I say, then I lead and they follow and we are in the living room looking out.

'Who's that?' Wahida says to me quietly, when she sees the back view of the slut who is still on the doorstep with Amir. I shrug and suggest that she is maybe selling something, though what she's selling is obvious to everyone. 'Oh no,' Auntie whispers to Samirah. 'It's not that friend who came round last time, is it?'

I shrug, and leave them talking about parking permits and I go out our back door, turn left out the garden gate and head down the alley quickly, where I press my back against the bricks and push my left ear out towards the street, to hear Amir say, 'Where?'

'To clean up for my daughter. She's coming soon. For the weekend before half-term. I'd hoped she'd be able to stay all week but she's only staying the weekend in case she catches any incurable personality traits from me.'

There is a long frustrating pause, and I can't see what they are doing, but eventually I hear the slut say, 'Can I leave you a spare set of keys? Because I'm gonna take Elle away for a few days. Holiday. Theme-park kind of jobby. Would you come round and check on the house for me, love? From Friday?' She says all this real quick, like it's just occurred to her, and when Amir asks her where exactly she's going she shrugs and says, 'Hey, I'm free. No job, no bloke, no responsibilities. There's a whole world out there. All those seas, all those fishes.'

My aunt's tapping on the window is so loud now I think she's gonna crack the bloody pane, and drag little bro dickass in by his collar through the broken glass.

But there's no point us getting angry. We've tried physical restraint and it don't work, just allows Amir to feel like he's the bold rebel, the freedom fighter. In fact I'd gotten way more grief off everyone about it than he had. We have to try something else.

'Yeh, some time alone with my lovely little daughter will be just the thing, Amir.'

'Yeh, sure,' Amir said and she hands over a set of keys. Then there is deep kiss on pink cheek, quick, despite the fact that Aunt is still tapping and Anaya is still watching and must have thought something of it, poor lass.

Amir is too drunk on the old slut to notice his family at the window.

As they say goodbye, Amir holds on to her hard for a too-long moment, like he is truly trying to wind me up. 'If I left the iron on, turn it off will you, love,' Jackie says as she turns to walk away. 'You don't need to worry about the house plants, though,' she gabbles on. 'You were right; they're already dead.'

He reaches for her, and she topples towards him.

'That's enough,' I shout and I appear behind them instantly so they both jump out of their slutty little skins. I put a hand on Amir's shoulder like he is seven years old and I pull him back along the pavement. Still he holds on to her for a moment too long, even when I am dragging him away. I am speaking softly now, as if to a dangerous madman, prising Jackie out of his grip, like she's a sharp knife.

'Yes he better go in, his stranger's getting annoyed,' Jackie says, smiling up at me, and at last Amir turns to the window and both of us see Anaya and her people, and our sisters and mother looking out at us, worried and wondering.

I see the shame on my little brother's face. I see the embarrassment and guilt I've put there perfectly. Which are both more powerful deterrents to badness than beatings. I've learnt that much from all of this. And I've learnt not to allow mixing. Last time she came round I made the mistake of allowing Amir's woman to get too close to our women, so that she could fashion herself as a normal friendly person, and so there was chit-chat and gossiping and sharing. But now as he looks from our family, worrying in the window at a distance, to her there in the street, it is quite clear that Amir must choose between her and us.

I lead Amir away and, like the dickless donkey that he is, he lets me.

Indoors they all turn to look at him angrily. I know that poor Anaya might not survive this experience, but she is too much of an absolute total babe for him anyway, and the despair that Amir will endure at having brought all this on his own family will help him turn himself away from the wrong path he is on. He will be ashamed of himself for a long time and the disgrace he has brought upon us all today will ensure that he punishes himself more than I could ever punish him. And eventually, one day soon, we will find a good woman who knows nothing of his true desires, and who he no longer has the will to refuse.

AMIR

Later that night, when I should be sleeping, I came over all texty, though I know there's no point and there've been too many false hopes, and when we did get the chance to be together just a few hours back, I screwed it up again. Though all the time that we did nothing on the wind-blown doorstep I was thinking how we could just run away together. Take our passports and go. Winter in a hot country. Return here when things have cooled down.

Then I remember my aunt's tapping on the window, the sound like a wind-slapped branch, and when I turned, puzzled, the troubled look on Anaya's pretty face. I think how Jackie tried to save us both from shame by inventing a holiday with her daughter because I knew she had to say something because we were being watched, and it was just something she had made up on the spot to save us from embarrassment. Like I did that day in April when I caught her with that tosspot royal, dressed up as a fluffy chick, and I pretended I needed her to bring in a hard-boiled egg. A hard-boiled egg! That seems so long ago, before we went mad, got written up by the newspapers and sacked.

There is no reply to my texts, and I start thinking that Jackie is like the green summer weeds, and the house plants, and my career, dead and gone, and I wake in the night sweaty with the discovery of her like a brown stalk in the sand on a yellow beach somewhere, and Halima met me on the landing and asked what was worrying me, and if I would like her to pray for me.

I think of Ashfaq travelling round Pakistan alone, visiting our distant relatives, giving money, telling them all how well he was doing, and them saying how proud Pa would have been of him, as I wander around the house like a restless ghost, thinking of her kissing me goodbye this afternoon, her hot left cheek pressed right up to mine and her slim body up against me right down to trembling ankle. Just like before. I wouldn't let her go and she's held there against me, real hard, though behind me, all the time, I could hear my aunt calling and shouting like she was trying to scare away a manky cat.

Then I returned to my room and thought how our thorny alley is a few seconds away though it is coming to the end of the year now and the weeds are dying back, the flower lights out, the smell not musty of pollen and honey but cold mulch and rot, and I feel stomach sick because she and I, we, missed the warm summer moment completely. Because I chose fear, and his friend control, over courage and commitment and there is now no going back.

At three am, the ceiling spinning like a disco ball, my phone lit up. 'Cum outside,' it said. I stared at the message for a moment. I know that she wants me to make love to me. It's just something I know for sure. And that's some rare, intimate certainty that I don't get, can't expect to get, from Anaya, no matter how breathtaking she is to look at.

So, against everything I knew to be right, I floated down the stairs wearing just my boxer shorts, and there she was standing in the street, in a moonlit gown that could have been a nightdress too. My heart thunders for the second time that day. I used to think the thumping in my chest whenever Jackie was near was fear; but no, this is something else entirely.

'Actually, I've been informed that it's going to be a bit of a problem for me to take Elle away with me for the weekend. I have to ask her father two weeks in advance apparently, and then a judge needs to agree to it, then the prime minister, then the head of the United Nations. And they all agree she has to spend half-term at her dad's. So I wondered if, er, well, if you would like to come with me next week instead.'

It is a wet and windy October night, and I am nearly naked, yet I feel warm as chips because I don't think a woman has ever asked me anything this directly before and I can't reply immediately though I have slept with two married women. Both white lasses that I met through work – customers, in fact. I know now that I went with them so that nothing could come of it. We would screw and then they would go back to their husbands and I would go back to my life, unchanged.

I put my head against the doorframe and close my eyes. 'Now that neither of us is working, and I've got a bit of money spare.' Jackie was speaking slowly and calmly and when she shivered she said, 'Somewhere hot, maybe. Just board a plane and see where it takes us.'

I think of my auntie this afternoon, and how she swatted her hand at me from behind the living-room window, repeatedly as if dismissing a grubby doorstep salesman. And poor Anaya narrowing her eyes, but trying to smile. Wahida and Samirah looking frozen still and scared. And all the other moments so far when I've been revealed to my people as the selfish, shameless, heartless little English bastard that I surely am.

'No,' I said, 'I can't, I can't, I can't.'

'Are you certain about that?'

'Yes. I can't. I'm sorry.'

'OK,' she said, and turned to leave, 'I just thought I'd ask.'

If it was a dream, it was one in which I was drowning, and from which I couldn't wake.

ELLE

All the first evening I held the telephone in my hot hand in case anyone called; but Dad wouldn't call because he expected me to be away for the whole half-term week, and Mum wouldn't call because she didn't think I was still there, and she couldn't use a phone anyway if she was dead and already being eaten by flies.

On the last Sunday she'd looked so lonely, and so sad. Something had happened, and though I really didn't want to know what it was, I did want to be with her to keep her safe. So I'd decided to insist and stay all half-term week at hers.

But several times as the first darkness fell, I thought of giving up and running home and telling the Steps that I had stayed one night home alone and now I had no idea where my mum was and we had to call the police. But clock Cherub rolling her vicious green-crusted eyes, 'Wow, one night in Slutworld. Big fucking deal.'

Plus it was half-term at Bitch Academy and the Steps would be home all day, all week, slinking around the house like huge hissing cats, rubbing up round their own true mum and purring for special shopping trips and ice-skating treats. And the thought of Claire raging about how she would have to get Dad to go back to court because Mum couldn't be trusted ever again now, and how Mum'd had her final chance, and how I could have been murdered by a paedophile or burnt to death on the oven or drowned in a too-deep bath.

If only!

And anyway the police might not be too chuffed about me being here alone. They had already spoken to Mum about her watching George, and then about what happened with George's daughter. It might be better not to say anything at all. And Dad would definitely not want to get back with Mum if he heard she'd left me on my own all night.

So zip it.

And when I realised how my silence was protecting Mum, and how lucky I was not to be at home with the Steps, the first few hours were actually totallyfantastic.com.

I found Magic FM on her super-loud new digital radio. I had half a packet of chocolate Hobnobs and a box of After Eights for my dinner. I poured a bottle of her luxury bath soak, into the deepest, most dangerous bath ever. And walked around naked, dancing, blooming with her best perfume, my toenails painted in a greeny sheen designed to drive any woman emerald with jealousy, then I watched the very rude comedy show that Claire says is totally forbidden at my age. I wanted to watch a violent horror movie but I didn't have a paper so didn't know what was on.

Which gave me the next idea: to investigate vibrator and porn on Mum's new computer. Porn was actually more than sex on TV. It could be anything you wanted, but was often lots of girls like Cherub, but with bigger bazookas, kissing, which was really funny and I went through loads and loads of the sexy photos looking to see if there was anyone I knew. It was very interesting, particularly if, unlike Ashanti, you've not seen a lot of willies yet, and even if it did make you feel a bit like the smelly old men that Claire said went online looking for schoolgirls it was fascinating, and usually cheerful and unusual, and all the girls are pretty, oily and bronzed as roast chickens with nice knickers and bras, and once you've seen one nice girl you get the curiosity to see another and another because you are doing quick sums as you look, adding and subtracting to discover where they are better, legs, bum or chest, and where you also score, then click click the whole evening's gone and you've not felt lonely or scared once.

And you learn things, like I'd never have guessed a vibrator was a pretend willy! As if I'd want one of them delivered in twenty-four hours! Though I had money. The secret twenty-pound note that Dad made me take during my every-other-weekend, just in case, was in my purse. I could further my interest in porn – because I soon learn it's like anything in life, you have to pay for the best stuff – or I could get a taxi home, just say I'd changed my mind. I could order a pizza. I could go to the cinema.

But where was she? Maybe she had gone to London for a job interview. To visit an old friend in another part of the country. Perhaps she'd picked up a guy and gone home with him. Maybe to see the Asian. And all the time, whatever I was doing, looking at the porn or having a bath, I listened for the key scratch, the lock rattle, watched the floor for the line of light under the door, saying that she's safe and home.

The freakiest thing was the objects in the house – how calmly they took the silent sun and then the moon. Though they were used to being alone, and I was not – never had been in my life – and I was restless, and unlike the sofa and the sideboard, the table and the lamps, I could not settle. Somehow, that first night I just fell asleep in all my clothes on her bed in the early hours with the curtains still left wide and the moon staring in at me, and I woke still worrying, half about the porn girls – maybe because it's cold outside and there's never any sign in porn of warm clothes, or maybe I'm just jealous because they all have each other in their happy porny world and I'm still all alone and mumless on a chilly morning, or maybe it's because sometimes the porny kids look like they're screaming in pain, even when they're just touching their bum.

I watched the morning news for news. Like when I was first removed full time to Claire's and used to worry Mum had had an accident or had died and I didn't know. Rolling news was my only reliable friend. Because how would anyone get in touch with me to let me know if Mum died during the fortnight that I didn't see her? How would they know I was even anything to do with her? At best there would probably be at least twenty-four hours between her dying and Gran being told – that's if Mum did have ID on her, which she wouldn't if she was out at a club with just her little silver clutch – and then Gran telling Dad and then Dad telling Claire and then someone maybe telling me. I used to think this a lot – I used to be surprised when she was actually alive, still there, smiling and breathing and waiting for me two weeks later.

All this was until I mastered my tricks – of removing her photos and her cards and notes, and to try not to even think of her while she wasn't there, to try and keep myself full up with other more meaningless things. So all the second day I kept looking at this letter in her pile from a man with the made-up name of Oscar Goldstein, Vice President of Membership at American Express. In a large silver banner it said: '*Put the American Express Platinum Credit Card at the top of your to-do list and start living a life less ordinary.*' There was a little pat of glue, like torn skin, where the card had been stuck. I wondered if his name was an anagram, but can't make nothing of it, so I thought of the Steps having their organic porridge with maple syrup and chopped bananas and of Caprice making gagging noises, and Cherub making secret calls to lads in her bedroom. And no matter how worried and lonely I was, it felt like I belonged here at Mum's and they belonged there at Claire's.

Plus, a whole day takes a lot of managing. By day three I had less time for sloshing about looking for familiar faces in the porn, for I was defrosting food and I was washing up. I worked out how to put the washing machine on, and though it's disloyal to Mum to praise anything about Claire, I have to say that she's taught us things about housewifery, which she takes very seriously, like it is some ancient forgotten skill like cave painting. For example, never end the day with a full washing-up bowl. Wash up, wipe the bowl and the sink, turn the bowl over, and fold the dishcloth on top. When you wake up the next morning it's like Christmas Day. I also know to lock the door and leave the key in in case there is a fire and you need to get out quick. Don't block hallways. I know to draw the curtains tight, and to iron clothes on a low setting and not to bother with a mop but to go at the kitchen floor first with the vacuum cleaner, then on your knees with a cloth. I know to check the oven and the hobs are off, and to clean them over each night with a spot of lemon juice.

Alone, I discover new things too: Elnett hairspray smells of Mum. Soft shower water sounds like Mum ssshing me to sleep, and that you get very smelly in three days of no washing. Then I started becoming a bit like Dad: worrying about grass in the gutter, the all-night drip drip of the cold-water tap, and what would happen if the toilet got blocked. And by day three things were getting forgotten; brushing my hair: no one was going to see me. Table manners: I ate my defrostings as a wolf would, suddenly and messily, in a heap of litter. Privacy: I left the bathroom door open when I weed. Was I finding my true Claire-free self? Or was I losing my true Mum-loved self? Whenever I panicked and cried I thought that too much time had passed now and either she had really died, in which case nothing mattered at all ever again and I might as well devote myself to online porn, or there had been some mega mistake, and if that came out she would be in terrible trouble.

So I had to just carry on. In the day I could control my worry-head with Claire's busy thoughts, but at night I dreamt Mum's dreams. I made a tent of the bedcovers, like a kid, and in there I sniffed my own ripening and thought how we imagine that our dreams come from within us, but what if really they come from without? What if they hang in the air, porny stories strong as smoky smells, waiting for any sleeping body to soak into? Because though I didn't know where she was or why she'd gone I dreamt of white sand and blue skies and sometimes the pornies rolling around kissing at the edge of the frothy blue water. In the morning I'd hear a crackling sound, like very close by someone was unwrapping sweets or walking on twigs, and I'd think this was her, yes, come back, until I turned around and there was no one there.

This is how you could go mad, by waiting for someone every minute with every sense in your body, who never comes. So on the fourth day I do go mad and I sleep in my clothes, in case anyone does come, unexpectedly, and I need to flee, or shine a sudden smile of normal. Though really with my mum gone I feel geekier and weirder than I do even at the Bitch Academy, though it doesn't matter because no one has seen me for days.

I knew for certain that I mustn't leave the house. Later, people would say how brave and sensible I was, but really it was only because I stayed indoors the whole time, waiting.

On the fifth day I humped the mattress from her bed down into the front room. That way I could keep an eye on every-thing; the street, the fish tank, the television, the telephone, the front door, the clock, the internet. Down there I could be more in control because whatever anyone says you only have yourself to rely on. I learnt this during my week alone at Mum's, and in the following months I would need that lesson more than ever. For example, weeks later, when this part of the story had just happened, my big manly doctor said to me, 'It must have been unbearable, Elle, simply unimaginable.' I said nothing, just looked sorrowful, because actually I had got over the shock and now rather liked the attention. 'We're always here for you, Elle. If you need to speak to anyone about what happened when you were left alone at home, anytime at all during the school day, or in the evening, my door is always open. Even if you want to just talk about how you spent your days. I'll tell the receptionist to show you straight in. No need to wait. Just say your name and she'll bring you straight into my room.'

Sure. Like he wants to know everything about online porn!

Then the week after, I stood up from my class and walked out when I heard some kids whispering about Mum being a mental slut. I walked to the doctor's two miles away. The door was open. I went inside and sat down right in the doctor's room. No one was there. I waited. I looked at the low table with the cut-in half plastic body, the empty vase, the clear sweep of the big desk, the tall bookcase with just a couple of books laying flat, the half pulled line of broken vertical blinds. The room smelt of bandages and dust. It was chilly and I could hear the waiting room happening way off in the distance, like I was sunk down, numb, unable to move, like in the final minutes before death.

The counsellor said later that feeling is called depression.

Eventually a woman appeared. 'Excuse me, who gave you permission to be in here?' she said, quite crossly. I told her I was looking for Mr Cooper, the doctor, and how he'd said I could come and see him whenever I needed. 'What about?' the woman said more crossly.

'It's private,' I said.

'Well, he's away sick,' she said. 'And he will be away for some time. So can you come out of there please, right now.'

Which is why people like porno so much, because you're on your own, baby; you'd better believe it, honeybunch. Adults in real life want to be kind and helpful more than they are able. Doctors go sick, teachers forget things, clowns can't keep everyone happy. Mums are sometimes so busy they are three steps ahead of themselves and things get dropped and forgotten and lost – even people. So take it from one who knows, you'll have to accept this because it's your lousy life.

AMIR

I managed almost a week until, unable to bear it any longer, I take the keys and walk through the lamp-lit drizzled late-night streets towards the goreh estate, with the mini-bikes still racing and the gangs of insomniac lads still hanging there damply in packs, yawning.

It's odd to realise the world hasn't changed, because I feel like a new man. Though I still walk with a dry mouth, hood up, head down, until I get to her dark house, shaking. I knock first, because I want her to be alive and in there, warm, nearly naked and waiting, dressed-up as a chicken, webbed-feet, ready to tweet. I have rehearsed what I will say, no jokes this time, no nerves, just that I am ready and have my passport in my pocket and I am hers.

So wild am I for her, I think I could blow the frail house down with one puff. But instead I ring hard on the bell. I don't see the little face gloomed behind the nets until I am about to use my key and go indoors. Then I notice a glittering that is both candlelight and panic and I see what at first I think is a small lad. Then I look closer and see it's Jackie's impish little lass who I'd first seen months back, then again more recently sulking round ours, then entwined with her mum at the fateful brides' event.

Flamelight is flickering the room to a dangerous shrine. It is almost midnight. 'Is your mum in?' I say and she shakes her head, stepping back like she is total afraid of me. Her face shrouded by net curtains like a spook. She probably thinks I'm a burglar, or worse. 'Where's your mum?' I say again, smiling and bending down low to her level. 'I'm a friend of your mum's. I'm Amir. You came to our house.' This time she pulls back the nets and pulls up her eyebrows. She points behind her, and I see a cityscape of candles on all surfaces, and a mattress dragged on to the floor, the cans and plastic bottles, the quilts and blankets flung around, the white screen of the computer.

'Is your mum in?' I say again, more desperately.

'Do you think I'd be living like this if my mum was in?' she shouts at the glass, and points behind her at the slummy room. I try to smile. She scowls at me, then her chin starts to tremble.

'Can I just talk to you?' Again she shakes her head, and frowns. 'Where's your mum?'

'At the shops,' she says. 'She won't be long.'

'It's midnight.'

'Actually she might be a little while,' she says.

'No worries,' I say. 'I'll wait.'

'No,' she says and shakes her head quickly. 'Big worries if you wait.'

It's the messiness of the lass's hair, and the way she's wearing her dressing gown over her crumpled jeans, that alerts me to trouble next and I think again that perhaps her mother has died so my heart is thumping. She is shaking her head and nearly panicking so I don't go in, but I find the number in my wallet, given to me months back at the mad Sunday dinner, and I ring Shirley on my mobile phone and tell her why she should come to the house. I have to hold the phone away from my ear to control the rage-blast of her reply.

Then I sit on the step and wait for the crazy old ma to arrive. And when, ten minutes later, in a cloud of fag ash and booze-breath she falls out of a cab, the first thing she does is ask me to leave. 'Where's Jackie? I want to just make sure she's all right,' I said, when Shirley came out of the house, her small pointy face white as peeled garlic.

'My daughter's never been all right and she never will be,' Shirley said, holding hard on to her moon-faced granddaughter. 'So I suggest you get used to that idea.'

'But just let me check that Jackie's safe.'

'Our Jackie don't want to be safe. She likes to be dangerous. That's why she got with you in the first place.'

'I want to know she's OK.'

'Why you worried about Jackie? This little lass's been in there for five days. And you're worried about *Jackie?*'

'Where is she? What's happened?'

'Look, love, just go home and forget about my daughter,' Shirley said, snapping her arms across her chest. 'Many men before you have tried to save her and it won't work. Stick to your own side, love, it's better all round.'

But it's not her iciness that makes me go, it's the sight of the little lass trembling, with her nose pressed to her gran's hand, scowling at me through her tears.

Two days later, on the first day of November, I get into the freezing shop at five am and Ashfaq is leaping between his mega dump bins grinning. He has laid all the newspapers out on the counter, and over the ice-cream fridge and some on the floor. He has two copies of each newspaper displayed, one with the headline, and then another copy of the same paper with the story spread open from the inside. 'It's her, innit,' he screams. 'Again!'

All before I even can focus on the black ants crawling before me.

'It's Amir's top tart. Her there, look, man! Arrested, innit. A criminal. Again! Just weeks after the last episode! Your putty-coloured balloon-tittied happy whore heading for the gallows.'

'These English have no shame,' Hamila says.

Trouble at Till for Busty Mum Dumb Blonde 'Forgets' Daughter 12 Home Alone Girl Forgives All Dash of a Sales-woman Ooops Where's My Daughter Mother Jets Off to Find OAP Lover . . . It all merged into one and I couldn't follow the story.

It was the first I'd heard about it. I had sat on the step until Shirley had turned up to rescue her granddaughter, then I had gone straight home, so all that I knew about Jackie's flit came in one big head rush now, from the papers.

To be honest, it was great just to see that face again.

Ashfaq gave a breathless commentary as I read the headlines. Like the showbiz agent who'd first discovered the tabloid star, he knew every report word for word, and as he read he exhaled proudly and grinned. Because ever since Ashfaq saw Jackie early that morning in April, the dick has not been able to forget her. The cat scrap at the bridal bash only made him more doolally. He tells me that not only has she been to his own house, but she has been into the shop many times, and so he could tell the reporters about the gori slag, sell his story. Then he says that I know her real well, and that I could perhaps flog my own gossip for proper good money. 'Buy your own shop, man, with the winnings. Make her compensate you for the humiliation you is suffering by knowing her.'

So he wants to know what I know, if Jackie ever told me anything real dirty, or suggested anything. But I can't speak a word. I just fall to my jelly knees and read the papers that are spread over the cold tiled floor. I feel watery-mouthed, throat-sick, then dizzy too. 'Now go and deliver them to our custom-ers,' Ashfaq says. 'I want everyone to know what this whore of yours is like.'

I refused. He sacked me. He told me never to come back to his house again. I went to the park and read all the papers over and over, more angry with every lie they told. As the light began to fade Ashfaq called me on my mobile and said the evening papers needed delivering and would I come back if he apologised.

He was too excited to let me go. I was like a faded failed celebrity still caught in my public's viscous jaws.

I made him beg and then I agreed, and over tea that night Halima laughed and called me a dope but Anaya, who had, to my surprise, been invited for another visit, said I was already thinking like 'responsible husband material'. Wahida called to say she was worried about me. Yasmin said she'd predicted something like this would happen. Samirah said I should make an appointment with the doctor.

At the end of the day I resigned. 'I don't want to be the manager of a newsagent's,' I told Anaya, 'I hate newspapers for a start. It's all lies.'

'But you must respect your elder brother,' Anaya says.

'I respect him, but I don't want to be him.'

'You don't know what you want. You've had your thick head turned by some slaggy white lass,' Ashfaq says when I tell him, though Anaya is there listening. 'You think you are in love with this world-famous tart,' and he holds up her grainy front-page picture and shakes the paper so she rustles and wiggles like a ghost in grey and white, 'but in fact you're just like one of those drivers who slow down when they see a car crash.'

'That's her who came to your house that time,' Anaya says, slowly realising the scale of the humiliation. 'That dog out on the pavement.'

'He's fascinated by the gorehs, when he should be looking in another, more heavenly, direction.' And Ashfaq stabs his fat thumb towards Anaya.

We both look at her and know that, despite her perfect prettiness, she will never make the papers for there is not one thing even faintly interesting or unpredictable or passionate about her.

'Is this all true?' Anaya asks, no longer shy and gentle. I nod and she calls me a sex-mad dirty bastard in Urdu, then she slaps me hard around the face as Wahida weeps and Halima claps loudly.

I knew from the news Jackie was back. There was a photo of her coming through Heathrow Airport, bug eyed by those huge mafia-dark sunglasses. She looked like a celeb returning from exile, and so badly did I want to call her I dialled several times before flinging my phone against a wall – I had to stop it; I had nothing to offer that could help her; I could only make things worse.

All the papers reported that the only thing she said to the waiting press was, 'No comment,' which seemed like progress.

One day later I received a text thanking me. It was short. It just said that: 'Sorry, Amir. Thank u 4 finding Elle.' And I managed not to reply, and then three days later I was busy with the visit from Harpreet, who was staying with my aunt and waking daily at five am to come round the corner to our house and prepare our family breakfast.

I knew Harpreet came so hot on the heels of Anaya that it seemed like a joke. It was a joke. I was the joke. Like Mum's favourite Englishman, Benny Hill, when he's being chased by those half-naked ladies. Yes, I was running for my life now too, because they were serving up the women faster and faster, tinkled over with gold and silver garnish, tempting me, wearing me down, chasing me to the final surrender – all to the jaunty soundtrack of sitcom music.

But it wasn't funny.

Harpreet was even more servile than Anaya though she dressed like she was right out of old Bollywood with perfect make-up and shiny styled hair. When I spoke to her she jumped.

'She acts like a nervous slave,' I say to Ashfaq.

'She's just pretending to be shy. Once you're married she'll be a ball-breaker like all the rest,' Ashfaq says.

'Great,' I say.

'Which is exactly what you need if you want to stay out of the *News of the World* yourself,' Halima adds. 'She's going to have to keep you on a very short rein.'

'She likes to be with you. And she is going to learn sewing at college,' my aunt says.

'I used to work in a fashion store, I don't want a wife to sew my clothes.'

'And she's wonderful with Ashfaq's children. That's enough, isn't it? It's good you lost your job at the store and then your job with Ashfaq,' my aunt continues. 'Now you've really got time to get to know a future wife.'

'What kind of woman wants an unemployed man?' I ask.

'At least you are no longer Ashfaq's paper lad,' she reasons. 'No woman wants to marry a paper lad.'

'Which woman wants a man who can't support her?' I beg.

'One like Harpreet,' Ashfaq says, 'with a father with his own businesses.'

'Yes. You have sinned and this is your punishment,' Halima giggles.

Ashfaq, like he's my social worker, tells me he's already 'made all the arrangements'.

They are all delighted by how badly things have turned out for me, and perhaps it does prove that Allah is watching over us and punishing the bad and rewarding the good. Our very distant 'Uncle' Hamid is a Mercedes-driving dour millionaire: rich and organised and therefore good. Jackie is a penniless single mum who forgot her kid: poor and dizzy and therefore bad. Where's the choice?

'Hamid is going to train you up to manager standard,' Aunt grins.

Our 'uncle' owns a chain of restaurants and has a policy of starting his dickless managers on the bottom rung of the ladder, serving dishes or washing up. This training can go on for years until the defeated employee has learnt all aspects of bending and scraping, and has had their independent spirit crushed. 'I've no experience,' I plead.

'You've been a batty-lad fashion specialist in one of Europe's top shops,' Halima smiles, 'you must have learnt something about flogging to the dumb goreh public.'

'Why me?' I ask, turning this time to Ashfaq. 'I'm too lazy and clumsy to be a waiter.' I can only picture myself slopping curry in the laps of businessmen, falling asleep on a mattress of naans, weeping into the washing up.

'Well, we all have to have a hopeless cause to champion,' Ashfaq says and then later that night, when I am itching to call Jackie and can't wait a moment longer, my aunt catches hold of me in the kitchen and says, 'I have asked Harpreet to stay for a few more days.'

This is how it must work when you are held the twenty-eight days for suspected terrorist questioning. Quite quickly you can't bear it any longer, you will agree to anything if only you can stop being asked the same questions about who you are and what you do and what you want, over and over.

So over the next two days I stop arguing. I let Halima do all the talking. I listen to the women and nod and everyone seems to love me more. 'It's true. I can see you and Harpreet growing old together,' Yasmin says. I don't reply because everyone, including my ma, is so happy, but the truth is that we've already grown old together; I've aged twenty years since Harpreet's been around and I can feel myself growing a beard

and reaching out a gym-muscled arm for the *Grocer* magazine.
'She will be good for you,' Yasmin says.

But Harpreet is one of the most beautiful and boring women
I've ever met. She is also an experienced hospital nurse, which
seals it for Ashfaq. I can't imagine any trouble she could ever
get me into that medication couldn't cure. So I decide to give
up and marry her. Then, just when I am about to propose, and
three weeks after Jackie got back, I get a text: 'Out on bail. If u
want 1st exclusive interview meet 4 coffee. PLZ.'

When I came into the coffee shop, she stood up and kissed me,
cheek cheek, then held my face in her cold hands, till I felt
faint. She thanks me over and over for finding Elle. 'My hero,'
she says, and when I tell her how I've been spending my days
since she's been gone she says, 'My hero the paperboy.' Then
she tells me how Elle had not cried once, through five long
nights, despite being afraid of fridge noises. She tells me how
Elle had cleaned the kitchen floor, defrosted the freezer,
stacked up the bank letters for recycling and done a full
half-term in the house all alone.

'Paperboy, eh? Now that is what they call downsizing, love,'
she smiles, when I tell her that while Elle has been a heroine I
have been working twelve-hour shifts for Ashfaq.

'It's called staying out of trouble,' I say. She is still holding
my fingertips, can't let them go, she says, because they are ice
cold.

'Your fingers are freezing too,' I say, and reach to take her
hand. 'Didn't you drive?' I have her fingers up close to my
mouth now and I am blowing on them.

'Repossessed,' she says and when I laugh because I think she
is joking she says, 'No, really. I've been rather overspending.'

But we need to get all the tabloidyness out the way so I say,
'Ah yes, and I hear you've been involved with the police since I
last saw you.' I had been worried about mentioning this, but

actually now we are together it does all seem quite funny and ridiculous, impossible that the law and the police and all the rules of the world apply to us.

Us.

'Well, I wouldn't say involved, Amir. It wasn't like we were formally dating. I could still see other guys,' she says.

Then she tells me everything, beginning with how she'd heard George had gone there on holiday, so, unbelievably, she went to apologise, and then how when she was on her Greek island she was approached by a man in regular tourist clothes. 'Can you confirm your name, age and address?' She thought it was a chat-up. 'Not when I'm almost sober, I can't. But I will if you'll buy me another drink,' she said. It was only when they said they were the police that she said she went cold in the way that a parent does. 'If anything had happened to Elle, my life would be well and truly over.'

'She's fine,' I say. 'She adores you.' And I hold her hand while she cries and tells me all about her daughter and how she survived and how she cooked and cleaned.

'Well, at least you're not in prison,' I say, after a while when all the terrible details are done.

'Yet. How are you with prison visiting?'

'I'm very punctual,' I say, which is true.

'More likely I'll get a tag. Ever had coffee with a woman with an electronic tag, Amir?'

'I'm good with gadgets. If you went off unexpectedly I could reset you.'

She is gazing at me now, and then thanking me again and again for finding Elle. She says that she should have been aware of the police coming after her because the day before a photographer had hurried up to her when she was sitting in the very same position outside the bar and he had taken pictures. Bobbing down low so her face must have been only visible through a fence of green bottles. Still, she was too bleary to object, though she'd wondered hazily later why he seemed so keen, and why he didn't offer to sell her any afterwards and why he hadn't taken any of anyone else, or bothered to speak a word to her.

She is confessing everything to me, like I am her best friend in the world, and I know I need to tell her about Harpreet, and the decisions I have made, and I am going to do so any minute now.

'You know your daughter's at home on her own?' the police said to her and Jackie had just replied, 'Whoa! Where the hell is her father?' 'He stopped living with you several years ago,' the policeman replied. 'She's been on her own for five days. Until your mother found her. She's been looking after herself every day. Making her own meals, lighting the gas fire.' Jackie demonstrated to me how she had closed her eyes and shook her head and pressed her fingers to her mouth, still astonished by what had happened. 'If it hadn't been half-term then the school would have rung the police before,' Jackie says. 'They do in these cases. It's standard practice. Sometimes they have to break down doors, because often when these kids see a police officer they refuse to let them in.'

She still couldn't believe that she was involved in a situation where a child, her child!, was left at home alone. She was not entirely woken from the hot yellow nightmare, and she tells me how on the plane she remembers that she had a kinky dream that she was handcuffed to a policeman – and she woke up and she was handcuffed to the policeman, 'Which is one way for me to keep a guy, Amir!' But I don't laugh. 'He said there's a chance I might just get a warning. But I told him, "Warnings don't work with me." I told him that I don't know why but they just don't. It's been that way all my life, Amir. The more I'm warned about something, the more likely I am to do it. And you know what he said to me, Amir? He said, "Mrs Jackson, that's the case with psychopaths. It's all part of

219

attention-seeking behaviour. Often in line with the personality-disorder spectrum." '

I say nothing.

'How does it feel to be having coffee with a potentially dangerous psychopath, Amir?' and she vampires me her teeth, so I have to laugh, and she thanks me over and over for finding Elle, and for a moment we can't help it, we hold each other.

'I didn't do anything dangerous. I just called your mother.'

'That's always heroic. Many men wouldn't dare to do that, love.'

'Perhaps if I'd stuck around, I could have . . . prevented it . . . the papers getting involved.'

And she strokes her hand slowly over my cheek and now I have to do it. I say, 'Jackie, things have moved on a bit while you were away. I've changed. I'm going to be getting married soon.'

I haven't got the stomach to spin it, so it comes out how it feels: like a piano out a window.

'Well, I guess it's no surprise,' she says, staring over my shoulder and letting her grip go loose on my hand.

'Her father's got a chain of restaurants and I need a proper job, Jackie,' I say, pleading.

'Haven't you heard of a job centre, love?'

'He's going to buy us a house. And my ma will come and live with us. She's called Harpreet. She's a nice . . .'

Miserably I tell her all the happy details.

'Don't marry someone you don't love, Amir,' she says when all the joy is done. There is a silence. 'Unless you have to, of coursc.'

'I have to,' I say, and she studies me, like an important letter. 'And I hope one day you will settle down too. I'd like to see you settled, Jackie.'

'Hmm,' she says, with a smile. 'Like a dog in its basket.'

For a few hot moments neither of us speak. She's right, I've not changed at all: I am so flaming warm for her I want to take all my clothes off though outside it's icy. 'Well, you're the one who said we are all animals, Jackie,' I say.

'Wild animals, love, not domesticated pets.' She looks down at the table, like she's thinking hard. 'No, you're right, Amir. I need to be tied down, because I'm like a balloon and I need someone to hold on to me or I just take off. If I'm going to keep out of trouble I have to stop falling in love and start facing my responsibilities.'

'Me too,' I say. 'That's exactly what I've been thinking.'

'Yes. Getting married might be a good idea for us both. Not to each other, of course.'

'Obviously.'

'But to a nice stranger.'

'Yes. And this time, Jackie, how about you marry a stranger who isn't afraid of you, but who loves and respects you?'

'Don't be silly, Amir,' she says, and I can see a little dampening of her eye that I can't bear to look at. 'Even I'm frightened of me. I'm terrified of what I might do next.'

We stay there for a while because neither of us have a job to go to, or a warm family home we are longing to return to. And though I really want to believe what Halima says, that family are everything, the source of the deepest and most meaningful relationships we will ever have, I know now that I believe something else equally: that strangers and bravery and daring and independence matter too. But I am simply not able to bring these two beliefs together and to act on what I believe and know.

Which kills me.

'Well, look at it the way I do, Jackie: at least you know you're not being married for your money,' I say eventually.

'Or my virginity. Or my career prospects. Or my unblemished police record.'

'Exactly, so you just need to work out what you want in a guy and find him. That's what we've done in my family.'

Which is the opposite of love, I know that for sure. To know exactly what you want from a person, but the alternative, to not know, to have no determination about what will happen, to just wander with adoration, isn't romance any more, just like Ashfaq said and Jackie proved: it's aimlessness and drifting and results in disasters for the children.

So we're both decided: we have to get married and nestle down in our own baskets, and when I leave the coffee shop I see that out there the snow is back, numbing the street with an icy fur.

PART FOUR

ELLE

W ell, if that's decided, then the world's our oyster now,'
she says, clenching her fist to a knot of knuckles and
then putting her whitened hand on my dress and stroking it. I
push her hand away roughly. I want to stop and get some
Coke and sweets, but I know she won't let me.

'You should tell someone,' I say, 'because it's all really
happening you know. You can't just snap your fingers, and
vamoosh. There's a fairytale wedding about to begin just a
few hundred metres from here and you, dear mother, are the
fairy.'

There is snow falling and ice hitting the windscreen like
sugar.

Mum had told me some of where she'd been and what she'd
done. She described this warm dark room, and I can picture
her standing by two single beds, each made up with a thin
white bedspread. On the walls faded photographs, limed green
round the edges, of Greek islands – and then her doing what
middle-aged women do in Claire's favourite Sunday-night
dramas – pulling on a sunhat and setting out to explore the
island.

Eventually she nods and says, 'Who shall I call?'

'Call Gran and tell her to go and make an excuse for you. Say you're sick or something – you are, don't forget, Unpredictable, Unstoppable and Unavoidable.'

'Will you call her for me, love?' Mum says quietly, stroking my hair. 'Please.'

Gran had refused to attend the wedding, and when I call her and say that Mum isn't going to turn up she screams in joy, 'I knew it! I knew it was a mistake from the beginning.'

'Will you call up and tell them for us?'

'No, she'll have to ring herself. I won't mop up after her any longer.'

There was some more bitching and she repeated the line about beds and lying in them, and then Gran slammed the phone down and I turned to Mum and said, 'Yes, she says that now you are famous she'd be delighted to help you and she sends her best wishes.'

'You know, when I was your age, I really did think I'd be famous,' she sighs.

'Robbie Williams on the radio said that the worst thing about being famous was that he couldn't go away for a week to Bridlington,' I say. As soon as I say the words Robbie Williams a big smile comes over Mum's face, either because she's relieved to hear her geeky tomboy daughter make a girly pop reference, or because she thinks of dear Robbie as a true friend.

'Bridlington!' she laughs and claps her hands together like a little kid. 'Elle, that's it!'

The driver puts the wipers on faster.

'Oh, Mum, just because a man suggests a thing doesn't mean you have to do it. Even if it is Robbie Williams.'

'Yes, let's go to the seaside,' she says. 'Yes, yes, yes.'

'In this weather!'

'We've done that before. Do you remember? After me and . . . well. In Devon?'

'It rained all week and you wouldn't let me go out because you said there was a paedophile in the caravan next to us.'

'But we had fun, sweetie.'

'We had cockroaches.'

'This time we'll have cocktails.'

I wonder if they have hedgehogs at the seaside; it doesn't sound very likely, but still I feel fizzed up with fear and excitement. 'Yeh,' I smile, because with Dad and Claire we go to these woodland leisure centres and it's OK but it's not the same as when me and her went to the seaside that time. It was mad. Always out of season, and with Mum you are never sure what is going to happen next; cock-ups, cocktails, cockroaches. 'We had meals out every night, and chips and the fair.'

She taps lightly on the dark partition window and the glass slides back. 'Would you drive us to the sea, pet?' Mum says in that way she has of talking to men who she wants to do unreasonable things for her, like they are foreigners and she has to speak with a little smile and her eyebrows raised and in this girly cutesy voice. 'We're not going to the wedding after all.'

'That's a lot of money, lady,' he says, shaking his head.

I am bouncing on the seat now, because she is not getting married and it is really going to be just me and her alone together all day and night. She'd told me how the Greek room was run by a small black-cloaked little dumpling with not a word of Mum's native language to her unpronounceable name – and I can picture that toothless wizened crone, and next to her my beautiful, lush, spike-heeled Winter Wonderland mother.

'Money is the one thing I do have,' she lies, and of course the newspapers had detailed all about her debts and found people from work who told how they had lent her money and never been paid back. I knew that each morning bank envelopes were the only letters she received.

'Debt Shame of Runaway Mum,' I whisper. 'What about careful planning and personal responsibility?' I say in Dad's deep, flat, worried voice, and she laughs and hugs me so I have to really shake her off hard. Nothing pleases Mum more than me slagging off Dad.

'Seriously, you can put personal responsibility on the credit card, love.'

On the motorway she tucks my shoulder under her armpit and strokes my hair and sings songs by her old friends: Madonna, Robbie Williams and Olivia Newton-John, while I sulk, then pretend to sleep.

I think how the Greek coffee looks and tastes like soil – and how one day we will go there together, just us. Clock Cherub's despair when I show my tan, my bikini, my porny sun-kissed hair.

We arrived two hours later, just as I woke. We were in Bridlington. This is how things were with Mum; an idea, a giggle and then wham, which never happened with Dad and Claire who planned things for months and then decided no, too expensive, too irresponsible, too exhausting – certainly too dangerous, and they would rather stay at home and work on the garden.

'Hedgehogs do exist, don't they?' I ask her, rubbing at my eyes. But she's not listening, just peering out the car, at shoppers hurrying with tinsel and mistletoe through a last-minute market, only a few bothering to turn their heads as our limousine slinks into town. A pile of Christmas trees were still available for a knock-down five pounds each and Mum said she would have bought one, piled it in with us, if the driver hadn't been saying he was in a hurry and would have to drop us at our destination and get back. 'Where you going to stay?' the driver asked. 'You got relatives here?'

'Not exactly,' I say, pressing my nose against the cold glass, keen to see the lights and the trees and the shoppers, 'though my mam's a great believer in loving thy neighbour.'

'So where are we off?' he says, getting annoyed.

'I'd like to say take me to the centre of everything, but I guess there's no centre to the middle of nowhere,' Mum laughs, and the driver snorts and I bounce on the seat.

'Robbie Williams didn't mention where he'd have stayed,' I say.

'Is there a big hotel?'

'No idea,' the driver says crossly, like he is our dad and we are the kids. Mum and I giggle, hands over lipsticky dry mouths, truly lost and together.

It seems so dumb that at my age I don't know absolutely about the hedgehog, but then again there's the duck-billed platypus, the seahorse, the unicorn to consider, and I wish Mum would go to the zoo with me, though it's probably shut at Christmas. I stare at a traffic light, and if it turns green before I count to five I will immediately know what to do. It turns. 'Take us to the seafront,' I say and when we get there brown waves are crashing out of a grey sea close to the sea wall and I ask the driver to head for the biggest hotel we can see, a long ugly block, painted in thick beige, called the Esplanade. It was coming dark and when we opened the limousine door an icy sea hail hit us hard in sparkles. In the distance I could see a great turning star and Mum suddenly claps her hands in delight. 'Oh my God,' she cries, 'that's a lighthouse. How romantic!'

I shook my head then put her hands over my eyes, because even a lighthouse would be no help to her, who saw the light all right but reckoned it advertised a clifftop club, and so sped on straight for the rocks.

In my stomach I tasted both fear and thrills, and some rolling rocked in my head. 'Can you wait a moment while we see if they have any rooms?' I ask, but the driver is really annoyed by us now, and says he only has a few minutes before he has to get back, it was Christmas Eve after all, and he had a proper family waiting for him. I try to reason with him in a flirty way but it makes him even more irritated and he refuses.

'Oh please,' Mum pouts and suddenly he's agreeing, when Mum bites her lip and flutters her eyelashes and leans forward so her udders swell out of her Winter Wonderland dress – offered to him as if on a tray. Yeh, OK, he would happily wait a few minutes longer.

I get out and slam the limo door and stamp my feet and slush slides off my bridesmaid's slippers, till I tap it out to watery pools.

'Are you bloody joking?' the porter says – pronouncing it 'jerking' when we pressed in through the revolving doors, Mum having to crumple her train in her arms to squeeze through and me shuffling in behind holding on to my freaking blush-pink costume against the wind. 'What do you think this is?' he gasps. I can smell his oily brown hair.

'Little Town of Bridlington?' I say, raising my eyebrows. He has those tiny red buds blooming in a rash on his fat chin, and he's damp like he's just stepped out of the snow.

'In Bethlehem the druggies hadn't turned all the accommodation into crack houses,' the porter says, in a growly voice. 'There's nowhere safe in this town for you tonight, love.'

'What happened to goodwill to all men?' I say.

'So where've you parked the donkey, eh love? And what about the three wise men?'

'You never get wise men around my mother,' I say, and she thumps me hard on the arm, laughing, and I squeal, there up on stage with her, the porter watching and smiling and I love people seeing how I make her laugh. That was another bad thing about being home alone, there was no one to see how brave I was being.

'The donkey's in the boot of the limousine, look,' my mum says and the man smears a hand over the misty windows in the bar and looks out at our limousine, which is still purring outside. He looks at us, real astonished, then through the window again. 'Feast your eyes,' Mum whispers. 'Upon our wheels.'

'Who are you two? Rock stars?'

Mum puts a finger on her lips in a slow shushing gesture and smiles at him. 'Keep it to yourself,' she says, 'but our show's been cancelled and now we need a bed for the night.'

'No, seriously?' the man says, though now he's really grinning at Mum. 'Are you off to a fancy dress or summat?'

'Nope. My mum was gonna get married again and then she realised it was another big mistake so at the last minute she changed her mind. And we had to flee. And that's the truth.'

'Are you two for real?' he says, not taking his eyes from Mum, though it's hard to know if this is because he suddenly recognises her. And though all the newspapers criticised Mum for having been married twice and having 'a string of failed love affairs' I didn't think that was so bad; some people couldn't get anyone to go out with them. Ever. Not that I intended to be like Mum, or like Claire. Not a tart or a housewife.

In the bar a couple of crumblies stared us out, perhaps remembering their own wrong weddings. 'I don't know what to make of this,' the porter who is now the barman sighs.

'I take it you don't know my mum, then,' I say, speaking to the whole room, and then he looks at me with a smile. 'Because it's exactly the kind of thing that happens to her.'

'Well, this place is fully booked, love. And unless we have a few deaths before dinner, which,' and he bends down to whisper in my ear, gesturing over at the old women in the corner of the bar, 'is not entirely impossible, then you won't get a bed here tonight.'

231

'Nothing even out in the stables?' Mum asks, her eyes wide, her face soft and pale as the angel on top of the tree. 'A bale of clean straw, a bucket of water – perhaps a quick tipple of ale – that's all we need.'

She was excited by this asshole, which was gross and worrying, but might also mean she could make something happen to keep us warm that night. 'We've only got a c-c-car park, I'm afraid,' the man stutters. 'You're going to have to take your donkey back. You'll not find nothing in this town tonight, love.'

'Not even if my mum was with child?' I say, so the barman looks confused. 'You know, having a baby. Big with ch-ch-ch-child. Up the duff. Bun in her oven.'

'Elle!' Mum makes to clip me round the ear.

'Well, you might be, mightn't you!' I exclaim. 'I thought that's what you wanted.'

I thought about it a lot while I was home alone, that Mum might have a baby. I imagined my little half-sister's seagully cries through the silent house. Though last week when I told Cherub Mum was probably soon gonna have a baby, Dad reassured Claire that it was 'impossible' because Mum was 'well past it'. Claire said, 'Except that in the case of your ex-wife the impossible disaster usually happens.' And one newspaper had written, 'Despite her peroxide-blonde hair, heavy make-up and teenage dress sense, Jackie Jackson is obviously another poorly preserved example of the bedraggled, bleary-eyed middle-aged mums who in the twenty-first century stagger in glorious denial of their age and responsibilities through our country's less salubrious nightclubs every week-end.'

I'd memorised all the reports. But I'd found no clues about the Asian, though I was always looking. They probably weren't allowed to reveal his identity. He might have police protection because he's gotten so famous off of Mum. Caprice says there's people famous for remembering the entire tele-phone book. Like that's useful!

'No, you'll have to go back,' the man says, rubbing a hand over his pink forehead.

'But we can't go back,' I cry out, like we are in a thrilling film, 'because Mum's fiancé is a baldy sales-rep psychopath, and he can barely read, and he will find us and make her marry him. He's a dumb beast.'

I don't mention the Asian. But he is out there too. And, because to do what he did he must be clever as well as cruel, he's probably more dangerous than Tony.

At last the man looks at Mum and laughs weakly. She smiles back, and I feel angry, and I go out to the toilet and scowl at the shock of myself in the mirror, then realise I don't mind looking like an urchin-lad most of the time, because being a proper bridesmaid makes you the insane big sister of Little Bo Beep.

If the toilet has loo paper in I'll stick with Mum, if it doesn't I'll call Dad and ask him to come and get me.

When I return Mum is sitting at the bar, sipping clear liquid through a straw and then talking quietly to the bar-man who was leaning over the counter on his elbows to listen to her. It looks an innocent enough chat; but with my mother what looks like water can also be gin and I feel a bit sicky with worry. 'Ach, so what didn't happen?' she sighs, straw sucked in mouth, her baby-blue eyes up to meet his, and I go and pull up a stool alongside this man-eater posing as my mother.

'My mum, you see,' I say, 'well, she has this problem. She docsn't scc pcople as they really are. I mean, she probably walked in and looked at you and instantly saw a really cool handsome successful sexy guy.'

'Well, happy Christmas to you too, love,' he says, blowing air out of his measly pink cheeks.

'Elle!' Mum exclaims, and I give her a long slow look – which says she's confusing me for a daughter who gives a damn.

'Which means she falls in love, when other women would just laugh and walk off.'

'You certainly know how to make a guy feel good about himself.'

'Well, that's exactly the difference between me and my mum. I don't have any interest in making guys feel good about themselves,' I say.

I let them absorb that. Mum stares at me, like she is amazed by me somehow. 'And I don't need them to make me feel good about myself either,' I say, and Mum looks at me kind of sadly. So I snapped on a quick nasty smile, climbed down from the bar and sauntered over to play the quiz machine. I might be unkind but I was deeply good at general knowledge. If I get the first four questions correct it means we'll have a safe bed for the night.

'Can't you ring round some other places for us?' I hear Mum say. It was not the thing to sexy-flirt with a total complete stranger in front of me, I could tell, but if a little touch of it was needed, I'd leave the man-eater to it. Anyway the Steps know nothing about my mum in Greece, and I don't want them to know anything either – because she is just mine and I don't have to share her with anyone now.

'Normally I'd more than happily invite you back to mine, love,' he says quietly. 'I usually live on my own.'

As I play the questions I try Mum's patter on my lips, let her voice fit my gob like a tongue: Come here, I love you. Don't go. You're everything to me. Come on, let me get you a pizza. Have you done your teeth? Don't forget to go to the loo, love. 'Oh God, and it's so overrated, isn't it?' she says. 'Living alone. So many women I know live alone nowadays. My mother, my best mate Marilyn, my ex-boss Orla. It's so common now, everyone wants their space, their self-expression, but hell I hate it. Me-time! Isn't that the saddest thing you've ever heard? Me-time! I get so lonely. I want us-time. I want to be with a guy, a friend, care for them, share my bed and mad, bad, one and only life with someone.'

She's right, and silently I mouth the words as she speaks them, babbling like a pot of water, boiling to keep up. Once, years ago, she'd told me she went out to clubs just to hear people laughing. I tick five questions: if I tick the next two Mum won't end up sad and lonesome.

Actually the worst thing about living alone – as I had in her house – was the way nothing changed, the way the cup you put on the table was still there when you came down from upstairs, the way the towels stayed slung over the bath, and the only squeeze-print ever on the toothpaste tube was your own. Ashanti says her mum likes living on her own, but how can that be true?

'But I've got my old mother for Christmas, love,' he says and I can hear him creak like an old piece of wood, with aching for her as I – champion! – get the next two questions right.

Yes, I am a genius, thank you. 'Excuses, excuses,' she says and sighs, falling forward a little so he stares down her lacy bodice and his breathing quickens. Men are just so easy: I can understand the temptation to meddle.

'I know, just my bloody luck, I meet a gorgeous woman and I have my incontinent mother staying,' he says and Mum laughs – can't help a bit more sparkle sprinkling out.

'We've driven a hundred miles to get here,' she says. 'Can we at least get another drink?'

'How long did that giving up last?' I call out from the machine without looking round.

'Oh, Elle, give us a break, love; I need a brandy to help me think.'

'I'll have another lemonade, then. And some crisps, and a

sandwich, if you've got anything like that. But no dried fruit.
Definitely no mince pies.'

Never mistake my mum for one who worries about little
things – like feeding her only daughter. Still, I am delighted
that I am there with her, just us two, in Bridlington on
Christmas Eve. 'We've never had a runaway bride before,'
he sighs. 'You're our first. So you can have this on the house,
compliments of the season.' And he hands me a plate with
sandwiches and crisps and a brown plop of composty salad.
'You seem like a good woman,' the barman says, serving Mum
another brandy, and smiling warmly so his eyes look deep and
handsome and his cheeks crinkle like cotton. It's true that
around my mum every man becomes better looking.

'I try,' she sighs and drinks it down in one, so he serves her
another immediately.

'But it's hard, right?' he nods, having a drink himself. The
elderly women in the bar are starting to melt away, leaving
only him and her, and in the shadows as usual, me chilling
with daughterly fear. Whenever a bloke is near. 'You're on
your own with a kid, bills to pay, disapproval from family and
friends, endless advice. It's the same for my ex-wife. She's on
her own with my son. I can't even remember why we split up.
Here, have another.'

'It must have seemed right at the time,' Mum says, trying to
sip her new drink slowly.

'That's the frightening thing,' the man grins, and pours
himself another too. 'It did.'

'To us,' Mum says, drinking down the lovely brandy, 'the
people who did what seemed right at the time.'

'I'll go and ring a mate of mine, but don't hold your breath,
love,' he says. 'It's mad, this.'

'I appreciate your help,' Mum says, reaching over across the
bar and touching his hand in what the newspapers would call
'a lingering caress'.

'Mum,' I call, when the fat barman is out of the room, 'can you try and remember that I'm not even old enough to watch sex on the television, never mind right in front of my own innocent eyes?'

Mum suddenly jumps from her stool and runs back to me madly, and tickles me under my arms and whispers in the manner of the bloke who reads the soccer news on Saturday teatime, 'If you don't want to see the score look away now.' I am kicking out at her with my feet, my meringue up round my waist, like I'm a crazy little toddler. She fights me, tossing me over her shoulder and under her arm because she's a lot stronger than she looks and can do anything Dad can do in the play way, and salad is strewn over the floor but she don't notice and I want it to go on for ever, but she stops when he appears.

'Nothing,' he says. 'And the tourist information office is closed and everyone agrees that you'll not get a room in this whole town tonight.'

'What about a women's refuge?' I say, breathlessly. 'They're there to help women like my mum, aren't they?' I continue to pretend to box with her and he watches us, but her heart's not in it any more.

'Well, usually women run from this town, not to it,' he says.

'Goddammit, we're running in the wrong direction, Mum,' I say, tragically and tearfully.

'Ach, story of my life,' Mum says and goes back to the bar and drains the last drop from her glass. 'Fill her up, barman,' she says.

I could tell the barman was wheezy too, because of the situation, and if Mum had been on her own then we might have it sorted by now – she must have been thinking this too because the next thing she says is low and breathy. 'It's my little lass I need to think of, you see. Me, I'd kip down right there behind the bar, it wouldn't be the first time, but a poor child needs a roof over her head.'

Poor child! Like it's my fault!

'Look, love,' he says, quickly wetting his lips with his tongue, 'this might not be exactly what you had in mind, but a mate of mine has a caravan up on the headland. There'll be no one in that tonight.'

'She shoots, she scores,' I say quietly, stroking the machine, as she starts blubbing out her life story.

'I've had a bad year. A lot of trouble,' Mum says, 'and I was about to get married to the wrong man. So at the very last minute I changed my mind. Ran away to sea.'

'To sea? To see what you could get away with, you mean,' I shout out, worried because now I have to lose the barman, get her out of the bar, and into the caravan.

'You did the right thing, love,' he says, ignoring me and reaching over and kissing my happy mum, firmly on the cheek, displaying what the papers would call 'a typical male's inability to resist'.

'Hey, mister,' I call out, 'take your hands off my mother. And if she asks you to go to bed with her take no notice; according to the newspapers she says that to everyone.'

'Elle!'

I want Mum to lift me up on her knee and cuddle me, but she never does now so I walk around the bar whistling and combing my two fingers through my hair, while the barman called his friend who came round an hour later with the caravan key. The friend owned a chain of fish shops, and was thin and pale as a chip. He looked at me and Mum and grinned, and I was sure he did recognise me as Whore's Daughter, because the two friends made some jokes that reminded me how men were exactly like spots: worse on a night out and in a group.

Then the limousine driver, who we had both forgotten about and who had fallen asleep outside, started beeping his horn. Mum put her arm round me and said, 'I'm lashed, love.'

'I know,' I said and held her up firmly from behind, like she was my cardboard cut-out disguise.

The lighthouse was working and every five seconds washed us in a wave of white, as Mum struggled from my grasp and hugged and kissed the barman and promised to stay in touch. He said he'd call her. I was so chuffed that she was leaving him behind and coming away with me. Then the limousine driver said that he'd had enough and refused to drive all the way to the caravan. He must have realised Mum was drunk, but he just said he had waited too long and had to get back, so he took us to the edge of the site, where Mum stuffed his palm with notes, and then we watched as the long limousine stretched away into the salty distance like a white cat in a dream.

We walked. I kept the caravan key in my drawstring purse, because already Mum couldn't be trusted not to drop the key in the long grass we were stumbling over. I run backwards with my arms aeroplaning out, howling because we are together and Tonyless, and even the Asian is nothing more than the Second World War; something mysteriously terrible that happened way back in history.

We came to a steeper place. 'Elle, carry me,' Mum giggled, 'it's too hard!'

'In life, dear mother,' I shouted to her, loudly and seriously and drunk with the coming wisdom, 'there are uphill bits and downhill bits and you have to learn to walk them all, alone. There's no one to carry you.'

'Oh go on, love,' Mum whined, 'please.'

And she ran and leapt up on to my back – remember she is nearly forty and puffed up as a fairytale bride and I am Little Bo Freaky Peep, so I stumbled and cried out and panted until we both fell over in the icy snow-shot grass and she tickled me wildly as moonlit silver clouds dashed through the black sky and I am squirming there, freaking out with tickles and chills. 'Stop it! Mum! See what happens when you rely on other people.' But she was not listening to me, just panting, laying on the spread of her white skirt, her face like a cherry on an iced bun. She was looking up at the stars. I felt the burning whips of ice-rain on her hot red face. Below her the white earth would be spinning and she would be wondering if she was going to vom up or fly.

'Is hibernation a real thing? I mean, how does that work? Can it be true that they survive asleep for so long?'

'I won't change, Elle,' she said, 'I can't. I mean, I won't go back to how it was with Marcel, or George, or Tony. I know that was . . .'

'And why do some animals do it and not others? What is it about the freaking hedgehog?'

'But I will keep relying on other people. I will. I know it.' I helped her up from the stiff snowy grass, spread down her enormous ivory skirt and wiped the ice-water from her hot face. She's got a smeared pout now, like lipstick punch.

It was five o'clock and dark. Sunshine Valley was a little town of dirty oblongs, fitted very closely together. Orange windows glowed against the ice wind. Red and white flags maybe left over from the World Cup clapped and slapped. I could see no shops or swimming pool or entertainments. Sloping away below us was the village we'd driven through – a single street with a couple of chippies, a dusty hairdresser's and pubs with boarded-up windows. It was the kind of village where in the olden days they'd have burnt Mum as a witch. Maybe these days too.

'Why are caravans always white, Mum?' Christmas trees and strings of fairy lights were looped around some doors, and when she looked at them Mum began to cry, which shows, not only the power of brandy, but that Christmas must somehow mean more not less when you get older – because I didn't feel at all soggy sentimental. I just had an urge to go online. The lighthouse turned over us strong and regular and I marched forward, though I was worrying too that I would have to soon call Dad and either lie or confess. In one long and complicated newspaper report, with no photographs, that Claire had cut out, there was a great block of words around a black line drawing of a child clutching her face and inside her skull two adults clawing one another. The bit I read spoke of my 'predicament' as 'indicative of the exhausting, and often terrifying, tightrope act children from broken homes must perform as they struggle to keep an uneasy peace between their warring parents'.

'Are you all right, love?' Mum says. 'Walking, I mean.'

'It'd look much better if caravans were all different colours,' I say.

Tomorrow I'll ask her if we can rent a boat and go find hidden sea caves. Maybe we can go to an amusement arcade, and she'll give me a tenner in coins for the games. I know she probably won't, but whatever we do I know for certain it will just be the two of us. Soon I will have to call Dad and tell him that I'm not coming home for dates and raisins. 'That's so wild to have Christmas Day on the beach,' I call out to her through the mist. 'Can we?'

'It's hardly the Caribbean.'

'It's perfect. Promise we can have a picnic.'

'If you change your mind we can go back at any time,' she calls out, and stumbles towards me with her arms outstretched like a kid in a game of blindman's bluff, which is exactly what life is like for my mum. Windswept, the drizzle on her bare pink face, her hair blown madly to a dandelion clock, her gob full of snow and I suddenly didn't recognise her as the legendary runaway mum, which chuffed me; I didn't want

241

her to become one of those celebrities who are most real in photographs.

'No, we can't go back, Mum,' I say, gripping her wrist hard. 'Dumb Tony's out there with his rifle, no, not a rifle, that'd be too complicated for Tony. A club! Hunting us down with a stone club. Grunting.'

And the Asian, I hadn't forgotten about him. But at least he'll stand out; we'll see him coming. 'Yes,' Mum growls and giggles, 'we have to stay out here for ever, together, until we get old and die.'

'You'll never get old,' I say, and whistle as we walk, her forwards, me backwards, gazing at her so happily.

I found the caravan easily, because each row was numbered clearly. 'Listen Up, Thieves and Robbers,' a sign on the window said, 'All Valuables Have Been Removed.' I slipped the small silver key in the lock and the door gasped open with a rubbery suck. Inside it was dark and damp-feeling and smelt plasticky and cold, but the lights worked and it seemed clean and even if there were earwigs I was too excited to remember to sulk. Picture the look on the Steps' fizzog when I tell them about this place! Where everything was flour-coloured and there were stiff lace doilies and a skirted corn dolly on the cold wall, pastel wild flowers on the matching plates and cups. No one expected this decorating to 'reflect your inner person', as Claire said decorating should do. Though Mum said if this was true, then Claire's inner was covered in stencils of daisies and seahorses.

I could taste a linger of chip fat and remembered I was hungry, so I told her, but she just skips into the bedroom and flings the light on, and throws her stole, her shoes, her necklace over the bed, and bounces and squeals like a mad little lass. It's kind of irritating but I don't expect anything else. 'Elle, this is perfect!' she cries, trying to big it up for the kids, which you have to do all the time if you are a parent, more if you are a guilty and useless parent. At least the bed is funny, with a slice cut from one corner so you can get into the tiny toilet. Caprice would die for that bed.

'Come here, love,' Mum says later, 'you must be really tired,' and I lay my head on her lap, my feet over the edge of the shallow beige sofa that lined three walls. She pretends to comb my hair with her fingers. If she keeps doing it until I count to five we'll be safe. I sniff up the caravan, look around our frail iron walls, and at the patches of light where the moon leaks in. Now she was making a plait out of sections of my short hair. It was Christmas Eve and we had no bedding and no food, not even a toilet roll. 'If you want to call your dad and say he should come for you then that's fine,' she says, mind-reading.

'Why don't you believe that I want to be with you?' I say, with my eyes closed now, feeling her pulling and nipping at my hair, the soft pads of her fingertips bumping against my scalp. 'Claire's really nice . . . but . . .'

'But Christmas at Claire's – it sounds like it'll be the real twinkly deal.' She is stroking my forehead as she did when I was a kid. 'Angels, mince pies, crackers, carols.'

She was in the mood for Claire-baiting and I didn't want to encourage her. 'It'll just be lots of raisins, let's leave it at that.' My eyes were closing slowly in Mum's lap. When I wake I'll have the thick folds of her satin dress patterned on to my face. 'And on Christmas Day we have to go to a church service and then to see her old mother – who is just the same as Claire but more wrinkled. And then after dinner we do the washing up immediately while Dad falls asleep in the chair.'

'Well shucks, honey, I don't wanna boast, but your father never fell asleep on an evening with me,' she says, in a funny sexy American voice. She's running her knuckles gently over my cheek now. 'Hell, no, never.'

'Mum, that's because he was too busy thinking up ways to kill you.'

'True.'

And though she laughs, I know my teasing has made her remember what the papers called her 'two disastrous early marriages, both ending in acrimonious divorces'. One paper even tracked down her first husband, who she never spoke of, who looked old and confused and said, like she was some terrible shame, 'I've put Jackie Jackson behind me.' No reporter went looking for Marcel though; no one found out about him at all.

Yet.

And the Asian never stood up to be counted. Then I start to worry that news will reach Marcel in Afghanistan and he will sell his story, that the whole thing will flare up again, maybe tomorrow, maybe the next day. Or the Asian is scheming away, trying to get a top eye-witness exclusive deal, and he's gonna give away all her secrets, and mine, to the highest bidder.

'I'll never regret meeting your dad,' she says with a sniff, 'because he gave me you.'

'Mum, can I just remind you we are in a Yorkshire caravan not an American feel-good movie?'

Her eyes are shut and she is smiling. 'I told you, I'm lashed. I'm plastered. I'm completely caned, love.'

'I know, Mum.'

She fell asleep first, of course, though she was the one supposed to be soothing me. I just lay on her lap and listened for crime noises between her snoring. Then I found a cigarette tucked up her leg-of-mutton sleeve and went to stand out on the balcony to choke on it. I wanted to go online but instead coughed like I had cancer, then called Dad on my mobile. 'I'm gonna stay over with Mum,' I say and his freaked response is what I expect, demanding to know my exact satellite location, and then, upon hearing my lie, insisting I change my mind and do as he and Claire say. It's just the same way everyone is about Mum: so scared and angry.

Eventually he calms a little and says, 'It's her wedding night, doesn't she want to be with her new husband?'

'Have you met him, Dad?'

'Now, now,' he says, laughing like Henry VIII because Dad's just the same: adores it when I'm cruel about her.

'Well, let's just say I've met Tony now and it's all the more reason to stay with her. I'm not changing my mind, Dad. I'm staying with her tonight.'

One thing I know for absolute certain now is that I had gone along too far in the past with how Dad and Claire wanted me to see Mum. When they had said Marcel was a danger to me because of his age and him being a squaddie I felt afraid. But I was only ten then, and had never stayed alone for even one night. Now I was stronger and braver, and soon I'd have all my own opinions about people.

Outside it is bitter cold and it's odd to think that no one but Mum knows where I am. For all the new technology and all the dinky gadgets, it's still easy-peasy to lie and lose people, to hide and deceive, to start all over again, unseen.

When I got back inside the caravan Mum's lips were parted, a spider-line of spit connecting her saggy mouth to the crunchy sofa. I was so chuffed it was just us alone together. She was booze-warm, just as she had been when I was a kid, when I went into their bed in the night sometimes. I tried to find sheets and duvets but all that was in the high cupboard was a scratchy blanket, which I put over her carefully. Then I found an itchy blanket for me and went to lie in the only bedroom on the bare mattress, because it'd be too babyish to curl up next to her. What kind of loser needs warmth and clean sheets and pillows and duvets anyway?

AMIR

It's ten pm on Christmas Eve and there's still no sign of Jackie Jackson. Instead her fiancé, gimpy Tony, was talking to me at the start of the unwedding reception. We were sitting in the designated corner of The Bar with the balloons and the banner Orla had insisted upon, darkly; GOOD LUCK TONY AND JACKIE strung up overhead. Only about six guests had made it along to The Bar, and they were all the groom's, plus Orla, who couldn't resist the climax of the disaster. The old tosspot had chosen me to talk to, I guessed because I was the only sober one left, and the first thing the half-head wants me to know is that there was just one night of knowing Jackie Jackson, two bottles of red wine and a tableful of cocktails before the marriage proposal. If there had been longer tosspot Tony says he wouldn't have made the mistake. He's a senior sales executive; so normally a very astute man. He'd have seen right through her.

I'd gone along in case Jackie appeared; dazed, confused and ready to dance. There was a chance: she weren't one to miss a party. I had tried her mobile but there was no response and now I was aching to go round to her house to check she was OK, and to celebrate her freedom, but I knew I should not. So there I was, in my usual gimpy way, loitering somewhere I

shouldn't in case she appeared, though in just a few days I was
going to propose to another woman entirely.

And all the while Tony was telling me how he'd only met her
ten times and the last nine times they'd just drunk, shopped or
shagged, though Tony admits there were clues. 'Have you got
a boyfriend?' Tony told me he asked her on that first night
they met in The Bar.

'My last boyfriend dumped me – but he had to flee the
country and get me arrested and charged before I got the
message,' she told Tony.

'Well, it's all over now,' Tony said, joking, and stroking her
back. He could feel the knuckled bumps of her spine through
her damp silky top.

'Apart from the court case, love,' Jackie said, and then she'd
laughed so hard it hadn't occurred to Tony that she had been
telling the truth. 'For a whole week, Elle, my twelve-year-old
daughter, cared for herself.'

But the way she turned, the drag on the cigarette, the smile,
the leather bar stool by her side, free, seemed like a pure
invitation. Tony knew she was drunk but assumed the tarty
lass was drunk for the same reasons he was, because there
hadn't been time for grub and she wanted to have a good time.
I could just picture it – her lip bitten, her folded snow-white
arms – and I wanted to hear no more, but the poor gora won't
stop talking and that watery-eyed face-lock was on me hard.

He really was no looker. Which should have pleased me, but
no, it just made me sadder for Jackie and for her daughter. He
said he'd hoped Jackie wasn't going to get out the Polaroids of
her kid and sob and I half wanted to punch him and really
thought I might, particularly as I was sober and he was lashed
and I could totally flatten the ugly gimp.

'Are you in trouble?' Tony asked her then because he said it
was hard not to always feel fatherly with women now, even
those he had dark intentions towards.

'Am I trouble?' she replied and smiled. 'You mean, after what I've just told you, you need to ask?'

I laughed at this – her joke, not his telling of it – but he thought I was encouraging him so I turned to look over the wet city. One wall of The Bar looked out over the entire glossy street; you could see churches and high rises and ice-topped buses crawling. Tiny people moving in clumps with balloons. Christmas lights were on, bulbs like sucked sweets in shapes of trees, angels, ivy, puddings, and every so often great balls of steel, wire and light suspended dangerously. It was the end of the year; now or never for everyone.

And why was I out again, sober with a bunch of drunk whites, when I should be at home with Harpreet flicking through the catalogue from Ikea?

He said it was when she offered him a shag that he decided he should leave: she was a nutcase; she'd be OK, and probably expected him to do it. He'd done it before to similar women, he says.

It is quite obvious Tony knows nothing about Jackie, and she's just hastily arranged herself a marriage to a stranger. Just like I suggested.

He tells me he doesn't really like women making the first move, and I remember Jackie in my street in her nightgown asking me to go away with me, and me shocked and afraid in exactly the same way as this half-head here now.

I am about to leave when he tells me his father has Alzheimer's, and I tell him that my mother has too, and Tony tuts and shakes his head, and I understand a bit more about why he really proposed to wild Jackie Jackson.

'Actually I'm not trouble as long as I don't go out the house,' Jackie had told him, smiling. 'Indoors I'm a pussycat – it's the cat-flap I have to avoid. If I'd not gone out I'd not have forgotten about Elle.' Then another bottle and apparently our Jackie was telling this dickhead how she lost her job and why.

Now that Tony lived alone he tells me that he'd seen all sorts on the internet but fighting between lasses wasn't his thing. 'I wasn't covered in mud and wearing a thong at the time, if that's what you're thinking. And she started it. And anyway that was months ago.'

'Do you live alone?' he asked her.

'Ach, if you can call it living,' she said in her deep voice, tarred as a black road with cigarettes, and he'd laughed. Then she stands up and goes to the bar, without asking him, and gets them each a free cocktail, some lavish concoction in an odd-shaped glass, with a sparkling white powder around the rim. When she opened her handbag (yes, he said 'handbag') he saw a thick litter of twenty-pound notes, making him wonder if she'd just robbed a bank.

Then he nattered on about how the chalky drink she had given him definitely tasted sourer than the others. And that grittiness, cunningly concealed by the salt round the rim. What the hell was he drinking? Why hadn't she paid for it? He was letting her poison him, he was sure. And plus, Tony tells me, it was hard not to feel she was saying all the things that the man should be saying, taking all the control away from him – 'which is not at all sexy in a woman'.

'There's a late bar at my hotel,' he said to her next. 'It's not far.'

'Closer,' she smiled, running the back of her hands, those nails, down his sandpapery cheek.

I thought of kind Samirah, and how she'd come up to me yesterday and said, 'What's happened to you, Amir? You used to be such a good lad.' And I shrugged and she smiled and took my hand and she said, 'I know. The same thing happened to me.' And I knew she was referring to the mysterious white postman who we never mentioned but who had haunted the margins of our lives for the last two years. 'What do you do? What shall I do?' I asked her. 'Whatever you think is best,' she replied. 'For who? It's the same old problem. Me or the family?' 'Well, maybe what's right for you is what's right for the family,' she says, smiling. 'After all, you can't go on like this, can you? You're no use to any of us in this state.'

'Jackie told me I was just the right age for her. She said she'd been in love with a lad much older and a lad much younger, and most recently a lad perfectly properly right,' the half-head says.

'What did she say about the man who was perfectly properly right?' I asked, leaning in to hear, as my heart bounded deer-like across the table.

'That he was already getting married to someone else.'

'Oh,' I said. Then to stop myself crying I added, 'Sounds like he had a lucky escape.'

'Apparently, yes. She said she didn't want to ruin his life. He was a good lad, too kind and considerate for her.'

Then Tony was telling me how he had a feeling at that moment that he should have got some money from the cashpoint. Surely Tony was going to have to pay Jackie Jackson for this . . . shag. Ah, that was it, he said. She didn't work in the store at all, she was a whore, a crack whore who pretended to work here. She was in league with the barman, who provided poisoned drinks for victims. Hence the money stuffed in her handbag. She mentioned the police not to scare him, but rather to falsely reassure him, to link her with authority and so security, to make her damned self seem safe. Maybe she wouldn't explicitly say that she was wanting money for the sex, but she'd want money for a cab, or some such thing. A little gift. A piece of jewellery. Perhaps she had that drug in her handbag. Her very expensive handbag, he notices now he's thinking of her in this way. A bag her last client bought her, no doubt. Tony's had that before, he tells me – the expectation of presents – 'like they're dating Father Christmas'.

He thinks I'm his mate now and he's loosening up, telling me all his seedy secrets. Gifts you have to give to them, he says, as their consolation for dating old, grey you. Ho ho ho. It's better if you are prepared, he tells me. Sometimes, if he picks a woman up in a shopping-centre food court, as he has done on several occasions, he's even had her immediately suggesting a meal, then leading him to a retail outlet and asking for a new dress.

I can't let Jackie have any more to do with this gimp. I am glaring at him, but Tony continues saying to me how he was preoccupied all the time she was looking at him with thinking how much money he has in his pocket. He laughs loudly, saying how he'd been working out how much she was worth. 'I need to get some money,' he'd told her, 'can we stop on the way? Is it far?'

'Near here,' she says again, 'near.'

He'd liked to have been more involved in making at least a few of the decisions about what they were going to do, he tells me. The way she was holding hard on to his hand, deciding everything before he's even got a word in, meant it was more like being with his mother than a lover. Which is a trap that he has fallen into before, he tells me. Then before he knew what was happening they had left The Bar and were in a darkly lit corridor – 'that womb,' the banshee leading him said. And so the family womb it was, right there before them, that picture of a man and a woman on the door each with a small child in hand, the lad shape a millimetre bigger than the girl shape. Each person shape with a lollipop head and a blank curve for a smile. She pushed him into the womb with, oddly, two toilets, one big and one small. It was the first time he had seen this – and I tell him they are why the store recently won an award for the finest toilets in Europe. The door slid shut and clicked perfectly. 'And then,' he said, with a big boozy gora grin, gulping down his lager before he starts his dirty tale.

But I didn't want to hear how her dickless future husband had shagged my friend and then proposed to her in the store toilet. How Jackie Jackson met her future husband in Europe's finest in-store public convenience.

ELLE

'Elle,' she cries, shaking my shoulder violently. 'It's Christmas Day.' She was offering me a small box, which, when I'd unwrapped it carefully, held a silver bracelet with my name on in curly capitals. She was pretending this was specially for Christmas, though I knew that yesterday it would have been my bridesmaid gift. She was pretending the wedding had never almost happened.

I tried to cover my disappointment as I gave her my present, which was a lottery ticket. 'I got it because I think your luck is gonna change, Mum. I just have this total feeling that you're about to get really lucky. If you stop drinking and going with men.'

I felt tired. I'd hardly slept because of the icy cold and because I was listening for male footsteps crunching through the clifftop frost. But we'd made it through a whole night without the appearance of any dangerous predators and daylight would be easier.

'There's cornflakes here, in the cupboard, but they might be a bit soggy,' she said, wiping away a tear. 'And we'll have to pretend that there's milk. Do you remember you were a baby and I used to pretend that cornflakes were crisps? I was determined to keep you healthy.'

'Well, you know what? I still eat my cornflakes without milk! How convenient!'

'I'll go next door and ask if they can lend us some bread.'

'But we've only got these clothes to wear,' I say.

'I'll have to say we've escaped from a lunatic asylum.'

'You have,' I say and Mum nods and looks at me deeply, surely remembering Tony like you do a monster in a dream: in tiny upsetting pieces. 'Hey, Mum, tell them that we always dress up as brides on Christmas Day!'

'Yeh, I'll say it's a family traditional thing.'

'Ah yes,' I say, mimicking Claire, 'and traditions are very important, they bind a family together.'

'Will you come with me, love?'

'Oh, Mum, you've got to get used to doing things for yourself.'

'Please,' she whines and pouts. Then just as we are going out the door she grips my puffed satin shoulder and says, 'Tony! We left him at the altar,' then she bites her lip and begins to whinny through her nose like a horse.

'I can't believe you're finding it funny,' I say, because sometimes her being happy and laughing about her sex life makes me angry. I want her to be sad and tearful and guilty about all the men she's been with, and especially about leaving me home alone, because then she might hold herself back the next time she gets the wiggle to do a fun thing.

'Oh, love, I can laugh about it now but at the time it was terrible.'

'What about him? How terrible must it have been for him! It's time you started thinking of someone other than yourself, Jackie Jackson,' I tell her, and she nods and apologises, snuffling a giggle.

'We're getting ready to go to a fancy-dress party,' Mum says on the doorstep of next-door's caravan. The escaping smell of

253

bacon frying makes the seagulls whirl closer to the door and their cries cut at the morning like sharp knives. They frighten me, but of course Mum doesn't notice.

'Merry Christmas, love,' the elderly man says, 'come in, come in. My wife's just doing breakfast, come in. You both look lovely, definitely in line for a prize.'

The guy smelt musty, like an old fur teddy, and the caravan was exactly the same inside as ours – same styles, colours and layout – and I found this nice too. The television was on and I ate my bacon sandwiches watching children's Christmas Day programmes. This would never have been allowed at Claire's because we always had to do about two hours of hard labour before we were allowed ten minutes of TV. Mum drank coffee at the table and smoked and told the man and the wife some of the truth of our life. 'You left him there,' the old woman said, 'that's wonderful!'

'Well, I don't know how I feel about that,' the husband said with a frown. 'Poor chap.'

'He'd have been poorer if he'd married Mum,' I called out from the sofa, and then added quietly, so they can't hear, 'According to the *Sport*, that's "Miss Penniless but Passionate" you're talking to there.'

'But she didn't love him, Reg! It would have been a sham. All her life living a lie.'

I look at each of them and say, 'Everything my mum has told you is true. In another woman it might appear unbelievable but my mother really does live like this. If you type Unbelievable Woman into Google a picture of my mum pops up.'

'And if you type in Very Rude Girl, a picture of my daughter comes up,' Mum says, trying to be annoyed, but snorting. I'm desperate to go online and whisper merry Christmas to the silky sun-kissed girls of the porn world, but they say they have no computer.

'Well, we'll get you some clothes to borrow,' the wife says instead. 'I could call my daughter and ask if you can come with us for lunch at theirs.'

I felt suddenly teary. Maybe for how rare it was that people were simply kind towards Mum, without suggesting solutions, or pretending to feel sorry for her, or offering her just a little bit less than what she needed. 'And we need some sheets too,' I say. 'We've no bedding.' Mum looks at me surprised, like she's never heard the word before, or as if such things as *bedding* never occur to her, ever. And she's wondering how she'd birthed such a freaky laundry-focused geek.

The old man comes and sits by me and I say, 'Do hedgehogs exist?'

'Of course,' he says. 'I've got a book somewhere.' And he comes back with a book all about wildlife and I read the section on hedgehogs while eating chocolates from a big tub. Then he tells me about the area and about the Vikings, which is something the other Elle, who lives with her father and goes to stately homes on day trips, is very interested in. He shows me pictures of longboats and hairy men in animal-skin cloaks and he says all about how the Vikings came to invade England at this exact point on the coast.

'What about the heating in the caravan, have you got all that sorted out, love?' the husband asks me, like he knows I'm the adult. I wish he would keep talking about the Vikings but he's thinking of Mum now and who on earth we are. 'Caravans can be deadly cold if you don't get the heating right. It's the floor. The floors can feel colder than a frozen lake.'

'Watch him,' the wife laughs, patting her old smiley on the shoulder, 'he'll take over now he knows you haven't got a man in your life.'

'I'm only trying to help,' he says, helplessly.

'They think you're an abused wife,' I whisper when I sit down next to Mum on the identical sofa. I was sulking still because of her cheerfulness and lack of apologies for her crimes, but really I was chuffed too, being with the oldies, because it was like pretending me and Mum were in a proper family. 'They'll probably call the social services about us. Haven't you seen those films where people pretend to be helping someone just to be stalling for time?'

'They are called Reg and Joan,' Mum says. 'And they're lovely.'

'The police have probably sealed off the whole park already.'

'They're a very reliable couple.'

'That's what they want you to think, so the authorities have time to act. She's probably on the phone to Dad and Claire right now.'

'Why are you so mistrustful?' Mum says, stroking my hair away from my face and looking movie-keen into my eyes. I go cross-eyed, and she twists my nose gently.

'He's been gone so long because he's directing the police who are scrambling a helicopter in case we try to run for it. Claire's out there with a rifle. Dad's got one of those tranquilliser guns they use on tigers.'

'Did I do that to you, love? Make you distrust love and tenderness?' I shrug and turn back to the television, but TV's so ordinary. I whistle out some hymns and Mum looks worried. 'Do you wish you were back at home?'

'I want to go on the computer,' I say, sulky because suddenly I so badly miss my porn life, those billions of pretty girls who were like my big naked family, plus I want to Google more stuff about the Vikings and Danes and ancient England.

'I mean with Claire and Dad?' she asks.

'Er, actually paradise can be a bit of a pressure,' I say, but suddenly feel worried that I'm going to have to call Dad again and make another excuse for another night.

256

'Wait until you get old enough to give hell a go,' she smiles, smoothing down her hair, 'now hell's really something else.'

Mother From Hell Leaves Daughter for Pensioner Lover She Stalked.

A whiff of old biscuits comes first, then Joan appears carrying a nest of wool and says, 'Summat here is bound to fit, and I'll get you a pack of safety pins to hoick it all together if it doesn't.' Mum lets her jaw drop a little as she takes the armful of jumbly chavvy clothes, wondering if she really, once, long ago, worked in one of Europe's chicest fashion stores.

If the old guy comes back before I count to twenty then Dad'll let me stay another night.

'Heating's all set,' Reg says, coming in with a shake from the cold.

'Now what else do the pair of you need? I've written down bedding.' Joan brings us each a slice of mud-brown cake and says, 'I seem to remember there's no TV next door, so if you want to come round and watch ours with us you're always welcome.'

'Since she was on it, we stopped watching it,' I say in a whisper, while Mum says endless thank yous and pokes me in the ribs. Then I shake my head and say, imitating Claire for Mum's amusement, 'I don't like Mum to watch too much TV. It gives her ideas. She's at a very impressionable age. Which, seeing as you ask, is nearly forty going on fourteen.'

Joan laughs and says, 'Well, I could lend you a radio.'

'That'd be much safer,' I say, nodding. 'It's her seeing the pictures that we worry about.'

'You can pick up Denmark on this,' Joan says, reaching into a box and bringing out a big brown radio.

'That reminds me of your dad,' Mum says to me, pointing at the radio. 'I often thought I was picking up Denmark when I tried to listen to him.'

'Men and women are scientifically proven to be on different frequencies most of the time,' I say. 'It's nothing to worry about.'

'As long as you don't try to have a conversation,' Mum laughs, and Joan smiles at her strangely.

Which reminds me of that old grandma holding us so lovingly, so sadly, at the Asian party.

Mum and I had our Christmas lunch together in the local pub, because Joan's daughter had too many at her house already. Secretly I knew Joan's daughter had heard of Boozed-up Runaway Mum and Her Determined Deserted Daughter and didn't want us there. But I don't say this to Mum because anyway I love the fact that for once it's just the two of us. If Dad was there it could be perfect.

'Why am I such a fool?' Mum asks the moon as we walk to the pub.

'You're only a fool for love,' the moon replies.

We are wearing tracksuit trousers held up with safety pins, under itchy ten-ton jumpers, and no one seems to care or stare and I wonder what is the opposite of porny, because that's how we look. I liked our weird style, though Mum had wanted to cut her million-dollar wedding dress off at the knees and wear that instead. Joan stopped her by saying, 'Don't ruin it, you might need it again,' and though I'd said that I bloody hoped not, Mum agreed not to cut the dress up.

Caprice says it's the worst luck to be married three times. But on TV an American woman said, 'Third time's the charm, honey.'

The pub was blue with illegal smoke, mildewy musty, oily hot with the boil of frying, over-decorated, screechy loud with oldie Christmas music, and I could smell the snap-burn of hundreds of cracked crackers. Some of the men were big as Viking bears with haystacks on their chins and I started to sulk, because it's embarrassing getting lemonades from the bar around men like that, particularly when I wanted her to suggest a wine or a beer, but I knew she wouldn't. I asked for a shandy and she won't even get that, and so I refused to even hold the cola. Then I got bored with myself and put Olivia's 'Summer Lovin'' on the jukebox. 'Happy Christmas,' I say and clink glasses as the record plays. 'To us,' I say. Around us, boozy big mums in tissue-paper crowns were standing up to sing carols.

Dad would have died.

The only space they had for us to sit was a small wobbly table underneath the super-sized television. Behind us is a red spotlight that shines through Mum's hair. In the cracker I got a joke that said, 'What happened to the raisin that drowned in the Christmas cake? Answer: it got pulled under by a strong currant.' A few years ago I wouldn't have dared show that to Mum because it mentioned drowning, but now I show her it and she just says, 'You know you're going to have to explain all this to your poor dad.'

'Why are you quite nice about Dad, but still totally horrid about Claire?'

'Claire's totally horrid to me,' she snaps back, like the class's biggest bitch.

'I thought you were trying to be nice about her.'

'I'm just jealous of her, because she has you so often and she's not even related to you. It just seems so unfair.'

And for the first time I realise that deep down she worries about Claire in the way I sometimes do: if Dad truly loves a woman like Claire, so opposite of me and Mum, how can he truly properly love me?

I kiss her soft warm shoulder. I don't think about it, I just do it. I know all about jealous fear; it's like a heat and a hunger and it's very ancient and hard to do anything about it, even when you know it's hateful and wrong.

'I'm staying one more night,' I tell Dad when I call him between courses, and for a while he freaks out exactly as I imagined he would, and then he tempts me with all my presents waiting under the tree, and home baking and tins of chocolates. 'But Mum has hardly seen me all year.'

'Is it any wonder?' he says.

'I want to make her happy.'

'There's many before you that have tried that,' he snorts, but I also hear a little hint that once he must have loved her, so I put the counsellor's soft voice in my dry gob and say, 'Well, I'm going to keep on trying. I'm staying here a bit longer, Dad.'

I go back in and tell Mum I'm staying. She blubs and I have to remind her I'm the emotionally scarred kid not her.

'I've smoked so much I don't think I've got long left,' I say when we come out of the fag fog and into the sea wind. 'Claire says passive smoking is legalised murder.'

'I'll have to go round and blow some in her face,' she says.

'That's the kind of horrible childish behaviour that has to stop, Mum.'

'I know.'

'There's nothing to be jealous of. She's just Dad's wife, not my mother. She could never replace you.'

'Let's go for a walk on the beach to clear our lungs,' and she puts an arm around me.

There were several families skimming stones in the water though already the thick purple darkness was falling. The tide is right in, lapping up against the white rocks. 'I don't really hate Claire,' she says. 'I'm glad she's looked after you so well. Imagine if Dad had married another woman like me.'

'There is no other woman like you,' I say truthfully, and she half smiles.

I fold my arms and stare down at the ground, looking for hedgehogs or original Viking arrowheads. Some teenage lads are climbing high up on the chalky cliffs, a small girl was building castles in the sand. I wanted to join them and adventure, but I was older now and since I had seen all that porn, I was somehow more shy. I wished I had a metal detector, though.

Mum walked ahead quietly collecting shells, and the man's adult anorak Joan had lent us being so long it came down almost to her knees. She looked younger and a bit mental and I almost felt sorry for her. Dad said to me last week that Marcel the soldier never knew how old Mum really was: he thought she was in her twenties. I walked behind her at some distance, making sure she had her space, till it was total proper dark and we returned along the narrow road back to the caravan park, washed sudden silver again and again by the steady beat of the lighthouse beam. I can smell her usual perfume, that sweet booziness, and it makes me sulk because she is all warm and woozy and I'm just the plain fat little kid, who no one would cast in porn, not in a million years.

It was her who spotted something first. 'Did you see that?' she said. I just rolled my eyes, but she continued, 'Really, there was something moving around our caravan.'

'Joan and Reg, they were bringing bedding.'

'No, it was a tall body. A man, I think.'

'Oh, Mum,' I say and I pull her to me, and from the side of the road we stared at the caravan. Recent events had taught me to watch like an owl, very closely, stop, then wait. Don't panic immediately. Stop. Check the situation first.

On the nights I'd been alone I'd learnt to make myself very still, holding the fear firmly like a bird in my hand, while hoping for the comforting splash by of a car. Listening in darkness for suspicious noises, footsteps, breathing. Eventually I could tell a fridge rumble from a boiler's churn, a wood creak from an electricity click. But when the white beam of the lighthouse spun round, the man-shaped shadow by our caravan did move up, then down again, as if some beast was stretching its legs and then sitting back down again on our step. 'It's not safe, we'll have to move on,' she says, not joking.

'We're not on the run, Mum,' I say. 'It's not illegal to decide not to marry someone.'

'It's really bad manners, though,' she says, 'and he'll be perfectly justified in being very angry.'

'There's probably nothing to be scared of,' I croak eventually, because my gob is dry as straw.

Cars were driving back along the road to the caravans and some people slowed down to smile or wave, thinking we were just moving out their way. It was Christmas Day, people were happy and helpful. 'Is it him, Mum?'

'We'll have to go back to the pub and . . .'

'We'll have to call Dad. I know you don't want to but it's the only sensible thing to do. Dad'll come for me, no matter where I am.'

'So why didn't you call him before, when you were alone at my house?' she snaps, her eyebrows in her hair.

'Duh! This isn't an adventure, this is Tony.'

'OK,' she says, and she must be really scared to agree.

So we turned and walked quickly along the black path. If we avoid every puddle we'll be safe. But someone was hurrying along behind us, splashing through the ice-mud, and I pulled Mum's arm and together we ran, holding on to our oversized tracksuits at the waist to keep our mad trousers up. 'Quick, it's him!' I say. The footsteps behind us were heavy and getting closer. I was dragging Mum almost, pulling on her anorak harder and harder until she was stumbling and crying out little gasps of panic when she fell into a puddle or against a rock.

'Can you see him?' Mum pants, looking behind as I drag her.

'Just keep running, run.'

'What if it's not Tony?' she says. 'It could be that bloke from the pub.'

'Oh great, Mum! Now I feel really safe!'

'Or the one with the chip shop.'

'Maybe it's Dad, maybe he's tracked us down.'

'Hey,' a voice calls, 'Jackie, Jack, it's me.'

'Run,' I shouted, 'run, Mum, run.' I was getting faster and breaking off up ahead. I kept my eyes on stubby headlamps, ran towards the pale strip of road and people and safety.

'Stop,' a voice cried, close to my ear, 'it's only me. Stop.' Mum speeded up and grabbed at me and pulled me to a stumbling halt. Then I was holding her firmly at my side in my arms. She was panting hard and her breath in the winter air came out in warm whisky clouds. 'Jackie, it's me.'

My stomach is an ice-bucket, and if I vom up it'll come out in frozen cubes, because there before me is him. Smiling at me, hoping, like last time, that this will stop me speaking. But I find Dad's deep voice in my wooden gob and say, 'Stay away from us. We're gonna call the police.'

'You know I thought that I had the wrong caravan and then I saw your wedding dresses side by side over the door of the wardrobe. So I waited.'

'Come on,' I say, tugging at her, 'just keep walking.' Someone has an elastic band around my lungs, and my lip is weeping blood. And though I'm tugging at her she's grinning at him. I start to shout like Dad, about how I'm leaving, but it's having no effect.

'The limo company told me last night. But I didn't decide until this morning that I should come. I was being cautious,' he lies.

'Never good,' Mum laughs.

'Mum, please don't,' I say, 'just run.'

'They told me their driver had dropped you at this caravan park, so I came. Looking. That old couple insisted they'd not seen you. But I could tell they were lying to protect you.'

'There's usually someone having to lie to protect Mum. From people who want to do her harm.' I am crying as I look at her, but I see she is lost to me again, so I say, 'Mum, he is the one who told the police and the papers about me. It's him.'

'Oh, darling, no,' she says, shaking her head. 'No, no, no.'

I should never have come out here with her. I should have known it would end in disaster. 'OK, I'm going to get help,' I say, and I run out into the darkness, the wind slicing at my face, and my legs leaping over little hills and slush puddles, and she is not following me and I hate her but I'm flying onwards, and far away in the distance I can hear her calling out my name but I keep slamming on, and when I get to the road I am surprised by how much energy I have and I keep storming down that road, my feet springing higher and higher, like a gazelle over a desert plain, the wind lifting through my mane, my heart moving up a gear so my knees bend and calves stretch and I have never run like this ever, as if powered by an engine, with skin so hot, I shed that anorak on the road, so the icy night can breathe over my arms, my hard stomach and chest, and I hate Mum more and more and even want to get run over by a car to make her feel bad. I want the Steps to have to come to my funeral and sob. I want Dad to hang himself because of grief. Birds see me galloping and gather in the air, and ponies startle in their field when I pass because I am young and fit and they are all old and done. Only when I am in the high street do I slow down. Blokes look at me and I look right back with superglued stares because if anything happens with a paedophile, then it will all be her fault. I want to be murdered so she has to get out of bed and come and identify my battered body. Or get hit by a car because it's a slippy night and the wet black road is sequined with red, orange, blue and green from overhead decorations. And I stand outside a hairdresser's next to a stinky-warm Chinky takeaway, where I can hear music from a pub, and pant.

I could see the way she was smiling at the Asian. If Dad had known about that he'd have said, 'How come you're going with blacks again?' Like Dad had said to her about Marcel. Then she'd just smiled at him and said, 'I dunno. I just do sometimes, Paul.' I totally understood why Dad hated her now. It wasn't so much what she did, it was more that she didn't apologise enough for what she did. And I knew what Gran meant too; that there was something insulting about not sticking with your own kind, not choosing people from your own community and your own side. It was like Mum was saying we, her family, were not good enough for her, we were too dull and narrow and past; she had to spread out further, no matter what any of us thought, or wanted.

There's a group of kids my age huddled in a knot beneath the dull orange street light and they look over at me. My legs are jellying and it's hard not to imagine they are dissing me because they know Mum is out there with the Asian. They are bruised by shadows so I have to look closely to see that they are really teenagers. They look at me, dozy and surprised, like I just crashed into the bedroom where they were sleeping. One lad is eating a girl's face, another lad runs his hands up and down the side of a girl like she is a tree trunk and he's checking her bark. The fat girl who has no lad feels me over with her eyes instead, making me headachy and alert. Seeing her sniffing me makes you know why girls get called dogs. And I understand again the joy of online porn, where everyone seems warm and friendly, caring only for oily strokes and wet kisses, and nothing like these real girls at all.

Every few moments there is a milky peak in the night light, which is the turning searchlight. The fat girl in a white tracksuit crosses the road towards me and says, 'Wha' ya staring a'?' The rain has started up again, tiny nails in the ice-wind, making my face sore. My heels are aching from the running. I turn round to look in all directions but Mum has not followed me. She's nowhere to be seen, though all my senses are extra-keen and if she was there in the gloom I'd detect her. Around the lads and girls lamplit rain-fizz comes down bronzed, like champagne. 'What's yer name?' the stroked girl shouts, like she really doesn't want to know, but rather wants me to notice her. The strangers look from my mucky wedding shoes to my wet eyes very slowly. 'She a gyppo?' the stroking lad says. ' 'haps she don't speak English.' They are all crossing the road now coming towards me, untucking balled hands from pockets and pulling back their coils of ratty hair to show faces weasly white. My stomach gripes against the cold because I am not brave. I have no coat and am shivering. I wish I was online. I hug my arms around myself and lift my shoulders to my ears. The papers and my gran and my mum thought I was a hero, but really it was only because I didn't go out of the house. I just got used to my box and waited because I am not a very brave girl.

'Can't yer speak?' the fat lass says and snarls her lip at me. 'Are yer lost?'

'I think she's been washed up on beach,' the lad says and the laughter's an icy shiver. 'She's driftwood.'

This is how the locals would have first greeted the Vikings, the moment before they began with stones and arrows.

Then from around the corner a splashing, a car. Me and the girls watch as my mum jumps out and starts screaming at me. I am very relieved but I ignore her and begin walking on my jelly legs, and she has to march after me and grab my thin wrist and I fight wildly, for the girls mainly but for the lads too, kicking and shouting, so even the kissing pair stop and watch as I am bending at the waist and yelling at Mum until she bundles me into the car like she is abducting me.

I keep the fight going, though I know it is only because she showed how much she loved me by coming for me that I am able to show the girls how bold and wild I am, and how

266

I hate her, and they are dazzled by my power, gaping like kids before a magic show. The Asian drives away calmly as I stare at the big fat lonely through the window and she watches my face pull away, but when I turn round again, she is still standing there, alone in the snowy high street staring after our car.

Mum is raving as we drive, until the Asian says, 'You know what this here patch of land needs, Jack?' But Mum continues yelling at me until he says, 'Its very own mega branch of Fags 'n' Fings, and Mum lets herself giggle.

'That's his brother's newsagent's,' she explains to me.

'How fascinating,' I say.

'They're chalk and cheese, love.'

'Like I need to know that,' I say. 'Unless we're all about to be related.'

When we get back to the caravan I refuse to get out. 'Let me talk to her,' Mum says to the Asian, and he nods and starts unloading shopping bags from the boot.

'Looks like he's moving in,' I say.

'He's brought some provisions,' she says angrily. 'Which is very thoughtful.'

'Mum, that is the man who told the police about you, who called the papers.'

But I'm weary and hungry and it's an effort to argue.

'Oh, Elle,' she says, hanging her head in her hands and groaning. 'Is that really what you think?'

'Yup. He went and called the papers. They think you should be punished for being an old slapper and a crap mum. And you can't see it.'

'That's totally wrong. It wasn't him who called the police. Gran called my work, and they put her in touch with a tour-rep who worked with George, and she called the police. Babs probably called the papers too. She's the one who doesn't like me. I work with Amir, we are friends.'

'Er, I don't see any of your other friends here.' She looks at me like she is suddenly naked before me, but not porny and proud, just totally embarrassed, nibbling on her lip, and I know that this man is her only friend. 'He's after you, right, Mum?' She shrugs and tries to stroke me and we sit there watching Amir arranging his shopping bags carefully on the doorstep, like he's our butler. Then he stacks a heap of old sun chairs from the balcony, and gathers the old plant pots into a group, getting busy while he waits for us.

'I'll have to go and let him in,' Mum says. 'I've got the only key.'

'Don't go,' I say. 'I don't want him in our place.'

'I have to, love, he's standing out there in the freezing cold.'

'Don't go.'

'Stop being so silly.'

'Don't.'

'Oh, Elle.'

'If you let him in our caravan I'm off back to Dad's.' She stares at me. Then between me and the Asian. 'He won't have hardly any money,' I say. 'He's too young.'

'Money never made anyone happy, Elle,' Mum says. 'It's not what matters in life, love. Didn't I teach you that?'

'Great,' I say, 'I'll just go and get some free food and free booze from the free shop.'

She doesn't laugh, just rubs her head and closes her eyes. The lighthouse beam passes over her three times, taking its slow photograph. 'Why don't we just drive off?' I say, pointing at the keys still in the ignition. 'We'll be home by midnight.'

She stares right ahead, thinking of her home; the laptop, the lamp, the letters from the bank – the patient waiting sofa, the loyal cushion, the friendly chair. I think of Dad asleep on our sofa in his new jumper and yellow paper crown, and the Steps in their matching red-velvet party dresses kneeling beside their great tower of expensive electronic gifts, watching the dancing on the TV, and Claire singing hymns in the kitchen and fiddling creatively with the leftovers. I feel the bump of the Asian unpacking more stuff from the boot of the car, and then see him striding purposefully past the window. Toilet paper too. And some washing-up liquid. Men were often giving Mum things, but hardly ever what she needed.

'OK, Elle, if you still feel like this later, then we will go home,' and she gets out heavily and leaves the door open, hoping I will come out too.

I hear the Asian say, 'Now, Jack, I've also bought you some clothes and sheets because I wasn't sure . . .'

The words trail away like smoke as they disappear up the steps of the caravan together. 'I'm calling Dad,' I shout out the door. A moment later I see them come down the steps again for more bags from the boot, and as she passes the window I hear her say, 'She just pretends to be brave, Amir. When she was in the house, she didn't go out at all. Just stayed in doing housework.'

'Isn't that sensible, given the circumstances?' the Asian replies, as he lifts a heavy box out the boot and holds it strongly under one arm.

'I can't see what's good about staying alone and doing housework for five days. If she hadn't been so scared she could have just walked over to her dad's.'

They walk back and disappear into the caravan as I call home.

I think about the fat lass in the high street. Perhaps they are all staying on this campsite too, and will come to find me. They will like me because I seemed damaged and emotional and wild, and they will want to know details of why I was screaming like that in the street. They will think I am a she-boy, crazy and tough, and want me to show them more.

'Dad,' I whine. 'I'm so bored.'

'I wondered how long that would take,' he chuckles, and immediately I hear a click, which is Claire picking up the phone in the bedroom and she says, 'Do you want us to come and get you, darling? I've done a special buffet for tea.'

'We can be over at your mother's in five minutes,' Dad says. In the background I could hear Cherub asking when I was coming back.

'I can put you a naan bread in if you like, and I've got those mini onion bhajis you like,' Claire says. 'And Cherub is really missing you. Shall I put her on?'

'OK,' I say, as the light goes on in the bedroom and I see the Asian shaking out a clean sheet. I see a chessboard pattern of perfect pink squares, like he's ironed the goddamned sheet. Then he snaps the light off and goes back into the kitchen area, and starts taking food out of the supermarket bags.

'Hiya,' Cherub says, impersonating a nice kid, 'I've got your present here. When you coming back?'

'Dunno, there's some real weird shit going down here,' I say to her, cool and confidential, and she says, 'Oh my God, you poor thing! Come back and tell me everything,' like we are true best friends. Then it's Claire saying there's a cake baking and they are about to carve the gammon. Mum is just standing against the counter with a glass in her hand talking to him, laughing, and Dad is telling me all about how amazing their Christmas is – but how terribly they are missing me. Claire says she has a stocking stocked up for me on the mantelpiece, waiting. Dad has frozen me some turkey. Claire has saved me the letter from Santa Claus.

I talked to them a little more. I felt older and able to decide who I loved for myself and when I put the phone down my breathing was normal.

'And he's not as young as he looks,' Mum says, five minutes later, tapping the knife and fork on the closed car window. 'Elle, he's in the process of having an arranged marriage.'

'Like that means anything! You had a marriage arranged until yesterday morning.' This makes her smile, because nothing can stop the rising happiness she's feeling now there's a handsome lad around, and her world has meaning again.

'No, not like me, love,' she says. 'His marriage was arranged by sensible people who don't drink.' She begs me to come in and I refuse and say she can take the food back because I don't want it, and she says it's too cold for her to stand out there while I sulk, so she's going in again.

Then he comes out and I say, 'You know my mum's had young black guys before.' He just stands there, with a tea towel over his shoulder. 'Are you here because you want to screw her?' He just gives me a half-annoyed half-surprised sigh, turns to leave, then stops and looks at me and says, 'It can be lonely being on your own, Elle.'

'Er, I think I know that actually!'

'I mean, having to decide to be on your own all your life, so that you don't upset anyone. I've got an awful feeling my sister Samirah might do that if we're not careful.'

I notice again his oval eyes, his fingernails like long shells and his melted-milk-chocolate skin. 'But Mum always chooses the wrong company,' I say and I'm glad he doesn't say anything cheesy like, 'Until now, honey,' or 'All that's about to change,' or 'Just watch this space, pumpkin.' Instead he just shrugs so I say, 'She went with a guy who was seventeen. A soldier. Someone she met in the park. Marcel. Did you know?' He shakes his head. 'That's why I had to leave home. Dad said it wasn't safe if that's the kind of guys she was going with. He was only seven years older than me. It was all getting a bit *Chat* magazine.'

'My brother reads that,' he says.

'Well, perhaps I'll meet this brother at the wedding,' I say, and Amir goes back to the caravan, smiling. And as he passes Mum zigzagging over the grass, I hear him say, 'Don't be so hard on her, Jack, she's a good kid and she's been through a lot,' and immediately Mum says, 'But she can be so bloody *mean*.'

'So, Mum. Is he only here because he wants to screw you?'

'Oh, he's already screwed me, love,' she says cheerily, placing one hand on the roof of the car so her excitement is steadied. 'Just the once, though, unfortunately.'

'Mum, the newspapers were totally right about you,' I sigh.

'Yep, I'm a slutty useless thoroughly modern mother,' she says, so all the caravan site can hear, 'who deserves all the trouble she gets.'

'Exactly.'

'But unfortunately for you, love, I'm the only slutty modern mummy you've got, so will you please come inside. Now!'

She's grinning. She's lashed again. I say, 'And oh, ever so sorry about being so mean, that must be why I left myself alone for five days.'

But my heart's not in it. Soon it will be a new year.

Mum curls back inside laughing. I wait and wait and she doesn't come back. I am dying with imagining what they might be doing in there. I do and I don't want to catch them at something. I've seen enough porn now to know that there's a lot of variety, and Ashanti has seen her mum doing it on the sofa, which must be far weirder than some strangers on your computer. I used to think she was lying about that, even though she had all the details, but now I reckon it was the truth. Ashanti's mother has loads of different boyfriends, even though she's even older than Mum.

So Mum could be worse; it's unlikely but possible.

When I start getting thumpy with imaginings I creep back towards the caravan and just peep over the metal rim. There they are, not glued together humping, but just smiling at each other and she is holding a bottle of wine, which he must have bought for her. I creep round and tiptoe in the door, and for a while I watch them, just sitting together not saying anything. They remind me of Reg and Joan: everything must have already been said. Still, I sit on the sofa to stop them being alone together. He gives superglue stares to her and her to him, on and on. Eventually I say, 'Sorry, am I interrupting your mind-reading?' Then when this fails to annoy, 'Is the staring competition open to anyone or is it loved-up adults only?' Then I just sit for ages, so they couldn't be themselves. Then I say, 'Well, Dad'll be here soon. And Claire.' They both snap round and look at me. 'I've just rung him and he's coming to collect me. He says he'll be here as soon as he can. He sounded quite angry.'

It's like a starting gun's been fired because Mum begins pacing around the caravan. Amir finds a cloth and wipes the coffee table, then he takes the plates and washes and dries them as Mum drags on a fag and gazes out over the campsite. 'If you want to go . . .' she says to Amir, but he just continues with the wiping and drying.

'Your wedding reception was rather good for Orla,' Amir says. 'She went home with Tony.'

'You're kidding me!' Mum says and they are staring at each, as if their foreheads are strong magnets, and then, 'I'm nearly forty. You're just the kind of mistake I keep making, Amir.'

'Sssh,' he says, stroking a finger over her parted lips. 'We never love the same way twice.'

'I'm still here,' I say. They both look right through me. I could set fire to the sofa and they'd not notice. 'Are you coming back with me and Dad, Mum?'

She looks at me then. Totally amazed. 'Elle, I won't be able to show my face round there again,' Mum says.

'Perhaps you won't want to, Jack. It seems pretty good round here. Fresh,' he says.

'Fishy.'

'Secluded.'

'That's what I was thinking,' Mum says.

'I've had a few funny terroristy-type looks, but generally it seems friendly.'

'They probably just think you're really brave – I mean to come on holiday with your mum,' she says and he throws the tea towel at her, then hugs her and kisses her.

They don't mention Dad. Amir finishes the washing up and sits down and gazes again at Mum, who suddenly stands up and says, 'Amir, you know I'm going to be appearing in court soon.'

The lie about Dad has gone round the tin caravan like a can opener, letting out all the secrets. 'Don't forget I was an accomplice to the crime, Jack. Perhaps I'll go down too.'

'We could ask to share a cell,' she says, and he must be in love with her because this idea makes him laugh.

'I'd beg the judge for a life sentence.'

'I told him about Marcel,' I say.

'Thanks, darling,' Mum says with a funny grin.

'So I know everything now,' he says.

'Apart from roughly twenty thousand pounds of debt,' my mother replies, and immediately presses her hand over her face.

Me and him look at each other and he shrugs and says, 'Well, they'll never find her here.'

'Yep, perhaps financial freedom's just a facelift away, Mum,' I say, and Amir laughs.

'Cut your hair, change your name,' he says. 'Yep, I think you are due for a change of name,' he says again, with a smile in his voice.

'What do you mean?' she says, but even I knew that he was offering her second proposal in a month. I remembered once hearing Claire tell her friend that she had to 'work very hard' to get Dad to propose. No wonder many women seemed to dislike my mum – boring bitch jealousy; it explained a lot in life, but already I was growing out of it, and soon it wouldn't fit me at all. Hell, in nine months I'd be a proper teen!

'He'll probably be here in about forty-five minutes,' she says firmly, looking at her bare wrist, like there's a watch there.

'No worries,' Amir says, not looking at all frightened. Then he says that he's going to go out and straighten up his car so that Dad's car can get in when he arrives.

I don't know what I expected to feel as I watched Amir out there in the icy night, but it wasn't this; dammit, I rather liked the guy.

While Amir was outside I was going to tell Mum the truth – that Dad wasn't really coming. Then I see how Mum is pacing around smiling, sipping on her wine, looking out at the squares of window-light spread over the dark cliff edge. This is how she likes life; washed with coming danger, a beat of fear to put her apart from that ordinary indoorsiness, that deadly Claire-ish cosiness. 'Come here,' she says, and pulls me next to her at the window so we are both watching Amir moving his car in closer to the caravan, and moving the steps so Dad can get in safely. He looks up at us and smiles.

'He's OK,' I say.

'You think so?' Mum says, and kisses me.

You weren't meant to want fear, excitement, thrills when you were a mum because it was dangerous for the children, but she straightens her back and flashes me, then him, a sharp, excited smile, and hugs me closer and beckons Amir to come in. Then she turns me, holds my shoulders, bows now to my level and tells me, seriously, exactly what sensible kind things she's going to say to Dad and Claire. I can feel her warm delight and I know whatever she's saying, a young man out in the snowy dark, a daughter firm by, a touch of soon-coming chaos; yes, that night my mum had everything she had ever wanted, and all that she needed, right there, all together.

I felt kind of happy for her. And a little further away from her.

So I go out into the night, without asking, alone. I walk from the caravan over the white ice-grass towards the growl and roar. The cold slaps at my chest and the ice-spray salts my laddish face and wind whips through my short hair. There will have been Vikings feeling exactly this way, excited and afraid and in terror-wonder of the moon and the sea and the new English life ahead. When I lay down my spear and lift my iron helmet I can see our caravan far in the distance, the window a tiny bright screen in the night, blazing some time-travelling show about two twenty-first-century people starting to fall in love.

I walk on to the shore, not like a Viking boy at all really; like a strange entirely new person, a little apart and above, my mysterious modern future unknown to anyone, and all ahead.

ACKNOWLEDGEMENTS

Thank you to Arts Council England for the International Fellowship to the Banff Centre, Canada, where this book began, and to the British Council and the staff and students at the University of Mumbai where this book was completed.

For invaluable insight, inspiration and encouragement, thanks to Deborah Rogers and all at RCW, and Alexandra Pringle and all at Bloomsbury. Special thanks to Victoria Millar, Gillian Stern and Sarah-Jane Forder for their perceptive suggestions and good judgment.

As always I am indebted to Andy, Kendra and Cleo for their patience, assistance, support and love.

A NOTE ON THE AUTHOR

Helen Cross was born in 1967 and brought up in East Yorkshire. She is the author of two previous novels: *The Secrets She Keeps* and *My Summer of Love*, which won the Betty Trask Prize and was made into an award-winning film. She lives in Birmingham.

A NOTE ON THE TYPE

The text of this book is set in Linotype Sabon, named after the type founder, Jacques Sabon. It was designed by Jan Tschichold and jointly developed by Linotype, Monotype and Stempel, in response to a need for a typeface to be available in identical form for mechanical hot metal composition and hand composition using foundry type.

Tschichold based his design for Sabon roman on a font engraved by Garamond, and Sabon italic on a font by Granjon. It was first used in 1966 and has proved an enduring modern classic.